FLIRTING WITH THE CEO

THE WHITLEY BROTHERS

LAYLA HAGEN

D1534303

Copyright © 2023 by Layla Hagen

All rights reserved. No part of this book may be reproduced or transmitted in any form, including electronic or mechanical, without written permission from the author, except in the case of brief quotations embodied in critical articles or reviews. This is a work of 'ction. Names, characters, businesses, places, events and incidents are either the products of the author[]s imagination or used in 'ctitious manner. Any resemblance to actual persons, living or dead, or actual events is purely coincidental.

CONTENTS

Chapter One

Colton

"**C**ome on, brother. You've got to stop being a grump eventually."

My youngest brother Gabe could be a pain in my backside, but as I cocked a brow and looked around at the rest of my brothers, I noted they all had smug smiles. "So, what, you all wanted to meet here to crawl up my ass?"

"No," Gabe corrected. "We wanted to celebrate."

"You're the one who brought the bad mood to the table," Jake directed at me. He was the second oldest and *usually* the least annoying of them all.

I had to laugh when my middle bro, Spencer, chimed in too. "Dude, come on. I left Penny to stay with Ben on her own to come here. You'd better put on a good face."

"You're the one who started this whole thing and asked about the reason I'm frowning," I countered with exasperation.

"One of these days, maybe you'll learn what a rhetorical question is," Gabe noted, then asked, "So, everyone wants shots?"

"Yes," I said. There was a nod of approval from the rest of my brothers too. The five of us had come here to celebrate Gabe's business, Whitley Distillery & Bar, being listed as one of the top five places to be in Boston. He'd only opened it a few months ago, but it was no surprise to me.

When my brother put his mind to something, he aimed to be the best. That was true for all of us Whitleys.

I downed the shot quickly. It burned my throat but had the calming effect I was looking for.

"You've got a great selection of booze," I praised my brother.

"Thanks. How much time do all of you have tonight?"

The bar was bustling with people. I couldn't see us staying for too long. I had an early day tomorrow, and so did the rest of my brothers. Besides, Gabe had his hands full with the guests. He was the CEO of the distillery by day and insisted on spending his evenings in the bar. He'd aptly named it Whitley Distillery & Bar because everything was in one place, the bar in the front and the distillery in the back.

"We've only just arrived, and you already want to kick us out?" Jake asked. Someone was in a good mood.

"I was just trying to figure out how drunk I can get all of you and how much time I have to do it."

"Not me," I said.

Spencer rolled his eyes. "He was just making a joke. Although, come to think of it, maybe getting you shit-faced would take the stick out of your ass."

"Why are you so convinced this shadowing thing will be a disaster?" Cade asked me. He was Spencer's twin, but the two had very different personalities. Although Cade was channeling Spencer right now.

"Because they're sending this Zoey Thomas to babysit me, and that won't do. I like to call the shots."

"Don't we all?" Cade responded.

We were each CEOs of our own companies. Whitley Industries was a mammoth in the business world. My father almost ran it into the ground, destroying all of our grandfather's hard work, but my brothers and I had done a great job picking up the pieces after he left. Father had a secret family, which was a long depressing story I'd rather not think about. So when the time came, we divided up the businesses. Cade had taken over the coffee branch, Spencer the publishing company. Gabe was running the craft distillery that he'd expanded in ways none of us could have imagined. Jake had returned to Boston recently and was in charge of Whitley Advertising.

So yeah, we all liked to call the shots. Me probably more than them. I figured it was because I was the oldest brother. I'd been working on a breakthrough in my biotech company for two years, and a few months ago, I'd finally succeeded. Now we were in the process of bringing the immune-boosting supplement on the market. Whitley Biotech didn't have a production facility—we were strictly research and development—so we had to partner up with another company to actually make it.

The business worked well, at least from my point of view. I handed off most of the internal and external communication to my managers. They'd contact me with emails, requests for meetings, and calls as needed. For the most part, I ignored it. I was an R&D guy and had to come up with the next discovery. It was what I did best.

But our partners, especially the ones involved in production, disagreed. They labeled me uncooperative and difficult—which was probably true, because I was busy. So we were given an ultimatum in order for them to continue to work with us: I had to bring in an expert in organizational management—whatever crap that was—and work with her for a while. Zoey Thomas was supposed to help me develop my organization and communication skills. In other words, she was going to babysit me, and I didn't like it one bit.

I turned to Jake. "Brother, I apologize again for hijacking your wedding with business talk last week."

"You didn't," he responded.

I felt guilty because the first time I'd found out Zoey was going to work with me was at his wedding. I'd been determined to avoid bringing up the topic, but my brothers could always tell when there was something on my mind.

"It's a good thing you did so we could give you shit about it. I still stand by my original point," Gabe said.

I was looking over his shoulder at his bartenders. They were scurrying about. Gabe was clearly needed, and we were in the way.

He turned to look at me. "At least she's hot."

I groaned. "That has nothing to do with it."

"You know, he does have a point," Cade added. "If you're going to fight with someone for a while, at least it helps if they're good-looking."

"Just make sure Grandmother doesn't hear about this conversation," Spencer said.

"Why not?" I asked.

"I'm 100 percent sure she'll somehow get the idea that she should matchmake you with this Zoey chick."

I waved my hand. "You're way off base. She hasn't even met Ms. Thomas. *I* haven't met her."

"That won't stop Grandmother," Spencer said. "I mean, look at her track record." He pointed at himself, then at Jake, and then at Cade.

A while ago, my grandmother decided she'd had enough of our nonsense and wanted great-grandchildren. Since none of us were in serious relationships at the time, she said she'd try to find matches for us. Her record was perfect, considering three of my brothers were now married or engaged. But she also had a great-grandkid now, so I was sure she would slow down, since she'd achieved her goal.

If I shared my thoughts with my brothers, they'd probably fight me on it. They seemed determined to fight me on everything tonight.

"If you're needed somewhere else, we can entertain ourselves," Jake assured Gabe. Clearly, he'd picked up on the fact that the bartenders were waving at our youngest brother in panic.

"I'll be right back," Gabe said.

After he left, Spencer said, "You know, Grandmother might try her hand with Gabe next."

"You think so?" Cade asked, nodding toward me. "I mean, he's way younger than the golden boy. Colton is going to be an old lone wolf soon enough."

I stared at both of them. "You two actually have conversations about this?"

"Only when shots are involved," Cade clarified.

"Or when we want to give you shit," Spencer added.

"Man, you make it so easy for them," Jake said, shaking his head.

"I think you're both nuts," I said before deciding to share my theory with them. "Grandmother has Ben now. She wanted a great-grandkid. That's why she started all this." I patted Spencer's shoulder. "You gave her what she wanted, so I'm 100 percent sure she won't continue her matchmaking project."

My three brothers were silent, and that clued me in that they thought *I* was the crazy one. Jake started laughing first. Cade followed him. But I was convinced I was right. And if not, she could focus on Gabe. Or on our three half brothers.

Spencer just chuckled. "Keep telling yourself that if it helps. But if you don't brace yourself, it's going to smack you right in the face."

"What is?" I asked.

"You'll see," Jake replied.

"Jesus, what's gotten into all of you?"

"Ah, Jake is right. You're making it easy for us to taunt you," Cade concluded.

I'd been so buried in work these past few years that I was kind of out of it when it came to my family. I'd joined them as often as possible but hadn't been there nearly enough. And I'd definitely lost my footing when it came to my brothers' bullshitting, but I'd get the hang of it again soon. I was sure of it.

"I think we should get out of Gabe's hair," I suggested.

Jake's smile faded. He leaned over the counter, glancing at Gabe, who was mixing drinks alongside his bartenders. Was he understaffed, or had a bartender called in sick? I had to talk to him about it. He was heading straight to burnout.

Takes a workaholic to know a workaholic.

"Why are there so many people here tonight?" Spencer asked.

"That list got published yesterday. Maybe people came to check it out," Jake suggested.

There was a long line to get drinks. Gabe and the bartenders were not going to be able to handle everything.

"How are everyone's bartending skills?" I asked.

"I can follow a recipe," Cade said.

"I probably can too," Jake replied.

Spencer shook his head. "I can't stay. Promised Penny I'll be home soon."

"You go home. You've got a kid, but the three of us can stay and help Gabe. Right?" I asked, glancing at Jake and Cade.

"That's a good idea," Jake said. "Let me just text Natalie."

Cade nodded. "I'll tell Meredith that I'm going to be late."

Guilt gnawed at me. I was used to calling the shots, but I wasn't a jackass. Of course they had other plans.

"Go if you have plans with your women. I'll stay here and help Gabe on my own."

"No, the girls will understand," Cade said.

I still wasn't used to three of my brothers having significant others. It had been just us for as long as I could remember. Obviously, we dated, but until last year, no one we ever dated had been part of the group. Natalie, Meredith, and Penny were considered family now, and I liked all of them a lot.

"Want to ask Gabe if he actually wants you here?" Spencer suggested. I knew he was only half joking.

"We all know you like to be in charge, Colton, but maybe double-check with him," Cade added.

I walked behind the counter, straight to my youngest brother, tapping his shoulder.

He looked sideways at me. "Sorry. I'll be right with all of you."

"How about Jake, Cade, and I give you a hand?"

"Are you serious? That would be amazing."

Gabe never pretended to have things under control. If we offered help and he needed it, he accepted it. Something that was more difficult for the rest of us. Especially for me. I hated asking for help.

I looked up at the rest of my brothers and nodded at them to come behind the counter.

Spencer waved and headed out, and Jake and Cade came right next to me.

"All right. You have recipes somewhere?" Cade immediately asked.

Gabe nodded. "Guys!" he called to his two bartenders. "My brothers are going to help. Here's what we're going to do. You two will take over any of the custom house drinks we have on the menu, and my brothers will mix all the standard cocktails. We've got the recipes right there." He pointed at a stack of cards that was hidden under the counter. I grabbed the box and put it out so we could all easily reach it.

"We're on it," I said.

Gabe winked. "You can take the workaholic out of the office, but you can't take the work out of the workaholic, huh?"

I rolled my eyes. "I'm not a workaholic. I just like to get things done."

"That's why we haven't seen you for, like, a million years," Gabe replied.

"Okay, less talking. Get to work," I said.

We all started prepping drinks, and it really reduced the customer wait time. Most of the orders were for a wine or beer, and that was easy to do.

As we worked, I got to thinking. It wasn't that I was a workaholic, just determined. After Mom passed away, I'd made myself a promise: my work would make a difference. And I'd kept that promise. I regularly had breakthrough ideas. In the biotech field, that was what kept the business strong. Some discoveries were easier than others to create and bring to fruition. This last one had been particularly time-consuming. But because I didn't give up, I now had something to show for it. I couldn't wait to see the new drug on the market. If that meant having to put up with a third-party employee breathing down my neck, then so be it. I'd dealt with a lot of crap in my lifetime. I'd deal with this too.

I could certainly put up with Zoey Thomas for a year. But I had a hunch she wasn't going to last that long.

CHAPTER TWO

ZOEY

Zoey

"Are you there yet?" Hans, my boss, asked.

"Yes. I just arrived at the address." Whitley Biotech was in one of the most gorgeous buildings on Congress Street. I had a thing for modern behemoths made of glass.

"All right, then. Good luck."

I liked Hans. He'd called to give me a pep talk, although he didn't need to. *I've got this.*

"Thanks. I'll keep in touch. Okay?"

"Sure. And if he drives you crazy, I can always send someone else."

I rolled my eyes. "I'm not a quitter, Hans."

"I know. That's why I sent you."

"All right. Let's do this. I'll send you a report," I said right before hanging up.

I sipped from my Starbucks cup, glancing up and down at the building. My boss warned me Colton Whitley would be difficult. Well, actually, everyone warned me. I'd spoken to several people from his HR department over the past month, and they'd all been slightly wary about this.

But I also knew why Hans sent *me* here. I was great at my job. I'd gotten into consulting right after college because it paid very well. Then I specialized in organizational management. Over the past few years, I'd narrowed my expertise to personal organization. I'd worked one-on-one with many CEOs over the years with much success. Now I kept getting more and more difficult customers.

I understood the clients' reluctance. I wouldn't want some stranger bursting into my office and breathing down my neck for months on end. But it was what it was. I didn't mind handling difficult customers because I had mad negotiating skills, and I could usually get them to see it my way. It probably stemmed from the fact that I grew up with two annoying brothers.

I walked in five minutes earlier than I was supposed to, and an assistant led me straight to the Human Resources office. Although I was an external consultant, not an employee, the HR manager was still my main contact. Half an hour later, I was ready to hit the ground running.

I liked the office they'd assigned to me. It wasn't big, but I had a perfect view of the water. I really liked the building and its decor. Everything was light and airy. I was told they had condominiums on the top floor, though I couldn't imagine why someone would want to live above offices. It lacked the coziness I liked in a home.

Over the first few hours, people kept peeking into my office, introducing themselves, which was nice and friendly. I probably wouldn't have much to do with any of them, but I was used to the curiosity.

The man himself hadn't shown up yet. At lunch, I was almost ready to bet I wasn't going to see Colton Whitley at all today. And that was fine by me. After all, I was here for a year, and having a day or more to learn the ropes only helped me understand how to best help Mr. Whitley in his environment.

On the way in, I'd spotted a nice cozy restaurant by the water, and I wanted to take myself out on a lunch date. Before leaving, I checked my appearance in the bathroom mirror. My dark brown hair was a bit unruly today and unwilling to settle down. It had been a windy morning, and I actually kind of liked the wild look. I thought it suited me and somehow made my green eyes more prominent.

I was wearing a dark green dress today, which had long sleeves and a black leather belt. Over the years, people had hinted now and again that dresses were too feminine. But this was my style, and I didn't much care what others thought. At thirty-two, I completely embraced it. Besides, being feminine didn't seem to get in the way of things, so why not follow my heart and sense of fashion? I could probably have gone with something more practical than stilettos, though. My feet were hurting already. But I wanted to make a good impression on my first day.

I returned to my office, grabbing my coat, then stopped for a minute just to look around my office. I loved it and decided I was going to send the HR manager a box of chocolates or something. I was 100 percent sure she'd had a hand in getting me my own office, and I could kiss her for it.

Just as I walked out and closed my door, I heard a booming voice.

"I don't have time for her today."

"Colton, really. You should meet her. It's her first day, and she's here for you. You'll like her. She's very nice."

That was Sandra, the HR manager and my favorite person at Whitley Biotech. And the loud, angry voice apparently belonged to the one who'd become my least favorite person: Colton Whitley.

"I've got a full schedule today, and I don't have time to be managed," he said.

"I've seen your schedule. But I'm sure you can arrange just five minutes of your time to meet her."

Footsteps approached, and then two figures rounded the corner.

This was Colton Whitley? That was impossible. I'd imagined someone shorter, for some reason, or maybe with a bit of a receding hairline.

Someone older, for sure. After all, the man wasn't just a CEO but also a scientist.

That's what you get for holding a prejudice against scientists, Zoey. Now pick your jaw up from the floor.

Surely he couldn't be this good-looking. I'd googled him when I first got the assignment but couldn't find pictures. HR gave me a packet that included his bio, it didn't specify his age.

"I said no, Sandra," he boomed. Yep. The voice belonged to him. There was no mistaking it.

Fortunately, neither of them saw me. I wanted to catch him off guard and be the first to greet him.

I cleared my throat. "Mr. Whitley. I'm Zoey Thomas," I said, walking a few short steps toward him with my chin held high, as if I hadn't overheard their conversation. "Pleasure to finally meet you."

Sandra looked from me to Colton, then walked away with quick steps.

Great, even his own team is bolting. That isn't good.

He obnoxiously sized me up and down. What was that about? I decided to take a closer look too. I hadn't realized from a distance that his eyes were so blue. For a few seconds, I completely forgot what I was here to do, and that never happened to me. I was a professional.

"I was just going out for lunch and wondered if you'd like to join me," I continued.

"My schedule is full today," he quickly answered, then added, "I hope my team made you feel welcome."

They did. Unlike you.

At least he'd realized he was a bit rude.

"See you around, Ms. Thomas," he said before going into his office and closing the door. Seconds later, I heard his voice again. He was on the phone.

All right, so at least he wasn't making up being busy. By the sound of it, this was a business call, so perhaps his schedule *was* packed. Still, his manners were atrocious. I gathered that he wasn't happy that I was going to be shadowing him for a year, but he could be more gracious about it. I'd never worked with someone who had such hostile manners as Colton Whitley... or someone who was as handsome. But that was beside the point. Looks didn't matter, not one bit.

Well... maybe they did, but I wasn't willing to admit that.

I hurried outside, determined to move forward with my lunch plans. I grabbed a burger from the restaurant and sat on a bench facing the water. No matter where I worked, I always tried to get outside every day for lunch, even if just for fifteen minutes. August was coming to an end, so we wouldn't have sunny, warm days for much longer. Spending a bit of time in the sun filled me with a lot of energy for the afternoon.

My phone beeped just as I finished the burger. I smiled. It was my brother Alex. He knew it was my first day on this new project. I answered after swallowing my mouthful.

"Hey," I said.

"How's your day? Is the new boss living up to his reputation?"

I'd shared with my brother everyone's comments about Colton, so he knew what I was up against.

"You know, I think he actually is. Though I only saw him for like two hot minutes, so I don't want to draw a conclusion yet."

"Your first hunch is usually right," Alex said. "You're very good at reading people."

"I know, but I don't want to be hasty. Although, he does have atrocious manners."

"You'll let me know if you want me to kick anyone's ass, right?"

"Oh yeah, sure." I laughed it off, although the crazy thing about Alex was that he completely meant it. I had no doubt that if I told him, or

Dean, that someone was giving me a hard time, they'd kick their ass, even if it would get me fired. It was just how they were. No one messed with their little sister. I loved that growing up. I still did.

I got up from the bench, though I was going to stay outside for a few more minutes.

"Did you check on Mom and Dad recently?" I asked.

"I spoke to them yesterday."

"Are they still in Copenhagen?"

"No, they moved on to Stockholm."

"Oh, okay." I was having a hard time keeping track of where they were these days. My parents were both painters and had a gallery tour of sorts going on in Europe. I was immensely happy for them. They were both very talented, and I was ecstatic that the world had finally rewarded them for it. It took many years of hard work, but they'd made it and now were invited to show in galleries around the world.

"Want to meet up tonight and talk about the bad-mannered CEO?" he asked.

"You know, let's do that, though I'm not sure if I can manage it today. It's my first week here, and I'm probably going to stay up late to familiarize myself with everything."

"Sure. Let me know when."

The thing about growing up with two brothers was that I related far easier to guys than to women. My best friend was also a guy. Sometimes I missed having a female BFF. Last time I had something like that was in college. But I had my brothers, so I really didn't have too much time for other friends besides Tom, who I hadn't seen in ages.

The afternoon went by the same way as the morning. I'd asked Colton's team to prep a PowerPoint for me, summarizing the ongoing projects so I was on top of everything. I guess I'd have to tackle the man himself, though, in order to get him to meet with me.

I was determined to make Colton Whitley like me—whether he wanted to or not.

CHAPTER THREE

ZOEY

Over the next week, I saw very little of Colton, but I was buried in prep work. Now that I'd gotten a sense of the ongoing projects and to-dos—with the help of his assistant—I was making headway.

I didn't typically like to work late, but in the very beginning of a project, I put in as much time as necessary to be on top of everything. It only made my work easier later on. That was why, on Friday evening, I was the only person left on the floor. At least that was what I thought. The last time I'd heard a noise was probably an hour ago or so.

I yawned and checked the time. It was eight o'clock now. I could still get drinks with Alex and sleep in late tomorrow.

As I got up from my desk, I heard a sound in the corridor and panicked for a brief second before realizing it probably just meant I wasn't the last one here.

I walked out with my jacket on my arm and came face-to-face with Colton.

"Ms. Thomas," he said. "I didn't know you were here."

"I thought I was the last one in the building too," I replied.

"If I knew you were still here..."

"You wouldn't have come out of your office at all?" I finished for him.

He narrowed his eyes. "I appreciate your commitment to our collaboration, but I'm not expecting you to work late."

"You know, I was wondering if you'd been avoiding me on purpose."

He had a white coat on, which only increased his sex appeal. The stark white contrasted with his blue eyes. I couldn't believe this hot-as-hell man was Colton Whitley.

"It's been a busy week, Ms. Thomas."

"Yes, I know. For both of us." I narrowed my eyes too. "So, do you usually stay holed up in your office, or is it just because of me?"

"I figured the less we interact, the better," he said without hesitation.

"Ah."

I liked honesty, only now that he'd owned up to it, I wasn't sure how to react. I'd had difficult clients before, but I wasn't used to this level of antagonism.

"Mr. Whitley, I know it must not be easy for you to have an outsider practically take up residence in your building."

"No, it's not," he replied in a cutting voice.

"Still, it would be in our mutual best interest if we were on good terms." It was on the tip of my tongue to say *amicable*, but no matter how much of an optimist I was, even I knew that was a stretch when it came to Colton. "We're going to have to work together at some point."

The corner of his mouth twitched. "I suppose we will."

"How come you're here so late?" I asked.

"I was actually going into the lab."

He tugged at his coat, and I saw his dress shirt underneath. The mix between scientist and CEO was off-the-charts hot.

"May I join you?" I asked before I could help myself.

"No. I don't allow many people in the lab." He looked like he was searching for the right words, then said, "Safety hazard."

"Then may we talk in your office?"

He didn't say anything for a few seconds, and I was sure he was going to shut me down, but then he surprised me. "Sure, why not? Come in."

We walked side by side, and for some reason, his presence over-whelmed me even though he wasn't antagonizing me right now. In fact, he wasn't saying anything, but he was simply an intimidating man. He was much taller than me, at least six feet two or more.

All I could think about as we went into his office was that he simply didn't look like a scientist. Or like a CEO, for that matter. Although the suit would trick you into thinking that. Even through all the layers of clothes, the muscles in his arms were defined. I was certain that his entire body was equally toned. His features were handsome but also rugged. His jaw was angular, as were his cheekbones, and his eyes were downright hypnotizing.

His office was a clinical white space. It looked almost like a lab too.

"Why do you have a whiteboard in here?" I asked.

"I do a lot of work on it. I have one in the lab too. Math and chemistry are my bread and butter. I figure out the formulas, and my team does the rest."

"Then why do you need the coat?"

"Sometimes I work with substances myself. Mostly when the math isn't lining up."

"You don't have an ongoing project now?" I asked, pointing at the whiteboard. It was empty.

"I wipe it clean when I'm done."

"Afraid someone might steal your secrets?" I taunted.

"I just like to start with an empty whiteboard. It stimulates my brain."

"You're working on something new right now?"

"Always. I've been here every evening this week. I've got some new ideas."

"Wow," I exclaimed. "But you just developed a new immune-system booster that's hitting the market next year. Do you ever take time to relax?"

To my astonishment, he smiled, and let me tell you, it was something to behold. Did he know how seductive his smile was? Was that why he flashed it so rarely? Was he trying to spare those around him from falling at his feet?

"Sometimes, but not for long. When an idea nags at me, I go to the lab and work it out. Sometimes it ends up being nothing, but most of the time, it evolves into something my team can work on."

"You do have a brilliant mind," I murmured. I couldn't even imagine developing or thinking to the level he apparently did. I mean, I wasn't an idiot, but his brain was performing miracles, more or less.

"What's that? You sound surprised."

I laughed nervously. "Never mind."

"Ms. Thomas."

I rolled my eyes. So formal. "I only answer to Zoey, okay? 'Ms. Thomas' makes me feel like my mom. I love her, but I don't want to be her."

He chuckled.

"It's just that everyone told me Colton Whitley is an extremely difficult man, but he's got a brilliant mind," I continued. "Almost like one thing excuses the other."

"Who told you that?" he asked, seeming a tad affronted.

I cleared my throat. "Never mind." Shit. It was Sandra who'd mentioned it, and I liked her. I didn't want to throw her under the bus.

"Zoey?" he urged with a firm tone.

"I'm not at liberty to say."

"Yes, you are. It was someone from my team."

"Now, now, Colton. Don't jump to conclusions."

"Zoey." His voice had an edge to it. It sounded 5 percent dangerous and 150 percent sexy.

I rolled my shoulders and made a gesture with my fingers, zipping up my lips. "Nope, you're not going to get it out of me."

He glanced at me intently for a few seconds that seemed to stretch into minutes, but I didn't give in. Damn, he was serious.

Eventually, he straightened up, looking away. "I appreciate someone who doesn't blab."

I winked at him. "That's me. I can keep a secret like it's nobody's business. Although, to be fair, your reputation isn't a secret at all. Everyone warned me."

"And yet you took the job."

I blinked. "Of course I did. I'm not afraid of challenges."

"So you think I'm a challenge."

"You're proving you are with every passing second. I'm not at the stage in my career to simply discard jobs based on the client's reputation."

He raised a brow. "Why even choose this type of work? I can imagine most of your clients are... resistant."

"I'm good at it. I grew up with two brothers, and they trained me well. I can give as good as I get."

"You're close to them?"

Wow, we're having a real conversation. Maybe this will all work out after all.

"Very. Buuut let's focus on you again."

Colton didn't say anything for a few seconds.

I glanced around. "So, what motivates you to keep developing new products?"

"I like creating something that helps people," he said in a clipped tone and didn't expand.

I was certain there was more to it than that, but I didn't want to prod. Besides, it was none of my business. I'd made more progress with Colton in these few minutes than I had the entire past week. I didn't want to look a gift horse in the mouth; I wanted to wave a white flag and get to the nitty-gritty.

"Listen, I understand this situation is uncomfortable for you, but I promise I'm very good at my job," I stated.

"I never doubted that."

I looked him straight in the eyes. Well, that was a mistake because it wiped away my every thought. I lowered my gaze to the floor, gathering my wits before making eye contact again. I was determined to be completely professional no matter how amazing those blue eyes were.

"Then I don't understand the problem."

"The problem, Zoey, is that I like to call the shots. Always. I run this place. I take responsibility for the successes and the failures and the messes. I hate the idea of anyone telling me how to do things."

I swallowed hard, trying not to fixate on how damn sexy that Adam's apple bobbing up and down was. "That's not what I'm here to do," I said.

"Aren't you?"

"No, I'm simply here to make your life easier. Everyone's life. My processes aren't meant to simply tell you how to do things. It puts everything in perspective, giving you *options* so you have time for more things. You know?" I pointed at the whiteboard. "Like creating that product."

I was getting a good sense of who Colton Whitley was. For the first time, I understood why people said he was difficult. It wasn't because he was an asshole or because he thought he was God's gift to Earth. It was simply because he liked to do things his own way.

I knew he would probably be my most challenging client yet.

But I also knew I was up for the challenge.

Chapter Four
Colton

Darla, my assistant, poked her head in at eight o'clock the next morning. "Hey, Colton. Mr. Browning is here."

"Tell him to come in." Browning was the only one who arrived at the office as early as I did. He was one of the board members and also my mentor, someone I looked up to immensely.

I walked over to greet him, shaking his hand as he came in. "Good morning, Browning," I said. His first name was Joel, but he liked being called by his last name. "What brings you here?" He worked from home most of the time, so it was nice to see him in person rather than a Zoom call.

"Haven't been here in a while. I wanted to see how you're doing."

Joel was like a father figure to me. He'd been with the company for many years, long enough to have known my mom. The two of them had been close. After she passed away, he took me under his wing.

"I'm well. I'm already working on my next idea."

He clapped his hands, smiling widely. "That's what I was hoping to hear. Your mother would be so proud of you and the dedication you put into your work."

His words meant the world to me.

"Thank you, Browning. Whitley Biotech is my life's work. It means everything to me."

We chatted for the next fifteen minutes or so about pending projects, profits, and budgets Joel was inspiring, and I really enjoyed spending time with him.

After we spoke of the competition, I could tell he was ready to be on his way. He nodded and then stood abruptly. "Well done. Don't let me keep you from your work. I heard a consultant started working here."

"Yes. You know that one of the conditions the production company had prior to working with us was that I become more responsive."

He scowled. "Everything seems to be running fine, but what do I know? If this helps you organize your time better, why not? Would you mind sending me notes on your ideas as soon as you have something finalized?"

"Sure." I often shared my reports throughout a product's development. Joel was pretty sharp in pointing out things to look for as I created the formulas. It also kept me accountable.

After he left, I went back to my desk. This was turning out to be a good day. I hadn't seen Joel in a while, and I'd been thinking about taking him out to lunch. If I didn't have a date with my grandmother today, I would have done just that, but I didn't want to cancel on her. I knew she was looking forward to it.

The first meeting of the day was with my lead scientist, George. I was updating him on my progress.

"Colton, this all looks great. But the team and I can do more prep work in the early stages of the research," he said toward the end of the meeting.

"Thanks, but I like to do the brunt of the work myself. I'd rather focus on the details and not manage the team's efforts."

"But I think it'd be quicker, since we could create the formula and alter it as we go. See right then and there the breakdown and reformulate it. I feel like a broken record at this point," he countered. "You know my arguments."

"Yes. But I don't want to change our system."

George narrowed his eyes, then opened his mouth but closed it without saying anything. We agreed on next steps, and then he left the office.

I understood why he thought working together on the formulas would be more advantageous, but I was a hands-on guy. I didn't like the team hovering around in these early stages.

Shortly before lunch, Darla came into my office again. "Colton, your grandmother is here."

"Show her in, please." I was surprised she'd come to the office. We were supposed to meet at the restaurant for our lunch date.

The door opened wider, and Jeannie Whitley stepped inside. My grandmother was ninety-one, but you wouldn't know it from looking at her. She was agile and sharp and liked to keep me and my brothers on our toes.

I immediately rose from my desk, walking to her and kissing her cheek. "Grandmother, did I get things mixed up? I thought we were meeting at the restaurant."

"Oh, we are," she said. "That's what we agreed on, but honestly, I got bored of shopping, so I figured I'd visit you here in your lair. I haven't been to Whitley Biotech in a long while."

Whitley Biotech was one of the original companies within Whitley Industries that my grandfather started up.

"I can give you a tour. Want to see the lab?"

She waved her hand. "No, I know you don't like many people going into your lab, but I would like to look around the offices for a bit."

"Come on. I'll show you around."

I took her arm, walking with her down the corridor, stepping in front of each office, and giving her a brief explanation of what the team residing there was doing. She smiled and nodded and asked pertinent questions. That was one of the things I loved about Grandmother. She never made small talk. She always had important things to say.

"Oh, you've done such a stellar job," she said as we moved back to my office. "Your grandfather is proud of you, you know?"

"Thank you." That was very important to me. It was one of the big motivators behind everything I did. I wanted both my grandparents to be proud. They deserved to know that all their hard work paid off despite the fact that my father nearly ran everything into the ground.

"Want me to make you a coffee?" I asked her. I had a coffee machine in my office. I consumed so much of it that I didn't want to go to the communal kitchen every time I needed a cup. Besides, that place was more of a gossip center. I took after Grandmother and despised small talk. "We still have time before we have to be at the restaurant."

"Thanks, but I already had two today." She looked around again, then back at me. "You know, your grandfather would probably enjoy it here too," she said. "He's getting bored at home."

"Boring is good," I replied. "It'll keep him sane and safe."

"Well, safe maybe, but I'm not sure about sane. It's driving him crazy."

Almost a year ago, Grandfather gave us a scare when he took a trip to the emergency room.

His health problems started when our father left us all, years ago. Grandfather had been retired by that time, but he came back to work, overseeing Whitley Industries right up until he had a heart attack. Doctors absolutely forbade him from working again after that, and he slipped back into retirement. My brothers and I did our best, taking the reins of the companies as we grew older. The only business that didn't have a Whitley leading it until recently was the advertising branch. It nearly went bankrupt. Grandfather decided to run it himself for a while, right up until his health scare. After that, my brother Jake moved from New York to Boston and took it over. Ever since, we'd made sure Grandfather had absolutely nothing to worry about. But the man didn't know how to take it easy. Of course he was bored. I would be too.

"Ready to go to lunch?" I asked. "I'm sure they can accommodate us earlier."

"Oh no, it's fine. I don't have to rush. I like being out of the house. I'm so glad that you're making time for the family now, Colton. We've missed you, you know."

I sensed her starting to guilt-trip me, but where could she possibly go with this?

"I apologize that I've been absent these past few years, but you know how I am when I'm working."

"Colton, you'll always have work. Especially with what you do. It'll always be easier to prioritize the development of a new product over your personal life."

"I'm getting better at balancing it," I said even though I wasn't.

Sometimes you had to tell people what they needed to hear. I didn't want Grandmother to worry about me.

"Your brothers have been so much happier lately."

I narrowed my eyes. I was starting to suspect where she was going with this.

"Everyone finds happiness in their own way," I said in a measured tone.

"Well, yes, but you have to admit that ever since they each found their better halves, Jake, Cade, and Spencer are much happier."

She was right, but if I openly agreed with her, I'd be digging my own grave.

"I'm glad things are working out for my brothers" was all I said.

Grandmother shook her head. "Colton, do I really have to spell it out?"

"No, I would prefer it if you don't, actually."

"My darling boy, when's the last time you brought home someone to meet us?"

"I don't even remember."

She nodded. "Exactly. Don't you think it would be good to have a woman by your side? Someone who can shake some sense into you?"

"Colton? I need—" Zoey said, stepping into the office before stopping in her tracks. "Oh, I'm sorry. I didn't realize you had company."

She looked at Grandmother, who rose from her chair with much more agility than I thought she had.

"Don't mind me. You can come in for whatever you need."

Zoey looked at me, and I nodded. She walked with quick steps toward my desk. She was insanely attractive in her pencil skirt and high heels. The sway of her hips did not go unnoticed.

"I've got a report with suggestions that will help you improve communication with your team and others. I thought you might like to review it."

I only took a glance at the stack before looking back up at her. "That's a big stack for one report. It might take me some time."

She cocked a brow. "We can go through it together if you want. I'll send you a calendar invite for an appointment to review it."

She was persistent. I liked that. Damn it, I liked her even though I disliked the fact that she was here at all.

"You're the new consultant, aren't you?" Grandmother asked.

I whipped my head to look at Grandmother. How the hell did she even know about this? One of my brothers probably blabbed.

"Yes," Zoey said. She sounded as stunned as I felt. "I've only started here, so forgive me, but I'm not sure who you are."

"I'm Colton's grandmother, Jeannie Whitley. Nice to meet you." She held out her hand, and Zoey shook it.

"You look familiar." Then Zoey snapped her fingers. "Oh my God, you look so much like one of Mom's favorite actresses, Gina Delaware. You could be her twin."

Grandmother smiled from ear to ear. "Darling, that *is* me. It's my stage name."

Zoey's mouth formed an *O*, and I felt a stirring in my boxers. Fucking hell. I liked to be in control of my business and my life, but when I was around Zoey, I didn't even seem to be in control of anything.

"I can't believe it. Wow, Mom would freak out if she knew I met you." She looked from Grandmother to me and then back to her. "Would you mind if we took a picture? It would truly mean a lot to Mom if I sent it to her."

"Of course!" Grandmother replied. I hadn't heard her sound so happy in a while. This was a rare thing. She'd been a theater actress her whole life, but while she'd done well, she wasn't what you'd call a household name. "Colton, will you be a dear and take a picture of us?"

"Sure."

Zoey handed me her phone, and then she stood next to Grandmother, who immediately put an arm around Zoey's shoulders, pulling her into a hug. Zoey hesitated for a moment but then returned Grandmother's hug. Damn, she looked cute. I couldn't believe she was so happy that she could do this for her mom. I snapped a few pictures before handing her the phone.

Zoey grinned. "I'm going to send this to Mom right now. She's going to be thrilled."

"Is she an actress too?" Grandmother asked.

"No, she's a painter. Dad is too. She always looked up to you as a fellow artist."

"That's lovely. Do they live in Boston?"

"Yes, but they're in Northern Europe right now. Their work is being shown at various galleries. I'm happy for them but also can't wait for them to be back." She pressed her lips together. "Sorry, that's way too much information."

I wanted to tell her that it was simply the Jeannie Whitley effect. Something about my grandmother invited people to open up. It had always been that way.

It was nice to hear that she missed her parents. In my book, that told me something about a person.

"It was nice meeting you, Jeannie," Zoey said.

"You, too, Zoey."

She stepped out of the office, and Grandmother looked at me pointedly.

"What?" I asked.

"You know, I always thought you needed to get out of the office more to find someone to date. You don't want to turn into a wrinkly old Grinch."

There was an audible gasp from outside the room. I was absolutely sure that was Zoey.

"But I was wrong. You could start by dating Zoey," Grandmother went on.

I walked toward the door, glancing outside. Sure enough, Zoey was walking with quick steps. I closed my office door, then, turning to Grandmother, realized this wasn't a coincidence. She didn't just run her mouth. She *wanted* Zoey to hear.

I cleared my throat, choosing my words carefully. "Grandmother, you cannot talk to me like that at the office."

"Sorry, I didn't mean to. Forgive your old grandmother. I just want the best for you."

That completely disarmed me. I knew she wanted the best. I just didn't like the way she went about it.

"Fine. But don't disregard what I said." Then I added, "I'd never date anyone working for me. I'm not Father."

Grandmother turned pale. "Of course you're not. It's not even the same thing."

True, it wasn't. My father led a double life. He was married to Mom, and they had five kids, but he also had a relationship with another woman, someone who'd worked for him. Then she moved to another city, but he continued his relationship with her, and they had three sons. That woman never knew Father was married. To this day, I will never understand how he managed to juggle two families. How my mom didn't suspect that his frequent trips outside the city weren't work related. How the other woman believed him when he said he didn't marry her because my grandparents didn't approve.

My brother Jake discovered the infidelity, and the family imploded. It was a tough time for us all. Father headed off to Australia, and my mom got sick. She passed away two years after. My younger brothers became troubled. I was in college at the time. It was a shit show trying to keep everything afloat. My grandparents handled us well and kept us on the straight and narrow.

"Colton, honestly, the things you say. You are a single, attractive young man, and she doesn't have any ring on."

I couldn't help myself. I burst out laughing. "You noticed that?"

Grandmother smiled. "Of course. It's one of the first things I look for."

"She could still be in a relationship."

It didn't matter if she was seeing someone or not. She was out of bounds completely.

"I think she'd be good for you."

"You've seen her for all of five seconds," I countered.

"And I already know all I need to."

"Humor me. What exactly did meeting her for that short amount of time tell you?"

"Clearly, she can go toe to toe with you. You didn't look at all happy about whatever it is she wants you to review, but she kept pushing."

"And that's a good thing?" I asked, not letting on that it was a trait I'd immediately liked about Zoey too.

"Yes. You definitely need someone who doesn't just—" The corners of her mouth twitched as she hesitated. "—do what you say."

"Right."

I was too stunned to say anything else.

"The fact that she immediately thought about taking a picture for her mother speaks volumes about where her heart is. It's in the right place, and I always appreciate that in people."

I shook my head, checking the time and getting up from my desk. "Come on, let's go to lunch or we'll be late."

Grandmother beamed. "By the way, I forgot to tell Zoey, if her mom wants an autograph, I'm more than happy. Can you tell her that?"

I laughed. "Sure, Grandmother. I will."

"Good. Will you give what I said some thought?"

"You're going to go on about this our entire lunch date, aren't you?"

She patted my arm. "You know me so well, dear."

Chapter Five

Zoey

"Sandra, can I corrupt you into a lunch date?" I asked.

She looked up from her computer and then rose to her feet. "Sure, let's go. What do you have in mind?" She grabbed her purse from her desk drawer and her coat from behind the door.

"The burger place on the ground floor. It's amazing."

She nodded. "True, it is. I usually avoid it because too many people from work eat there."

"We can always take our burgers and sit on the pier."

"I'd like that," she said.

"We can soak up some sun too. Who knows how long we'll still have these beautiful days?"

As we went downstairs, I kept looking around, wondering if Jeannie Whitley was still here. I could not believe she actually said that to Colton and he hadn't given her a snappy comeback. I liked that he respected his grandmother even when she gave him a hard time. I almost burst out laughing when she called him a wrinkly Grinch. That was... I didn't even know what to think about it, but I was so proud that I didn't actually laugh. Although I suspected my loud gasp gave me away.

"I met Jeannie Whitley today," I told Sandra after we picked up our burgers and went outside. finding a quiet spot farther away on the pier. "Does she often come by the office?"

"No. Actually, I think this is the first time I've seen her in person. But from what I understand, Colton and his brothers are alternating taking her out to lunch every week," Sandra answered.

"That's thoughtful."

"Apparently she meddles a lot in the boys' lives."

I wanted to know more, but I wanted to be casual about it, not obvious about my intentions. I didn't want Sandra to think I had a personal interest in Colton. Because I didn't. This was all work related. Mostly.

"I even heard a rumor that she called herself the family's matchmaker," she added.

I laughed. "That doesn't even sound like a rumor, more like accurate information."

Sandra blushed, biting into her burger.

"Whitley Industries is very interconnected," she said after she swallowed her mouthful. "I know the HR people from other companies, too, and, well, people talk. All I know is that last year, all the Whitley men were single, and now three of them are married. Or wait, is it just two and one is engaged? I'm missing some of the details."

I liked Sandra. She was a bit of a gossip, but not in a mean way. She wasn't judging, but I still chose my words carefully.

"So, she had a hand in that, huh?"

"Apparently so. I'm wondering if she has something planned for Colton too. I mean, if she does, good luck with that. The man never leaves this place for a minute. He lives for his work. I've never seen commitment like his."

"Yeah, he seems driven in a way that few other CEOs are," I said, taking another bite of my burger. "I wonder why that is."

"Oh, I know why it is," Sandra said nonchalantly.

"Really? Why?"

"His mom passed away when he was in college, and he switched majors after that so he could take over Whitley Biotech."

"Oh my goodness."

"Yeah, the poor woman just had shit luck. First, her husband was a total asshole, and then she got sick."

I frowned, not following Sandra. Apparently I didn't know the whole story. "I guess I'm missing something. Why was he an asshole?"

"You don't know?" She sounded stunned.

"Know what?"

"About the Whitley scandal."

"No." I thought about everything I'd read in preparation for the job, but nothing came to mind. "I did some research on the company, but I don't remember there being anything about a scandal."

"It's not recent. This happened a long time ago. Their dad had a secret second family."

My eyes bulged. "What? Are you serious?"

"It was years ago. He left the boys and all the businesses high and dry, so there was a leadership crisis in Whitley Industries until his sons took over."

Several things started falling into place. I knew Whitley Industries was an older, established company—on the third generation—but I had no idea how all this transpired. I now had a renewed sense of admiration for Colton and his brothers.

"Have you made any headway with Colton?" Sandra asked.

I smiled sheepishly. "It's not going as well as I'd hoped, but I know how to pace myself. I gave him the first documents to get started."

She grinned. "Don't hold your breath. He'll probably get back to you next month. He really doesn't pay attention to anything that isn't directly related to his research."

"My plan was to bust into his office once I was back from lunch and read it with him." I laughed at my bravado. Yes, I'd go to his office, but there would be no bursting through the door, though it sounded good.

Sandra blinked. "You know, that's a good plan." She sipped her drink and added, "Better you than me. He's used to me nagging, but maybe it's more effective if you do it. I mean, that's why you're here, and you don't seem intimidated by him."

I shrugged. "No, I'm not."

She laughed. "I think you're the first person who can say that within a week of working with Colton. It took us mere mortals anywhere from one month to two years to get to that point."

"Well, my time here is limited. I've got to make headway with him quickly so he can develop his organizational skills and be comfortable with the process." There was also a difference that Sandra wasn't realizing. Colton couldn't fire me. If he didn't want to continue working with me, I'd still be employed by The Consulting Experts, and they'd assign me to another client. "Besides, I've got experience with stubborn men. I have two brothers who I cut my teeth on."

"Ahhhhh, that explains it," Sandra said.

I grinned and wondered if we had enough in common to become real friends and not just work buddies.

"Want to get something sweet for dessert?" she asked. "Something to give you the strength to ride the boss's ass?"

I laughed. "I like you, Sandra."

"Back at you."

We ended up sharing a slice of chocolate cake, and she was right, it gave me a boost of energy. I wasn't sure if Colton was back yet, but I was already preparing a speech in my mind. I didn't want him to feel like I was trying to manage him because I wasn't. My job was to help him communicate with his team more easily as well as organize his workload. Over the years, I'd developed certain methods of collaboration and organization that he could benefit from. It was just a matter of how I presented my ideas to him, and I knew I had a very short timeframe to convince him before he'd shut me out.

I passed by his office on the way to mine and saw he wasn't back yet. Oh, to be a fly on the wall at his lunch with his grandmother. I was betting that Jeannie Whitley had more wits and sass to share with him.

I was so grateful she'd taken that photo with me. I'd immediately sent it to Mom, but she hadn't responded yet. I knew it would make her day. Jeannie was an inspiration to her.

Back in my office, I paced around, rehearsing what I was going to say to Colton.

I'd checked his calendar before lunch. He made it available to everyone, and he didn't have a meeting. I had half a mind to send him a request for a meeting but then decided against it. He'd have a harder time physically removing me from his office.

I couldn't believe my "great plan" was to ambush him.

I startled when I heard his booming voice in the corridor. I opened the door to my office, listening to see if I could hear Jeannie's voice, but I couldn't, which meant he came back alone. I straightened up, wishing I had thought about checking my appearance after lunch. I ran my tongue over my teeth. It didn't feel like I had anything stuck between them. I smoothed my hands over my skirt, second-guessing the white blouse I was wearing today. I thought it looked too clinical, but whatever.

Okay, this is my moment. I'm going to ambush him before he gets the chance to start working on anything else.

But as I approached his office, I noticed someone else going in. *Damn it.* I checked his calendar again. It now appeared he had meetings until the evening. When on earth had that happened? I would just try to catch him after the last one ended, though I didn't have much time because I was getting together with my brothers for drinks.

At six o'clock, I practically jogged to his office, knocking at the open door before stepping inside.

"Colton," I said with all the confidence I could muster, "I need five minutes."

He glanced up at me in surprise. "Come on in."

At least he hadn't immediately excused himself, saying he had something else going on.

Walking with determined steps, I didn't sit down, just pointed at the papers I'd laid in front of him earlier today. He'd pushed them into the corner farthest from him.

"I want us to go through these."

A smile played on his lips. No, wait, it was more of a smirk. "And you can do all that in five minutes?"

I shifted my weight back and forth on my feet. "Maybe seven."

"I like that you're persistent," he said.

"Oh good, you're not throwing me out. I'll take that as a win. So, may I begin?"

"On one condition."

"Name it."

"Tell me something. Did you overhear what my grandmother said after you left the office?"

Well, shit. That was the last thing I'd expected him to ask. I knew Colton would be demanding, but caring about a social conversation didn't even cross my mind. To be honest, I'd almost forgotten about it after the info dump on the family Sandra had given me, but now his grandmother's comment was front and center in my mind again.

I tried to gauge if Colton was mad that I'd overheard or if he was amused. His expression was unreadable. The man needed to loosen up a bit. I decided to give him some sass.

"It's up to you, Colton. Do you want the truth or not?"

Chapter Six

Colton

"I always want the truth," I said.

I was making a huge effort not to look at her hips. Something about the way her skirt hugged her figure was far too appealing to me.

"Fine. Then yes, I overheard. I didn't mean to. I simply stopped in front of the door to send my mother the picture we'd taken. I wasn't expecting to hear anything. Least of all that."

"My grandmother is a character. I know she has my best interest at heart, but sometimes she can go about things the wrong way. I'm sorry you were exposed to that."

She waved her hand, but I detected a blush on her cheeks. "Really, it doesn't matter."

"I'd like to make it up to you," I said.

She grinned. "Oh? That's unexpected."

I sat up straighter. "Listen, I don't want you to feel uncomfortable."

She laughed. "You think your grandmother made me uncomfortable?"

"I know she made *me* feel that way."

She looked down and then back up. She seemed thoroughly amused by the situation. "Okay, yes, I was very uncomfortable."

"Hence my effort to make it up to you."

She came closer, sitting down opposite me. "Okay. I want you to take twenty minutes to go through the documents with me."

I whistled. "You're very good."

"I know."

"All right, hit me," I said. "Do you want to come on my side of the desk so we can both look at the documentation at the same time?"

"Yes, that's a good idea," she said.

She got up, and I moved her chair to my side of the table. Her perfume caught me off guard. She smelled delicious, and all I wanted was to get closer, inhale deeper. From where I was standing, I had an excellent view down her blouse.

Fuck, I don't need this image in my mind. I looked away quickly, noticing her fingers moving through her brown hair, pulling it to one side, baring her neck. Its curve beckoned to me, and I wondered if it was a sweet spot for her. Exploring this woman would be a privilege, and no question, I'd be very thorough about it. I wouldn't leave one inch of her untouched or unlicked.

I snapped my gaze up from her neck to her eyes. She darted the tip of her tongue between her lips, and I nearly groaned. My brothers always pointed out that I had an excellent poker face, but right now, I couldn't pretend.

The last thing I wanted was for her to feel uncomfortable around me. I had to get my shit together. This was unacceptable behavior. I wasn't my father, and I was determined not to follow in his footsteps, no matter how different our circumstances were.

"So, a big complaint from your business partners is that you're not responsive. That it takes you a long while to reply to an email, phone call—any communication, for that matter."

"Yes, but I get a lot of correspondence every day," I said. Heck, my own family had this complaint about me.

"Why don't we start there? I can go through your emails with you and help you separate things according to priorities and work. You'll be amazed how effective this type of communication management is. That will also help you with prioritizing phone calls, texts, and the rest. Make sense?"

"You want access to my emails?" I double-checked. I wasn't sure what she was thinking, but that was private company information.

"Don't say it like that. It makes me sound like I'm the bad guy here."

"That is a big ask. It's confidential information."

"Colton, I've signed NDAs. I can sign anything else you want to make you feel comfortable."

It was great that HR had her sign nondisclosure agreements, but that didn't mean I was okay with all of this.

"If it makes you feel more comfortable, I do this with all my clients. I would never share or use information in an untoward, let alone illegal, way." Zoey seemed a little upset with me, and I got it. My hesitancy came across like I was accusing her of something, and that was not my intention.

Yeah, your people skills suck, Colton.

"Okay. I could use help with my inbox," I said. And that was the truth.

She took a paper out of the stack she'd left me earlier. It was a screen-shot of an inbox with what seemed like a million labels.

Maybe this wasn't going to be a total disaster.

Her shoulders sagged a bit, and she breathed out as if this weighed on her. Had I been that much of a pain in the ass that my agreeing to one little thing made her sigh with relief?

"All right, I might need some information from you in the beginning, so it might feel like you're wasting time."

I had opened my mouth to reassure her when she continued.

"But you won't be, okay? In the long run, it'll save you time. Just give me the benefit of the doubt. I only ask for one week to get this set up."

"Fine," I agreed.

She grinned. "We should call your grandmother here to embarrass you more often if it means I get my way."

I stared at her. "Embarrass *me*? Right. You didn't hear everything, did you?"

"No, I left when she started berating you on why you're not dating."

"Then you missed the part where she suggested I date you."

I didn't know what possessed me to say that, but her face changed. She parted her lips. Her cheeks turned red. She brought her hand to her neck, rubbing her fingers on her bare skin, and swallowed hard. She was so expressive, it made me wonder if dating Zoey would indeed be a good thing.

"Oh my God, that's why you said you wanted to make it up to me. It made no sense to me." She laughed nervously. "Now it does."

She glanced at the stack of papers and then at the screen in front of me, where my inbox was open. Her blush intensified. "Where was I?"

Damn, she was cute.

Her voice was high-pitched. I was enjoying this immensely. Until now, she'd been the one who rattled me, but for the first time, I was able to do the same to her. And her reaction was delicious.

"I believe you were telling me my grandmother should embarrass me more often so you can get your way."

"Oh yeah," she murmured.

She looked from the screen to me. I was certain she was going to start talking about my email, but she seemed to be bursting at the seams with another question.

"Whatever it is, just say it," I said.

"Why would she even say that? I mean, why me?"

I laughed. "It's very hard to explain how Jeannie Whitley's mind works, but I think it boils down to the fact that she likes you."

"I like her too. She seems to be a very warm person."

"She is," I said. "I owe her everything. And Grandfather too. The two of them dealt with a lot."

"After your father left?" she asked. I felt cold. I never spoke about my father. "I'm sorry," she murmured. "I just found out, and it's still messing with my mind."

"You didn't know before you arrived here?"

"I truly didn't. I only read the recent history of the company, and it never occurred to me to look into the family. Anyway, I'm sorry for bringing up the topic. It's none of my business."

It wasn't. I could simply shut her down, but I didn't.

"Our grandparents are amazing people. And I indulge Grandmother a lot."

"You're a good grandson," Zoey said in a soft voice. She glanced back at the computer. "Let's get started!"

She didn't push, didn't press, or ask anything further, and I appreciated that more than she could know.

We spent the next twenty-five minutes going through one hundred of my emails, and that was a good start. On every email, she made notes about the sender and the project.

At the same time, she walked me through all the papers.

Frankly, it was a miracle that she managed to do all that in twenty-five minutes, but for the first time since I found out she was going to spend some time with the company, I didn't think this was a total waste of time. I could see why this would be beneficial, and I couldn't deny it: I liked being in her presence. She was smart, witty, and definitely didn't shy away from going toe to toe with me.

"All right, Colton, I have a flag system set up in different colors. Over the next few weeks, I'll monitor your inbox and sort it according to priorities in this folder right here." She pointed to the left of the screen. "How does that sound? That should shave some time off your workload while getting you to address the most important topics in a prompter manner."

I got another whiff of her perfume. Now I was obsessing over it. It was a honey smell combined with something more, but what was it? I didn't recognize it.

"That sounds good," I said.

"I also think there's some potential in reducing the number of email responses. I mean, you come into the office anyway, and some of these things are more efficiently discussed in person."

I narrowed my eyes. "No. Going to someone's office is pointless. A lot of time is wasted with small talk."

She glanced away, but I was certain she was suppressing a smile. "Not a people person, huh?"

"Not one bit," I admitted.

"Good. All right, then! I think we're done. Thank you for your time."

"Which ran up to half an hour. Not twenty minutes."

Zoey smiled sheepishly. It was an adorable look on her. "I'm a good negotiator, am I not?"

"What if I had something important planned?"

"You didn't. I checked your calendar. I'm respectful of your time, Colton, and the work you do. Really, I'm not the enemy here."

"I'm starting to accept that."

"Yeah," she laughed. "Accept it. Okay, well, I guess it's progress, so I'm going to take it. Now, where were we? You owe me one, right? Because of your grandmother's comments?"

"Yes," I replied, wondering why she was bringing it up again.

"So I can ask anything, and you'll agree?"

"No, that's not how this works."

"I knew I shouldn't have pushed my luck," she murmured.

"What do you want?" I asked. I figured she probably wanted to leave earlier or maybe take a day off, but her request took me by complete surprise.

"I'd like to see your lab."

Chapter Seven
Colton

"Why?" I asked, standing straighter and rolling my chair a few inches away. I couldn't think straight. That damn perfume was messing with my senses and my mind.

"Because I think it will help me understand how you think. I've never worked with a CEO before who was also a scientist. A lot of your emails deal with your lab work."

"I don't allow many people in my lab."

She ran a hand through her hair. "I'm not going to give away any company secrets, Colton. I just think it would help me help you, but if you insist that it's not something you want to do..."

I abruptly rose from my chair. "Let's go."

"Wow, that was fast." She jumped to her feet. "Let's go before you change your mind."

There was a risk of that. Very few people had ever been inside the lab. It was a place where I could simply be quiet with my thoughts just as much as it was a place of work for me. Sometimes I did non-research work there too.

I led her out of the office. She walked in front of me, and I drank in the way her ass and hips swayed. She looked delicious in those high heels.

She's here to help you manage the workload, Colton, and that's it. Don't mess things up.

I needed to have a serious chat with my grandmother. She couldn't go around saying stuff like that. Apparently, her words got stuck in my brain, and I was thinking things I had no business thinking.

Maybe 5 percent of my employees had ever stepped inside the lab. There was simply no need for them to do so. The research facilities were on the second floor, and all the scientists had their own private work areas. There was rarely a need for anyone to come into mine.

I activated the biometric security with my retina, and the door opened. Out of reflex, I took the white coat from the hook, then put it back.

"Do you need to put that on? Do you need to give me something for protection?" Zoey asked.

"No, that was just a reflex."

She looked around the room. "I was expecting something different."

I laughed. "I think most people would when they think about a lab. This is where I do all of my research work, sometimes even other types of work."

"How come none of your other brothers got involved in biotech?" she asked.

"I was the only one with an interest. Besides, Whitley Industries is large enough that we needed all of my brothers to cover each company. And my half brothers too."

She glanced from the whiteboard to me. "Half brothers?"

I scrutinized her. She was genuinely curious. "Yes. I've got three."

"Would you prefer to change the topic?"

"That obvious?"

"Your tone just got more clipped. You've suddenly got about 5,000 percent more frown lines. If that's not a sign, then I don't know what is. So, let me see if I've got this right. In case I don't find you in your office, I should come here and search for you?"

"Or you can just text me."

"You've got a signal in this bunker?"

I nodded. "Yes. I don't like to be cut off from the world. Sometimes I spend hours here. If something happened to my grandparents, or there's an emergency, I need to be available."

Her features softened. She came up next to me at the lab table, putting both her hands on the edge and leaning slightly forward, glancing around the room. From that position, I had a good view of her from above. Without even trying, I could see down her shirt, and she looked amazing.

I quickly snapped my gaze away. Fucking hell, I needed to get myself under control. I simply couldn't lust after Zoey. I wasn't my father.

She turned around, sitting against the edge of the lab table and crossing her arms over her chest, which pushed her breasts upward.

I drew in a sharp breath. She glanced at me, but I didn't look away this time. All thoughts blurred. I didn't care about my rules. Hell, I couldn't even remember them at the moment. All I wanted was to taste her, capture her mouth, possess it. I tilted forward, and she parted her lips, eyes wide with surprise.

The second my lips connected with hers, she opened up to me.

Fucking hell, I needed this. I needed her.

Her mouth was warm and inviting, and I couldn't get enough. She tasted amazing. The sounds she made were downright delicious. Her moans were low, but they vibrated through my body, going straight to my cock. I was going to get hard if I kept kissing her, yet I couldn't stop. I wanted to deepen the kiss and increase her pleasure. The more I explored her, the more I wanted to keep doing it.

A groan tore through me, though I wasn't sure if it was hers or mine. I put a hand on her waist, moving slightly upward, brushing my thumb on the lower edge of her bra. She rewarded me with the most delicious moan and then gasped, pulling her hand back. I swallowed hard, looking at her.

"Colton," she murmured.

"Zoey."

"I don't know what to say."

"I don't usually do this."

"What, kiss women in your lab? Is this your secret spot?"

I took a step back. "No, I've never brought a woman here."

She narrowed her eyes. "I'm tempted to tease you that that sounds like a line, but I'm sensing that you're really getting upset. You just gave me a smoking-hot kiss, yet all those frown lines are right back where they were before."

"Zoey." I moved closer to her again. "I don't do this."

"Yes, well, we all do things we're not supposed to," she murmured.

I wanted to explain, but the words didn't come easily to me. I wasn't used to having to explain myself to others. Usually I did as I pleased and didn't care what others thought about me, but I didn't want her to think I was an asshole. "Do you have plans for tonight?"

"That escalated quickly."

"That's not what I meant." She was too full of sass, but I couldn't deny that I liked it. "Why don't I take you out to dinner and explain?"

"Why you're still brooding despite the smoking-hot kiss?" She grinned. I had the feeling that nothing could deter her. I'd never met someone who simply rolled with the punches like Zoey, joking at every turn. "Unless you want to have your ass kicked by my brothers, tonight's not a good night."

"Why not?" I asked.

"I'm going out with them for drinks. They wouldn't take it lightly if I cancel at the last minute, and especially not if I do that because I want to get down and dirty with my newest client."

My cock twitched on the word *dirty*. I drew in a sharp breath and then kissed her again. I needed another taste. This was even more delicious than the one before.

She pressed herself into me, putting her hand on my shoulder and running it up until she reached my neck, then dug her fingers into the back of my head and groaned. I realized she was pushing herself forward on her toes so she could reach me better. She was much smaller than me.

I lifted her off her feet, putting her on the lab desk and spreading her thighs open, then stepped closer to her. Something tore, and then she gasped, pulling back.

"Holy shit." I stepped backward, and she jumped right off the table. "That's my skirt." She ran her hand over her thigh. "It's okay. Just a small tear at the seam."

"I'm sorry about that," I said. "I didn't realize."

"No problem," she said. "No one's ever kissed me so hard that I forgot what I was doing. That makes you the first one."

I swallowed hard, barely keeping myself from pinning her against the table.

"Let me make it up to you," I insisted.

"Oh, you will, don't worry. And if you forget, I'll promptly remind you, but right now I really have to go. I need to change, or my brothers will ask what's wrong with my skirt."

"I'll walk you to the elevator."

She beamed. "There's no need for that. Besides, you look like you're having dangerous ideas."

"Fucking dangerous," I confirmed as she backed toward the door.

"See?" She opened the door. "Good night, Colton."

"Good night, Zoey."

Chapter Eight
Zoey

I was meeting Dean and Alex at a bar on Kingston Street, and I texted them to let them know I was coming twenty minutes late. I had to go home and change; I knew I couldn't pass off the idea to my brothers that ripped clothes was a fashion choice.

At home, I quickly changed into pants and put on comfortable flat shoes. My feet were aching from wearing heels all day. Then I Ubered to our meeting place. I could have taken my bike, but I was going to have a drink or two, and I knew for a fact that my balance would be affected.

When I stepped inside the pub, I glanced around slowly, searching for my brothers. Dean waved at me from the corner opposite the bar. Alex held their two drinks and had already ordered my favorite margarita. I practically ran toward them.

"Hey, nugget," Alex said. That was his nickname for me, since I was the youngest in the household. He'd called me that when I was one year old, and it stuck. I didn't mind it.

I kissed them both and gave them hugs as well.

"I can't believe they're already making you work overtime," Dean said.

Alex cocked a brow. "Knowing our sister, no one's making her. She's volunteering."

"You've got to take it easier," Dean insisted.

I took a sip of my margarita before putting it back down. "I didn't work too late. I just wanted to go home and change. I had a mishap."

"What happened?" Dean asked.

I could have just avoided the topic or made something up, but I was bursting at the seams to share this with someone.

"Well, funny thing. Colton was showing me around his lab. One thing led to another, and he kissed me. Then things escalated, and... well, I forgot I was wearing a tight skirt, and it ripped."

I looked up from my glass a few seconds later because neither of my brothers were reacting. Their expressions were almost comical. Dean's mouth was agape. Alex was blinking rapidly and shaking his head slightly, like he was still trying to process what I said.

"You what?" Alex inquired.

Now Dean shook his head. "You're pulling our legs, right?"

"That's the same Colton with the reputation of being a hard-ass?" Alex asked slowly.

I nodded. "Yep, the same. Turns out the man can kiss like nobody's business."

Dean straightened up. "What the fuck? He cannot take advantage of you."

I tilted my head. "How did you even come to that conclusion?"

"He's your boss."

"No, technically he's my client, and I was very much into the kiss. I mean, obviously he took me by surprise, but..."

My brothers exchanged a glance.

"I've got no idea what to tell you," Alex said.

I heaved out a breath, taking another sip. This was one of those moments when I wished I had a sister or a woman as a best friend. Some things really were best discussed with another female.

"Sorry, I didn't want to make you feel awkward," I said. "I just had to share it with someone, and you two are... here."

"Now, doesn't that make you feel special?" Dean asked.

Alex was silent for a few seconds, taking a sip of his drink.

"So you're now going out with him?" he asked finally.

My eyes widened, and I held up a hand. "Whoa, hold your horses, Alex. We just kissed. We didn't talk about anything else, although he did ask if he could take me out tonight. I told him he would risk you kicking his ass if he did that."

"We might do it anyway," Dean said, "on principle."

"Just so he knows he shouldn't mess around with you," Alex added.

I winked at them. "I'll let you know if that's necessary."

Dean drummed his fingers on his glass.

I pointed at him. "You're sitting on something. Spill it."

He grabbed the glass, taking a huge drink. I knew he was just buying time. "I don't know, Zoey. Do you think that's smart, going out with a client?"

I bit my lip. Dean was never one to rain on my parade. I knew if he voiced that doubt, it meant he was seriously worrying.

I frowned. "I don't know. There's no rule or clause against it... but on the other hand, there is common sense."

"Yep," Alex quipped. "I agree with Dean."

"Oh, you two. I don't know why I told you."

Alex grinned. "Because we're your brothers and you like to stump us."

I laughed. "It's true. You should have seen your faces."

Dean cleared his throat. "But in all seriousness, you don't think this could bite you in the ass?"

"Dean, you always overthink stuff. We just kissed. There's a chance we're going to pretend nothing happened. I don't know. It was a spur-of-the-moment thing."

I decided to change the subject. "Do you think we've got a chance in hell of seeing our parents anytime soon?"

"We could meet Mom and Dad somewhere in Europe," Alex said.

"That's a great idea," I said. "I think they'd be happy if we went to one of their galleries."

I had to review my account to see if I could afford an overseas ticket. If I bought it well in advance, maybe I could find a deal. I was making good money and had a decent nest egg. But growing up the way we did, I always had a deep fear that I might end up without any money at all.

"Do we know if Mom and Dad are actually selling anything?" Alex asked.

I took another swig of margarita as Dean cleared his throat. "I asked them, and they avoided the topic."

"Do you think they might need help?" I inquired.

Alex shrugged. "Could be. You know how these things go. Everyone thinks that if your stuff is in galleries, you're making bank. But most of the paintings just move from one gallery to the next. That doesn't put money in their pockets."

We knew that well. When we were growing up, our parents struggled to make ends meet. They held down small side jobs while they tried to achieve a breakthrough with their art. We got evicted many times.

As kids, I'd shared a room with Dean and Alex right up until they left home. I respected Mom and Dad for never losing their passion, but it did make life more difficult. Now we were all in a position to pitch in and help whenever they needed it. My brothers had solid, well-paying jobs.

"And they don't always tell us stuff," Alex said.

"I can try and get it out of them, then. I think I might just offer to pay for their next hotel or something," Dean said.

Out of all of us, he was the best one at finding ways to help our parents without them realizing what he was actually doing. They never said if they needed money or not, but we liked to help whenever we could.

"All right, so we've talked about our parents and about me and my crazy life. What's up with you two?" I asked.

"Work's fine," Dean said quickly. He was an investment banker, so work was taking up most of his life. "I might have started seeing someone."

"Might?" Alex asked.

Dean glowered at him. "I'll share details at some point."

"How can you not be sure?" Alex said.

"Hey, stop badgering him. We each go at our own pace," I said. "And not everyone lets their client kiss them until their skirt falls apart at the seams—quite literally."

Alex shook his head before saying, "Dang, you're making me blush. Well, *I* am dating someone."

"Since when?" I asked, perplexed.

"It started last week."

He sounded so confident that I wondered if he was going to introduce her to us soon.

I stayed with my brothers until late into the evening. Then they waited until I got into an Uber before calling their own. They always did that whenever we stayed out late. I was a little bit tipsy, since I'd ordered a second margarita before we ate our fried chicken, and it went straight to my head.

Dean's words were playing in my mind. Was I stupid for kissing Colton today? It wasn't like I'd planned it, but still, I could have stopped it. My God, I didn't want to. The second his mouth was on mine, I'd completely forgotten where we were and what we were supposed to be doing. I didn't regret it, not at all.

When I arrived home, I took a long shower, and that completely woke me up. Afterward, I pulled my wet hair into a bun. It was my favorite trick to make my hair wavy.

Instead of going to bed, I went to the living room, turning on my TV and putting on one of my favorite Netflix shows about detectives. I had no idea how watching people commit murder and others solve it relaxed me this much, but I could practically feel my legs getting lighter as the scenes grew more intense.

My phone screen lit up just as the lead detective made an important discovery. I pressed Pause, not wanting to miss a moment. I'd forgotten to confirm to my brothers that I'd gotten home and figured it was them and that they were worried. It was probably Alex calling. The number on the screen was unknown, but I answered anyway.

"Hello!"

"Good evening, Zoey." It was Colton.

I shimmied in my seat, grinning. "Hey."

"What are you doing?"

"Watching my favorite TV show. And I'm also trying to order a gift for Mom's birthday, something that will be delivered to Stockholm and not cost an arm and a leg."

"When is her birthday?" he asked.

"Next week. My brothers and I decided to surprise her with a tent. My parents like to go camping. We used to camp a lot as kids too. How about you?"

Wow. I had no idea why I'd just told him all that.

"We never did that. Although, my half brothers did mention once that Dad took them camping."

His voice was a bit tight. Crap, how had I stumbled straight into an obviously bad memory for him?

"Do you get along with your half brothers?" I asked.

"I'm trying to," he said. "I'm not doing a very good job."

"Are they in Boston?"

"Yes. They grew up in Maine, but after they finished college, my grandparents asked if they wanted to move here. They manage some of the branches of Whitley Industries."

"So each of your brothers and half brothers is running a branch of Whitley Industries?"

"Yes. Jake runs Whitley Advertising. Cade, the coffee branch. Spencer, the publishing one. And Gabe covers the distillery, which he expanded by leaps and bounds. And of my half brothers, Nick is running a very successful fitness and sports chain. Maddox designs office spaces. And Leo runs a security company. But I'm not very close to them."

There was a lot of respect in his voice when he spoke about his half brothers' accomplishments.

"Do you *want* to be closer to them?" I asked.

He seemed to hesitate again. "I think it's unfair for me to hold resentment toward them. After all, it wasn't their fault any more than it was ours. My other brothers, especially Gabe, but also Cade and Spencer, have a much closer relationship with them. It's just me and Jake who have had a harder time, but Jake is coming around. They're good people, and that's all that matters. It's important to my grandparents that we all get along."

I thought it was very endearing that this grump who was used to running everything with an iron fist and everyone bending to his will was so hell-bent on pleasing his grandparents.

"I think your grandparents are very blessed with all of you," I said.

"Grandmother likes you. And she is very rarely wrong about people."

"I see. So that's why you're warming up to me?"

He let out a growl. I laughed.

"All right, I need to get back to my show," I told him. "It's gotten to a really good part."

"Am I distracting you?"

"Yes, you are."

"I wanted to hear your voice," he said. "Make sure we're on the same page."

My heart rate accelerated, but I decided to play it cool. "About what?"

He hesitated before murmuring, "Everything."

Oh dear God. That one word was so loaded.

"We are," I said even though I wasn't exactly sure what I meant. When he didn't reply, I said, "Good night, Colton."

"Enjoy the show."

I sighed as I disconnected the call. Then I noticed a message.

Colton: I wish you hadn't left the lab.

My pulse went faster. I hovered with my fingers over the screen for a few seconds before answering.

Zoey: Why? What else did you plan to do to me?

I saved his number quickly. Just as I finished, another message popped up.

Colton: So many things.

I crossed my legs, already feeling an ache form between them.

Colton: I meant what I said. I don't do this. I've never taken a woman there before.

Zoey: I believe you.

Colton: I still owe you an explanation.

I frowned. *What for?*

Colton: Are you free Monday evening?

Zoey: Yes.

Colton: I can't wait to see you.

My face exploded into a grin. I couldn't wait either.

CHAPTER NINE

ZOEY

The second I sat down on Monday and opened my computer, I went into Colton's schedule and frowned. It was much fuller than I remembered from last week. Actually, last week he'd had multiple meetings every day. Now he just seemed to be in one meeting from morning until late in the evening each day. I was supposed to go in his office at nine, but I didn't see an opening now.

I grabbed my phone to text him and found I already had one from him.

Colton: Change of plans. The production company is here to finalize some details, so I'll be meeting with them the whole week. Dinners too. Sorry. I was looking forward to our nine o'clock meeting.

Zoey: My tactics are growing on you, hmm?

Colton: YOU are growing on me. I wanted us to pick up where we left off on the phone.

Zoey: Not where we left off in your lab?

Colton: That comes later. I was looking forward to spending time with you.

What was that feeling in my chest? Oh yeah, my heart was sighing.

The rest of the day was extremely busy, and I didn't get to see Colton at all. But our collaboration was coming along. I was diligently reading through his inbox every day. Most of the email senders were the same people, which made it easy.

The other part of my job was to implement communication and organizational best practices that would help the company as a whole long term. I got an idea of who the key players were and who needed more instructions than others, but I was taking everything one step at a time. I identified that one of the easiest ways to process paperwork was to install digital signature software.

I went straight to HR with that idea.

"Oh, we have one company-wide," Sandra said. "Except for Colton."

"How come?"

"I pitched it to him once, and he seemed completely disinterested."

The corners of my mouth twitched. "All right, I'll work with him on it."

She smiled. "I love having you here. You can be the bad guy."

I laughed. "Yeah, that's usually when most people like consultants. They can blame everything on us. I don't mind taking that role."

I heard his voice for the first time that week on Tuesday afternoon, but he was flanked by a group of people, so there wasn't much I could do. But on Wednesday I saw my chance when I heard him go to his office. I popped in right away.

"Colton," I said in the most professional voice I could muster.

He hadn't even sat down yet and was in the process of rolling up one of his sleeves. He looked tired. But somehow, exhausted Colton was sexy as hell to me. He looked up at me, and his mouth curled into a smile. I felt victorious.

"Zoey!"

"I won't take too much of your time."

He tilted his head. "Pity."

I felt my cheeks heat up. "Listen, the whole company's got digital signature. Yours is the only one that's missing."

"I think Sandra might have brought it up at some point."

"Yes. There isn't much for you to do. I'll set everything up, and then I'll just need your actual signature."

"Just my signature?"

"Yes." I was sure I was winning him over.

This was one of my strong suits. Before I pitched an idea, I thought about what the other person could possibly have against it, and then I tackled those points first. I knew that for Colton, it was important not to waste any time filling out forms or whatever. I was sure that Sandra would have done the same thing I was about to do, but it was all about presenting it to him the right way.

He nodded. "Fine."

"Colton," a man's voice called from the corridor.

I blinked, shocked. "Wow, you already need to go back in the meeting room?"

"Yes." He frowned, coming closer to me. "How is everything around here? How are people treating you?" he asked as he closed the door to the office.

I sucked in a breath. It felt like we were miles away from everything going on outside his office.

"Good. Everyone's cooperative." I smiled, deciding to lighten the situation. "Even the CEO everyone warned me about."

"Hmm," he replied. "Are you warming up to the CEO?"

I grinned. "More than that. Let's see... Well, he kissed the panties off me."

He growled, "Zoey."

I pressed my lips together. "Oops, I slipped up."

He looked at my lips intently. "What are you doing tonight?"

I bit the inside of my cheek. "I have a long-distance call with my parents. I haven't talked to them in a while, but I can postpone it."

"No, take the call. The group will probably want to go out for drinks anyway. Who knows how long that's going to take."

We were both silent for a bit.

"You smell delicious," Colton said.

I bit my lip again.

"It's my favorite perfume," I said. "Honey by Marc Jacobs. Although it's running out. I've been thinking about trying something else, though." Realizing I was rambling, I took a breath to get myself together. "Anyway, I won't keep you."

"Colton." The voice calling from the corridor was stronger.

"I'll see you around, Zoey," he said right before opening his door, then slipping out.

I was used to teasing and rattling others, but I wasn't used to the reverse.

On Thursday, I found a package on my desk. I carefully took off the wrapping paper.

It was a perfume. Black Opium by Yves Saint Laurent.

I sprayed it on my wrists, inhaling it. Wow, the scent was strong. It smelled floral but also had strong hints of vanilla. I loved it, and I knew who'd sent it even though there was no note. My heart rate picked up as I texted Colton, sending him a picture of the perfume.

Zoey: Thank you. When did you have time to get it?

He answered right away.

Colton: Last night, after drinks, I went to a department store, and this scent reminded me of you.

Heat pooled between my thighs. I got up from my chair, pacing up and down my office.

Colton: How was catching up with your parents?

I grinned. He was asking me about that? Aww, I didn't see that coming.

Zoey: It was good. They're both so happy. They said they're probably going to extend their gallery tour. I'm happy for them, of course, but I miss them a lot.

Colton: You're damn cute. About that perfume... I want you to wear it.

I wanted to tease him that I didn't like to do as I was told, usually just the opposite, but I did want to wear it.

Unfortunately, I didn't get to see Colton that day at all to prove I had it on.

The next morning, I sprayed it on my wrist and neck. I was getting addicted to the seductive smell.

As I was sifting through Colton's emails, I found one that was from a sender I'd never seen before: Maddox Whitley.

I frowned. Whitley? That meant he was related to Colton. It wasn't one of his brothers, though. Then I remembered it was one of his half brothers' names. That meant it could be something personal, not related to Whitley Biotech, so I didn't open it.

I clicked on it with the intention of flagging it as personal but ended up opening it accidentally and saw the first line.

Hey, guys, I'm forwarding this email I got from Dad.

He'd sent it to a number of recipients. Crap! I really hadn't wanted to snoop.

I put Colton's email aside, focusing on completing the plans for the digital signature.

At nine o'clock, I heard his voice in the hallway. For once, he seemed to be alone. He had a meeting in five minutes, but what I needed from him would only take three, so I darted out of my office, careful not to make my steps too large because I was wearing a snug dress and didn't need this one ripping too.

I knocked as I opened the door, and he quickly looked up.

"Zoey," he said. "Come on in. Close the door."

"Um, you only have a few minutes until the meeting starts."

"You're right."

I looked at him and said, "Listen. Two things. One, I'll finalize everything for that digital signature today. I'll need your actual signature later on."

"I can sign now."

"No, it's better if we do it during the last step."

He nodded. "Okay. And the second thing is?"

"Did you check your email this morning?"

"Not yet."

"There's one from Maddox Whitley, and I was wondering if I should make a folder for personal emails. I'd recommend automatically forwarding personal emails to another email address. I can set it up if you give me a list of personal contacts."

His expression changed instantly, the corners of his mouth turning downward. He took out his phone, staring at the screen. His nostrils flared, and then he looked up at me.

"Yes, that's a private email. No need to label it. Maddox doesn't have my actual private email address, which is why he sent it to the office, but I'll sort it out."

How could his mood have changed so fast? I could practically feel him turning into a grump. An alarm clock sounded, and I startled.

"Sorry, that's my phone. A reminder that I need to go to the meeting room. I'll catch up with you later."

As he made his way past me, he stopped in his tracks. "You're wearing the perfume I gave you."

I swallowed hard. "Yes, I am."

"You've been wearing it all week?"

"Yes."

He drew in a deep breath. "You smell delicious."

"You should go." I murmured.

"Yes, I fucking should. Before I close this door and kiss you against it."

I stood rooted in my spot, blushing even after he left.

Chapter Ten

Colton

I'd always been aware of my strengths and weaknesses. I dedicated myself to things that relied solely upon my strengths, and that was one of the reasons I was so successful at everything I did. While working with Zoey, I started to realize that my team had always been left to pick up the pieces when it came to my biggest weakness: organization. I already had a much clearer overview of my inbox.

Zoey insisted that the most efficient way to deal with the emails was to open and read a message and immediately decide what to do with it versus letting them pile up. That had been my modus operandi for years, and the truth was, I never circled back. Emails remained at the bottom of my inbox, and someone else picked up the slack. Today I managed my inbox in the morning.

The one area where I wasn't making headway with delegating was with lab work. My team of scientists had been begging me for years to delegate more to them, but I just couldn't.

After yet another meeting, I looked at Maddox's email again. I hadn't read Dad's actual message.

Hey, guys, I'm forwarding this email I got from Dad. I haven't spoken to him in years, so I'm not sure why he's contacting me at all. As is obvious from the text, he needs financial help. I haven't

replied yet, and I think we should decide together how to react to this.

I minimized the message, intending to completely ignore the situation and just go about my work. My brothers would figure out what to do about it. The less I saw or heard, the better. I couldn't care less what they decided.

Ten minutes later, I could no longer ignore it. Damn it, I wanted to know what this was about. How the hell did he even dare to write to any of us, asking for help? And why didn't Maddox simply delete his email?

I knew I was being unreasonable. Maddox had actually handled this well. It was a mark of loyalty to the family that he hadn't dealt with this behind our backs. Instead, he wanted us all to know about it and decide together.

So Maddox hadn't spoken to him in years. That was good to know. I'd always wondered if my half brothers were still in touch with him. I scrolled to see what he wanted.

Hi, Maddox.

This is Dad. I know I haven't reached out in a long time. I wasn't sure if any of you wanted to hear from me at all. You all knew more or less where I was. My business profile is online. I assume that since no one contacted me, you all didn't want anything to do with me.

How the fuck did he dare give Maddox shit to make him feel guilty for not keeping in contact? He'd ruined both our families.

Recently, I've attempted a business venture of my own. Unfortunately, it failed, and I've gone into quite a bit of debt. Now, I know all of you are doing well, and it pains me to ask for help. I've exhausted all other options, and this is my last resort. Here is my phone number in case you would like to hear more about this. I'll be waiting for your call.

Father

I immediately deleted the email. Why the fuck hadn't I done that in the first place? Rage built inside me, thrumming through my chest and in my veins. My airways felt obstructed, making it difficult to take a deep breath.

The nerve of him!

I pushed my chair back, getting up and turning to look out the window at the city. The view usually grounded me. It was the quickest way for me to get out of my head, out of my thoughts. Not right now, though.

He'd attempted to build a business again. Had he really not learned anything from the mess he made at Whitley Industries? We were doing well now, but no thanks to him. In fact, we were doing well *despite* him. He'd left these companies in shambles, and it had taken a lot of effort over the years to bring them back on track and turning a healthy profit.

He'd all but destroyed our legacy, and now he wanted money? This was the most insane thing I'd ever heard. I'd never help him, not in a million years, and my brothers had better not either. We didn't want to open that door for him to be in our lives.

I turned my back to the window, glancing at my desk. There were a ton of things I wanted to get through today. I wanted to get back to my finance team, and I had to pull myself together. I sat down, staring at my computer screen, and immediately realized it was no use. I needed to get my mind off this and get in the ring.

Heading out of the office, I stopped by Darla's desk.

"Hey, Colton, we need to change your calendar a bit," she started.

"We'll talk about it later," I said. "I'm heading out."

"Oh. Oh, right." She frowned, looking at the calendar. "But you've still got a few meetings today."

"Cancel tem. I'm going to the boxing ring."

She just nodded. Everyone knew if I canceled a meeting to go to the ring, then shit had hit the fan. They also knew I wasn't to be bothered with phone calls when I was boxing. Darla was a champ for keeping everyone at bay. "All right, consider everything canceled."

"Great. I appreciate that."

<hr />

Zoey

It was six o'clock by the time I finalized everything for the electronic signature. If I got Colton's actual signature before seven o'clock, I could even wrap it up today. Grabbing my iPad, I hurried to his office, but he wasn't there.

Strange. I checked his calendar. He didn't have any meetings scheduled.

I texted him quickly.

Zoey: Hey, where are you? I just need two minutes to get your signature, and then I can finalize the digital signature process.

I waited for a few minutes before checking the phone again. Not only hadn't he answered, but he hadn't even seen it.

Damn it. I really wanted to make this happen today.

I decided to ask his assistant where he was. She had her own office right next to his, and I knocked at the open door. Darla was in her fifties with a straight bob. Her hair was jet-black, and the style looked great on her.

"Hey, Darla."

She looked up and smiled. "Zoey, how can I help you?"

"Do you know where Colton is? I desperately need his signature."

"He's gone training. He won't be back today. Can I help you? I was about to leave as well."

Crap. I bit the inside of my cheek, and Darla went back to her laptop.

I moved closer to her desk. "Any chance you can tell me where he's training?"

She glanced up at me. "Trust me, you don't want to get on his bad side. That's the only place where he completely disconnects from work."

"I want to finalize it today, but I can't do that without his signature." I was finally making headway with Colton. I didn't want to risk him closing up completely and not giving me the time of day. "So, you know, what comes first, the chicken or the egg? Why don't we do this? You tell me where to go, and I promise I won't tell him that you gave me the address."

"Girl, I'm not worried about myself. Everyone knows where he's training. He just doesn't like to be bothered there."

"I'll take my chances," I said.

"All right. This is the address." She wrote it on a yellow Post-it.

I snapped a picture of it with my phone so I had a backup in case I lost it. "Thanks. You're a lifesaver." I sent her an air kiss before I hurried out of her office.

I took an Uber there. I tried to limit my use of the service because it wasn't great for my pocketbook, but I could put this one on the company's bill.

I hadn't bothered to Google the address, assuming it was a fancy fitness club or something, so I was shocked when I arrived in front of a building that looked a bit decrepit. If I hadn't known this was the address, I would have walked right past it. It wasn't very inviting. There was a sign with the name above the door, but it was small enough that you could easily miss it if you didn't know what was here.

I stepped inside and blinked, double-checking the address. Surely I was in the wrong place. This wasn't a fitness center. This was a boxing club or something.

I was about to call Darla when I spotted Colton at the far end of the room and nearly dropped my iPad. He was in the ring, wearing boxing gloves and punching his opponent with precision.

My feet carried me forward. I needed to get closer. Part of my brain still thought this wasn't Colton but simply someone who looked like him. It was impossible for this CEO and scientist to also be boxing. Somehow all those things couldn't be used to describe the same person.

I looked at him, transfixed, keeping my iPad close to my chest. There was no one else in the room except the two of them. They didn't even notice me come in.

Holy shit, Colton's body was insanely hot and fit. There was a tattoo over his torso, he had a six-pack, and his shoulders, arms, and thighs were perfectly sculpted. Even his back was sexy.

I had no idea how much time passed until his opponent took three steps back and said, "Colton, you always give me a run for my money." Then he noticed me. "Oh, hello. I'm Theo. How may I help you?"

Colton's head snapped in my direction. "Zoey." His voice was even rougher than usual, probably from all the exertion.

"I work with Colton," I told Theo, proud that I'd found my voice.

Colton walked toward me, and I swallowed hard. How could he be so damn hot? The ink on his chest was amazing. Sweat trickled down his skin, and somehow that made him seem even sexier.

"I'm going to change," Theo announced. "Colton, you're good?"

"Sure." He looked at me.

"You know how to lock up in case you stay here longer than I do," Theo said.

Colton nodded at him but didn't take his eyes off me.

"Um," I fumbled, turning the iPad around. I needed to stay professional. "I've got everything ready for the digital signature, but I need your actual signature to finalize it today."

I handed him the iPad pencil. He took it from my hand, brushing the backs of my fingers with the tips of his, and a tremor went through me. His skin was slightly humid. I crossed my legs and sucked in a breath. He handed me back the iPad. Clutching it to my chest, I looked up.

"You're the first person from the office to come here," he stated.

"What did you do? Forbid everyone to come here? Why do they know the address, then?"

"For emergencies. They know I don't want to be disturbed here. I come to blow off steam."

My shoulders sagged. "This morning bothered you that much?"

I was doing *such* a good job. I was maintaining eye contact, and I hadn't let my eyes drop to his chest even once since we started talking, but God, I wanted to. More than that, I wanted to reach out and touch him.

His nostrils flared, but I didn't think he was angry.

"I'll change and shower quickly. And I believe I owe you dinner."

I laughed nervously. "That sounds like a chore."

He swallowed hard. "That couldn't be further from the truth. It would be a pleasure."

"I'll stay here and initiate the process of... Never mind, I'll just do my job. Take your time."

After Colton disappeared through a door—probably to the locker room—I quickly accessed the platform, uploading the picture with his signature. Within five minutes I'd sent it in. Then I had nothing left to do.

I put the iPad in my bag, looking around. A door opened, and I sucked in a breath, but Colton didn't come out. It was his sparring partner.

"Zoey, I need to get home to the family. There are no more clients scheduled today. Colton knows how to close up the place. Tell him to do it, okay?"

"Sure," I said.

The guy looked at me with a knowing smile. *Oh God. Don't blush now, Zoey.* Could he tell I wasn't here just for work?

"Sorry to bust in like that earlier. I just really needed Colton in person," I explained.

"Yeah, yeah." He winked at me. "You two have fun."

What did he mean? Did Colton tell him something? Was it written on my face that I wanted him?

It was a good thing Colton would come out fully clothed because I didn't think I could be around him if he was naked, sweaty, and all tatted up and not jump his bones. Forget kissing. I would *literally* jump him.

He came out a few minutes later. His hair was wet. His shirt looked different from this morning, like it was a bit too small and had stretched. But even though he was fully clothed and I couldn't even see a hint of his tattoo, the image of him shirtless was dancing behind my eyes. I couldn't forget it.

"Theo left. He said you should close up."

He nodded. "Sure."

"How come you've got the keys to this place?" I asked.

"I'm one of his oldest clients, and we're very good friends. I helped him set this place up. In turn he gives me the keys. That way I can come even when there's no one here."

"Who do you box with when that happens?"

"A punching bag. It's a very efficient workout."

"I'll say," I replied.

He chuckled. "Would you like me to take off my shirt so you can see that tattoo better? You couldn't take your eyes off it earlier."

I sucked in a breath, nearly swallowing my tongue. "I, um... well, okay, so that was obvious."

"Yeah, it was."

I was just becoming more awkward by the second, which was so unlike me.

"I didn't think anything could stump you," he replied.

"Neither did I, but apparently you have special skills." I frowned. "Look, sorry for ambushing you here."

"Don't worry about it, okay? I appreciate you taking this stuff seriously. But it's late. You don't need to put in overtime."

I shrugged, pushing a strand of hair behind my ear. "I usually don't, but seeing you motivates me."

"Oh?" he asked, cocking a brow.

I rolled my eyes. "I didn't mean it like that. I meant that I've never seen anyone who puts so much effort into what he does. It's inspiring."

"Some call it obsessive."

"Those things aren't mutually exclusive," I quipped.

He glanced at the bag I'd put on one of the benches and then back up at me. "What are you in the mood for?"

"Pizza, maybe," I suggested.

I had so many questions for him. When did he start doing this? Why did he need to blow off steam after an email from his half brother?

He looked at his phone and said, "All right, I don't know any of the restaurants around here."

Still scrolling on his phone, he took my bag from the bench. Putting it on my shoulder, he brushed his thumb across my clavicle. My lips parted, and I exhaled sharply. Colton looked up from his phone, zeroing in on my mouth. He repeated the motion before running his thumb up and down my neck.

How could that turn me on so quickly? I felt as if he was touching my nipples or drawing a straight line from my navel down to my clit.

I swallowed hard, trying to breathe in deeply.

"So damn sexy," he said.

I was certain he knew exactly what he was doing to me. He knew I was a puddle of mush at his feet, that he could do whatever he wanted and I'd be fine with it.

He put an arm around my waist, pulling me closer. It was all the invitation I needed. I immediately put my hands on his rib cage and moved them up. I'd been dying to touch his chest, and it didn't disappoint. It was even harder than I imagined. He smelled like a pine-scented shower gel. I needed him to kiss me more than I needed anything in my life. And he did, but not in the way I expected.

He lowered his mouth on me, placing small kisses from my earlobe to the corner of my mouth. He groaned, pressing me even closer to him. Then he kissed me ferociously with the same passion I'd seen in the ring. He gave me everything he had, and yet I wanted more. I wanted all of his passion, and I wanted it right now.

I was often impulsive, but not reckless. But with Colton, I wanted it all.

Chapter Eleven

Colton

Colton

She tasted even better than I remembered. I was hungry for her. I'd been starved for days. Ever since I'd kissed her in the lab, all I could think about was doing it again. I wanted to kiss her until her entire body shook and she begged for more. I wanted to give her everything.

Earlier today, I barely restrained myself from shutting the door to the office and kissing her against it. But I knew if I did that, there would be no stopping. I'd never let her out. I'd bend her over the desk and have her right there.

Now, I kissed down her neck slowly despite being desperate. I wanted to feel every single reaction. I wanted to learn her body and file away what turned her on.

A small tremor coursed through her, but it wasn't nearly enough. I wanted to make her come.

I moved down to her chest, tracing the neckline of her dress with my mouth, going from her right clavicle down toward her cleavage. I dipped the tip of my tongue just a fraction of an inch, and she gasped. Smiling against her breasts, I started kissing my way back up.

"Colton," she murmured.

I traced her neck with my mouth, up to her jaw, and then I straightened up, taking her in. Her eyes were shut tightly. Her breath was shaky, and so was her body.

Slowly, she opened her eyes, looking up at me.

"I want you, Zoey. So damn much."

"I want you too."

Completely forgetting where we were, I kissed her so hard that she stumbled. Walking her backward until I reached the nearest pole, I pressed her against the metal, and we kissed and kissed until she moaned against my mouth.

She put her hands on my chest, and for a split second, I thought she was going to curl her hands around my neck. Then I felt a tug at my buttons.

Fuck me! She wants to take off my clothes.

I only vaguely registered that we were at the ring. This wasn't the right time, and it sure as hell wasn't the right place. But none of that mattered.

She moved her hand farther down and placed it on my belt buckle. I stilled. My cock twitched as a groan tore through my chest.

"Zoey, you keep tugging at that and you'll see me lose control."

"Yes, yes. I want you so much."

Need took over at her words, instinct overpowering rational thought. Tonight, I was going to make her mine.

I steeled myself, touching her cheek with the back of my hand.

"Are you sure?" I managed to get out. I didn't want her to regret it.

"Yes." She nodded. "Do you have condoms?"

I nodded before devouring her again. This time, I turned her around. She held the post with both hands as I pushed her hair to one side, kissing the back of her neck. Then I grabbed the zipper of her dress and tugged it all the way down.

"Careful," she said in a teasing tone. "Don't rip this one too."

"Not making any promises." I pushed the dress off her shoulders. It fell to her thighs, and she yanked it all the way down and pulled it off.

I groaned when I noticed what she was wearing. "What are those?" I asked.

"Tights that have a silicon band to stay up. Never mind." She made to push them off, but I stopped her.

"I want to do it," I said. "Straighten up, Zoey." She stood ramrod straight with both her hands on the pole again. She was shuddering slightly.

"Are you cold?" I asked.

"No, not at all."

Fuck, so that was her reaction to me.

While I got rid of her tights, I kissed her ass cheeks, first one and then the other. They were round and taut and fucking perfect. I couldn't get enough of her curves. I kissed up her back, moving my hands on the sides of her body and brushing her bra on the way up. When I stood upright behind her, I unclasped it.

"You're beautiful," I whispered in her ear.

I let the bra drop to the floor and then turned her around, looking down at her. My cock was straining in my pants. As if knowing exactly what I thought, she palmed it over the fabric. I dropped my head back, groaning. I felt her lips on my neck, and then her hands tugged at my belt again. I didn't stop her this time. We both took off our shoes.

I took care of my shirt while she unbuckled the belt, then the button and zipper. I threw the shirt next to us before grabbing my undershirt at the back and tugging it over my head. She yanked my pants off next, and I stepped out of them. Then her hands were on my torso, mapping the ink.

"You went to all that trouble to get dressed earlier," she teased, "and now you're naked again. We should have just started this waaaay earlier."

"I still had to shower."

"Mm," she said. "I quite liked seeing you that sweaty. It was hot."

Smiling, she brought her lips to my chest, twirling her tongue around my nipple. At the same time, she grabbed my cock. It felt like a shock to my system.

But I couldn't lose my control. Not yet. I wanted to explore her.

She went farther down, mapping the ridges and lines to my navel. She moved back up, still pumping her hand up and down my cock, and then I took over. I grabbed both her wrists in one hand, lifting them over her head, holding them against the metal pole.

"I need total control," I told her.

Her eyes widened, her mouth parted, and she simply nodded.

I traced a straight line from her temple down her cheek, biting the lobe of her ear. Letting go of her hands, I moved down her body, wanting to map every inch of her with my fingers and my mouth. I needed to know her body intimately.

She sucked in her belly when I went below her chest. I looked up at her.

Her breathing was quick. "I don't exactly have abs."

"You're fucking beautiful. I love your curves. They're amazing. Fucking sexy. I want you to relax with me, Zoey. Completely."

She exhaled sharply, and her body went lax.

That's it. I didn't want her to think for a second that I didn't like any part of her body. I slowed my pace when I traced my mouth over her belly button, then down to her pubic bone. She tilted her hips slightly. I was going to grant her wish. I pushed down her panties and touched her pussy with my fingers, strumming over her sensitive skin. She was already dripping wet.

I teased her entrance and felt her entire body tense up. Then I put one of her thighs on my shoulder, kneeling in front of her.

"Colton," she murmured.

I was teasing her entrance with my thumb, drawing it up to her clit and then back down. Then I grabbed her ass with both hands and tilted her pelvis slightly upward.

Taking her clit between my lips, I worked it with my mouth and fingers, internalizing her cries of pleasure. Her entire body was vibrating. She was close, I was sure of it; I could feel it in the way her body tensed on every lash of my tongue.

I could make her come like this, but I knew exactly what she needed to intensify her climax. When her cries became louder, I slid two fingers inside her. My cock was so damn painful that I could barely breathe. I curved my fingers inside her, and she went over the edge the next second. She didn't seem to have control over her body anymore.

It was beautiful to watch her surrender to me. Her right leg shook violently. I put both hands on her waist, keeping her steady and safe as I rose to my feet.

"Colton, that was—"

She didn't manage to finish that sentence because I kissed her the next second. She even kissed differently now, after her orgasm. Like her entire body was still processing the pleasure.

She pressed herself into me so my erection was stuck between our bodies. Then she moved up onto her toes and back down onto her heels a few times before I realized she was doing it on purpose.

"Fuck me." I was barely hanging on anyway.

"Where is the condom?" she whispered.

I blindly reached for my pants on the floor. Finding my wallet, I took the condom out, rolled it on, then looked around. I wanted a place for her to be comfortable.

"Let's move to the right."

When we reached the mat section, I grabbed a few towels and spread a bunch of them on the mat. She grinned at me.

"What are you thinking?" I asked her.

"I'll tell you later. Now, get back to what you were doing before. I was thoroughly enjoying it."

Good. I needed to be inside her, but I wanted to make sure she was ready first.

I went to my knees on the mat and pulled her into the same position. Once we were facing each other, I skimmed my hands from her shoulders down to her breasts, touching her nipples. They were like hard little pebbles.

She moaned lightly. "They're so sensitive," she said. "My whole body is."

I lowered one hand between her thighs, intending to wake up her clit again. Then I realized she was soaking wet. Fuck, she was ready. She was more than ready. And so was I.

I lowered her onto her side on the mat so we were still facing each other. Lifting one of her legs with my hand, I propped myself up on an elbow as I teased her clit with the tip of my cock first.

I watched her face as I slid in, inch by inch. She was so damn gorgeous. The look of shock was exquisite, like she couldn't believe that much sensation was possible, and I hadn't even started. I was planning to turn her world upside down tonight.

I liked this position—I could watch her, caress her, touch her body, and pleasure her at the same time. I moved in and out of her with long thrusts. Her inner muscles clenched around me with each one. There was nothing like this feeling in the whole world.

I put a hand on the side of her waist, splayed my fingers on her rib cage, and leaned over her, taking one nipple in my mouth. I licked it as I thrust faster.

"Colton," she exclaimed, then shifted on the mat. It took me a second to realize she wanted to touch herself. I nearly exploded.

"Wait a second, beautiful, and you'll have all the access you want," I said as I moved her so she was on her back.

I put my forearms behind her knees, lifting her ass in the air. Her lower back brushed my thighs, and she circled her breasts with her hands. Then she shut her eyes when I flicked my thumb over her clit, clenching around me so tightly that she nearly pushed me out. I slid in and out, then felt her hand next to mine on her clit: I looked down between us, mesmerized by the sight of her touching herself. Her fingers grazed my cock on every thrust. My entire body was on hyperalert, my muscles tightening while I chased my climax.

I watched with immense satisfaction as pleasure overwhelmed Zoey. She squeezed her eyes shut and rolled her hands into fists at her sides. She was so overwhelmed that she couldn't even bring herself to touch herself anymore. But I was going to make her come hard.

I stilled my movements and rubbed her clit with my thumb in slow circles. When I felt her orgasm rolling in, I began thrusting again. She came even harder, completely unrestrained, crying my name out loud while scratching at the mat. She pressed her heels into the sides of my body. It was almost painful, but I fucking loved it. I pushed in until I felt her relax, and then I stopped fighting my own climax. It took over until I was no longer in control of anything—not my muscles or my mind or my senses. Everything blended. The only thing I was aware of was the incredible sensations coiling through me and the feeling of Zoey's soft skin as I leaned over her.

Still on my knees, I planted my arms beside her shoulders, resting my forehead between her breasts. After I pulled out, she threaded her fingers in my hair. Her breathing was ragged. I wasn't doing any better.

Slowly, our surroundings started filtering in. I lifted my head, glancing at her. She yawned, looking at me with a sated smile. I straightened up. Her skin turned to goose bumps, and she pushed herself into a sitting position, glancing around.

"Well, this was unexpected," she murmured.

"Yes, it was," I admitted.

"I didn't think you'd maul me right here," she teased.

I grinned. "Maul you?"

"Well, what else would you call it? Seducing me?"

I tilted my head. "That was the plan, but you... derailed it. Thank fuck there are no cameras around here."

She gasped, covering her mouth. "I didn't even think about that."

"Don't worry, I did. I would never have exposed you."

She grinned. "First you kiss me in your lab, then you fuck me in the gym."

I leaned over her. "Zoey, you keep saying that and we won't be leaving this place anytime soon."

She laughed. "You aren't even joking, are you?"

"Not one bit."

Chapter Twelve

Colton

Colton

"Let's go freshen up, and then our evening can start," I told Zoey. "It's already off to a good start."

After showering, we dressed quickly.

"Kudos for not ripping off my dress. The zipper is still working," she said. "Why are you looking at me like that?"

I smirked. "You look even sexier than before."

"I have post-sex hair and lips, so yeah."

"Are you hungry?" I asked.

She nodded. "Yes, but I don't feel like going to a restaurant."

"We could go over to my place and order in," I suggested.

She perked up. "I'd like that."

"Then let's go."

"Where do you live?"

"One of the penthouses on top of the building."

"Wait, which building? This one doesn't have many stories."

"No, our office."

Her eyes bulged, and then she quickly looked away. "Okay."

"What?" I asked as we stepped outside the gym, and I locked up. "Did you drive here?"

"No, I Ubered. I figured I could charge it to the company."

"My car's here. Come on."

I watched her as she got in. She was still holding back, I was sure of it. She was ready to throw some sass, and I was going to find out what it was.

Once we were both in the car, I said, "Still waiting."

"For what?"

"For you to tell me why you're so shocked that I live above the office."

She cleared her throat. "When I found out there were penthouses above there, I kept wondering who in their right mind would want to live in an office building. It feels so impersonal."

I frowned. "It's efficient. That way, I don't lose any time commuting. And if I have an idea, I can go straight to the lab and work on it."

"Now I understand why your grandmother was worried about you. The term *workaholic* is thrown around a lot, but I think your picture should be in the dictionary next to the explanation."

"You're even sassier tonight."

"It's probably from the two orgasms," she said with a grin.

A few minutes later, we were entering the garage of my building. Her stomach was rumbling.

"We should have already ordered something," I said.

"Or I can just feast on you while the food comes."

I laughed. "Wait until we're upstairs."

After we got out of the car, she headed to the elevators that went up to the office.

"No, Zoey," I called, stopping her. "The residential elevators are in a different area."

We walked over to the far end of the garage. Stepping inside the elevator, I inserted a special card that would take us directly to my floor.

Zoey gaped. "I've only seen this in movies—people having special cards for the elevator."

"There are only six penthouses, each on a different floor. The cards take us to our respective floors," I explained.

"I feel like I've stepped into an alternate universe. I can't wait to see it."

She was so cute and sexy, and I was way more into her than I should be.

"Wow," she exclaimed when we stepped inside my place. "This is breathtaking."

The penthouse was dimly lit. The lights were activated by motion sensors and gradually lit up as we moved through the room. Since it was completely dark outside, we could see the brilliant Boston skyline through all the windows.

"It's huge. Much bigger than what I needed, but as I said, convenience comes first."

"Colton, I take everything back. I was super judgy. This place is cozy. It doesn't even matter that it's on top of an office building. I don't know why I automatically assumed it would look like a workplace or something. Oh, and you've got pics of your family," she said, pointing at the mantelpiece above the electric fireplace.

The living room was enormous, with two separate sitting areas with leather couches, an integrated home cinema, and a dining area adjacent to it. Everything was done in shades of brown and white. I'd instructed my decorator to only use old wood when possible.

She went straight to the pictures. "Who's this adorable little nugget?"

"Nugget?" I asked. She grinned. "He's my nephew, my brother Spencer's son. Ben."

"Is he the only kid in the family so far?"

"Yeah."

"I bet Ben gets spoiled."

"He's a bit too young for that, but that's the plan."

Her stomach grumbled again.

"Let's order food," I said.

"There's a Chinese place somewhere around here. We've had it delivered a couple of times at the office."

"Go ahead and order," I said, giving her my phone.

She looked at me with wide eyes. "You want me to use your phone?"

"Yes. Since I didn't manage to take you out for dinner, I can at least treat you to Chinese."

She tapped on the screen quickly and then abruptly said, "You've got a notification. I didn't read it or anything." She sounded nervous all of a sudden.

I looked at the phone. "It's one of the apps reminding me of my daily fitness level. You want to add anything to the order?"

"No."

I clicked the green button, adding a portion for me before finalizing the order. "Should be here in twenty minutes." I put the phone in my pocket. "Now, are you going to tell me why you were so nervous?"

"What do you mean?"

"You looked at me like I was an alien when I gave you my phone."

"Right. It's just that... well, most men are cagey with their phone, and it's taboo to even glance at their screen."

"Only if you have something to hide."

She swallowed hard, pushing a strand of hair behind her ear, and glanced away. It was the first time she'd been vulnerable in front of me.

"I guess you're right. You know, I actually broke up with my last ex because he was cheating on me with multiple women. Emphasis on multiple. I found out because I grabbed his phone one morning instead of mine to check the weather, and he had a lot of notifications from Tinder."

"Fuck, that's shitty."

"Yeah, and guess what? He blamed me. For snooping. He was like 'Oh, if you trusted me, you wouldn't have looked.'"

"What the fuck kind of logic is that?" I exclaimed. "Sounds like a guy who doesn't have his shit together."

"He didn't. I felt like I was nothing."

I stepped closer to her, cupping her jaw, "You're an amazing woman." What kind of idiots had she dated who could possibly make her feel like she wasn't important?

"Colton," she murmured, patting the back of my hand. "You're like a puzzle. The more time I spend with you, the more you surprise me."

I lowered my hand, kissing the side of her neck quickly, then her forehead before saying, "Do you want a drink?"

"Do you have wine?"

"I've got a whole fridge of it. You can choose one."

"Did I mention I love this place? Serves me right for being judgy. Do you have a home office?"

"No, I don't want to bring work home, ever."

She scoffed. "So you do have boundaries with work? Ha, the joke's on you because now you brought me home from work."

I growled, pulling her close to me and walking backward with her until I plastered her against the fridge door. "I'm crossing all boundaries when it comes to you, Zoey, but I can't help myself. I've been fighting with myself ever since you stepped into my lab."

"Why?" she whispered.

I caressed her cheek with my fingertips, tracing the contour of her mouth, then swallowed as I stepped back.

"You already know my father had another family."

Her eyes dimmed, and she nodded.

"The other woman was someone he worked with for a while," I continued. She rolled her shoulders back, interlacing her fingers in front of her. "She moved away after a bit, and he always used work as an excuse to fly over there and be with his other family. They lived in Maine—" I shook my head. *Why the hell am I even talking about this? She doesn't need to know all the details.* "Anyway, long story short, I promised myself that I'd never start something with a woman I worked with. And here I am, breaking my rule. I can't help but draw comparisons between me and my father."

"Colton." Her voice shook as she walked to the kitchen island. "I don't know everything that transpired. But even though I've only known you for a short while, I can tell with certainty that you're nothing like your father."

"You can't possibly know that."

She smiled, poking my chest. "Yes, I can. I have a sixth sense when it comes to people, and you are not a jackass. Grumpy and a workaholic, yes, but not a jackass. That's the difference," she said, turning around. "I want that wine." She pointed at a bottle of Maxwell's pinot noir.

"Great choice." I took it out of the fridge. It had two dial controls, with separate temperatures for white and red wine. I immediately uncorked the bottle, then poured it in two glasses.

"To a great evening," she toasted as we clinked glasses.

"For the start of something great. This evening did not go as I'd planned, but I have the rest of it to make it up to you."

She smiled, taking a sip. "Just so you know, I think we're off to a fantastic start."

"You deserve more than sex in a gym, and I'm going to give it to you. I just lost my head completely."

"That is music to my ears," she said. Her stomach grumbled loudly as she took another sip of wine. "This will go straight to my head, but I have a feeling you'll take advantage of me anyway."

"Zoey," I growled.

"I'm totally on board with that, in case you were wondering." She pushed her ass back, straight into my crotch, and then rubbed herself against me briefly. I was already getting semihard.

"Woman, goddamn it. I already mauled you in the gym."

"So you agree?"

"Fuck yes," I said. "It's not very gentlemanly of me."

"No, but it will be so satisfying."

Zoey was something else completely. She loved life and having fun and was determined to enjoy herself every moment. I was sure she'd had her fair share of rough times, too, but she wasn't letting that get her down.

"Tell me more about your family," I said.

"Well, as I told you, there are three of us. I'm the youngest. I've got two older brothers."

"That must have been interesting growing up."

"Oh, it was," she murmured in a soft voice. "The boys are super protective of me."

"I agree with that. If I had a sister, I'd be protective of her as well."

"We're also close because we shared a room for years."

I frowned. "You shared a room?"

"We didn't have much space, so we couldn't each have our own room. My parents wanted to give me their room when I hit puberty, but no way could I let them sleep on the couch. Anyway, we came up with creative solutions so we could have some semblance of privacy. My mother painted this gorgeous partition for me and put it in front of my bed. I still have it in my apartment. My parents always had artists' souls. They did their best to take care of us, though we never had a lot. As soon as my brothers and I were of legal working age, we also pitched in to the family finances."

There was absolutely no accusation in her voice or resentment about her parents' financial situation. I was surprised about that. Some would be very bitter.

I'd never met someone with such a positive outlook on life.

"I'm happy that they stuck with their art because now it's paying off. I think. My brother's trying to figure out if they're really doing well, financially speaking, or if they need our help. When we were kids, it was easy to tell if things were good based on how much food was in the house."

I stilled. "What?"

She nodded. "We had some really tough years when they went through a bit of a dry spell. They took other jobs to be able to support us, but it wasn't really enough. They both studied art—that's actually how they met—so they didn't have any other marketable skills. But we made it through. I'm so happy they finally found some success. They're both very devoted to their art." She tilted her head. "Why are you looking at me like that?"

"I didn't realize you had such a tough time growing up."

"Well, maybe we didn't have a lot of toys and things, but our house was full of love. We had one another's backs. My parents gave their very best, and that's all we can ask of someone, isn't it?"

"I'm not used to people having your positive outlook."

She grinned. "You'd better get used to it. Anyway, my brother is better at gauging the situation than I am. I'm meeting them both to-morrow, and we'll see what Dean has to say."

"You see them every week?" I asked.

She shook her head, and I leaned in, kissing her shoulder. "Depends on how much time we have. How about you?"

"I'm actually meeting my family for breakfast tomorrow at my grandparents' place. It used to be a regular thing, but now with a few of my brothers having families, it's not as easy to coordinate."

"And they all got help from Jeannie, huh?" She smirked.

I raised a brow. "Why do you find that so amusing?"

"I don't know. I would have enjoyed having a meddling grandma. All my grandparents passed away when I was young. Jeannie seems like fun. My mom was so happy about the picture."

She straightened up, tilting her head from one side to the other.

"More wine?" I asked.

She nodded. "Yes, please. I like that you can anticipate my needs."

I wanted to do more than that—I wanted to anticipate *and* fulfill them all. I'd never had this impulse to take care of anyone who wasn't related to me before, but Zoey had this inexplicable effect on me. I didn't want her to go without anything. She wanted to look after her parents. I wanted to take care of her.

The food arrived quickly. I tipped the delivery guy generously and brought the food to the kitchen counter. Zoey immediately took it out of the cartons, opening it and inhaling deeply.

"Ahhhh, I love good Chinese," she said. "Although Greek food is my favorite."

"How come?"

"I went to Crete once to visit a friend from high school, and I fell in love with the food. Revani cake is my favorite dessert ever. But now let's eat. I'm starving."

I'd ordered mushroom pork. She'd ordered something with chicken. I put it in two bowls, and we ate right there at the kitchen counter.

She grinned. "I wouldn't have taken you for someone who enjoys Chinese."

"Why not?" I asked.

"I don't know. It's not very fancy."

I pinched her ass. "Are you calling me a snob?"

She pressed her lips together. "No, not at all. I don't know, I guess your fancy shirts with cuff links suggest you're not a Chinese takeout type of guy."

I lifted a brow.

She grinned. "Am I wrong?"

I kissed her cheek, wrapping my fingers in her hair. It was so damn silky and smelled so good. I wanted to bury my nose in it and lose myself in her scent—in her.

"Colton," she said, "your food is getting cold."

"I know, but I haven't gotten nearly enough of you."

She shuddered. "Hmm. I'm so tempting that you even forget your food, huh?"

"You're so tempting that I even forget my damn thoughts, what I'm doing, or what I'm planning."

She straightened her shoulders, looking up at me and licking her lips. I kissed her forehead and then returned to my food.

"Do you want to talk about the email from your brother?" she asked.

I took a mouthful of pork and, after swallowing it, said, "Sure. Why not? Maddox received an email from Father. He's... asking us for money. Maddox just forwarded it so we're all aware and can decide what to do."

"Do you often hear from your father?"

"Never. As far as I know, he hasn't been in contact with anyone for years. I'm surprised he reached out now. And also pissed."

She nodded. "So you're mad at your father, not at Maddox."

"I think Maddox reacted well by informing all of us."

"Are you going to do something about it?"

"I have no intention whatsoever of ever seeing or hearing from Father again."

"You got tense in the past few seconds," she said.

"How can you tell?"

She put her hand on my back, pressing between my shoulder blades. "See? Right here."

I could feel that the spot had cramped up. But I completely relaxed when the heat of her palm seeped between my muscles and loosened them.

"Huh. I can feel you relaxing. The wine is helping, isn't it?" she asked.

I turned around, taking her hand, and kissed the back of it. "No, it's you."

She grinned. "You know, normally, a guy sweet-talks a woman to get in her pants. But you were a total grump before and are charming me now. I don't know what to make of it."

Neither did I. But talking about other men, in any context, didn't sit well with me. Not one bit.

"But you do things your own way, huh?" she asked.

"Hell yes."

Chapter Thirteen

Colton

The next morning, I went straight to my grandparents' home for a late breakfast. I appreciated that everyone had time this Saturday, even though I was exhausted. Zoey and I hadn't slept at all.

I was the first to arrive at their house in the Dorchester neighborhood. They'd lived here since I was a kid. This place was practically home for me. I'd spent many hours on this porch. The green facade and white window trims had been refurbished three years ago, so the house was in good condition. I made it my mission to anticipate any necessary restorations to take the load off my grandparents' shoulders.

"Darling, want coffee? You look like you need a little pick-me-up," Grandmother said as she welcomed me inside the house.

"Jeannie, don't pounce on the boy, for goodness' sake. He just walked through the door," my grandfather added.

I nodded. "Coffee would be good."

I looked around with a critical eye. It was a habit. First, I scrutinized my grandfather. He seemed healthy enough. My grandmother was her usual energetic self. One thing that bugged me and my brothers was that she refused to have any help managing the household. We convinced her to employ a cleaning company back when Grandfather was recuperating, but once he was fit, she insisted they had everything under control. It was beyond me why they didn't want to make things easy, but it was their call to make, not mine.

I went to the kitchen, making myself a coffee. Grandmother was hunched over a platter with toast, bacon, and eggs. From now on our get-togethers needed to be for breakfast; it seemed far easier for her to prepare rather than the feast she always cooked if we met for lunch or dinner.

"Grandfather, what are you up to lately? We haven't seen you in a few weeks. Is your fishing partner—what's his name—Darren still coming every week?"

My grandfather put down the newspaper he'd picked up from the living room. "No, he's got the flu. It won't go away, so he hasn't been coming lately."

"So what have you been doing when we go out with Grandmother?" I asked.

Fuck me. Did Grandmother mention this and I totally blanked out? I was trying to listen to my family, be more engaged, and not just think about work lately.

Grandmother gave me a meaningful look, and I decided I was going to talk with my brothers about this. We'd been worried about Grandmother all this time because Grandfather always seemed to find someone to visit him and keep him occupied. Besides, he'd been housebound while getting his health back in order, but now we could take him out fishing or even to lunch. Grandfather needed our attention, too, but he'd never come out and say it. I was surprised, though, that Grandmother hadn't mentioned it.

When he walked back out with his newspaper to the living room, I immediately approached her.

"Don't start," she warned.

"I just wanted to ask why you didn't mention that he was lonely."

"Because the old stubborn mule absolutely forbade me to."

"And since when do you do anything except what you want?"

She looked at me out of the corner of her eye, shaking her head. "He's my husband. I will always stand beside him. I only fight you youngsters." She was so sincere that I couldn't help but burst out laughing. "What's so funny?"

"That you admit all of this so openly."

"I never hide my intentions. Anyway, now that you came to that conclusion, I think he'd enjoy it if you boys came by to see him now and again."

"I was just thinking we should do that."

"You're all such good boys. Maddox did take him out last week, and he seemed to enjoy that."

I stilled at my half brother's name. "Grandfather told them?"

"No, they just caught on faster. I think Maddox wanted to tell Spencer at their weekly tennis match, but I don't think they discussed it."

Talking about my half brothers wasn't my favorite thing to do. I knew I was being stubborn and hardheaded, and my reticence was causing friction in the family. My brothers were all on much better terms with them than I was. But I was determined to make an effort for my grandparents' sake and my brothers' too.

"Oh, I think a few more arrived."

She was right—there was a lot of commotion at the front door. When I looked out to the entrance, I saw Jake and Natalie were here along with Spencer, Penny, and Ben. My nephew was growing up fast. Some days I still couldn't wrap my head around the fact that my brother had become a father so unexpectedly. But he'd grown with the responsibility and adjusted remarkably quickly. He was an excellent father, and I respected him for that.

"Dude, you look like crap," Spencer said. "Were you holed up in your lab all night?"

"No, I wasn't at work," I replied.

Jake straightened up. He was about to whisper something to Natalie, but now they both had their eyes trained on me.

Spencer cocked a brow. Penny was looking at him questioningly. Even Ben stopped making baby sounds and was staring up at me. I felt like I was under a magnifying glass.

"So, what happened? Did you have an emergency or something?" Jake asked.

"No," Spencer replied. "He spent the night with someone."

I looked at my brother with fascination. "How can you tell?"

"I couldn't place that shit-eating grin before, but now I can. Good for you."

I quickly looked around the room. "But don't tell that to Grandmother."

"Don't tell me what?" Grandmother said, stepping into the living room with two plates full of toast and eggs and bacon.

"Never mind," I replied.

Someone was laughing behind me. Jake or Spencer. My money was on Spencer.

"Come on, let's all bring in the plates," I said.

We passed Grandfather, who brought a few mugs full of coffee. Jake, Spencer, and I took plates from the kitchen cabinet.

"Dude, that's not going to work, so you better fess up to Grandmother," Jake said.

"She'll forget all about it by the time we go back to the living room," I said confidently.

Spencer whistled. "Keep telling yourself that, dude. You'll have peace of mind for like ninety more seconds."

He was right. As soon as we stepped back into the living room, Grandmother asked, "Colton, what exactly are you hiding from me?"

I sometimes forgot that Grandmother liked to know everyone's business. She'd been meddling more than usual the past few years, but I'd ignored it. I'd been thinking about work every waking second, including when I was with my family.

"Grandmother, any chance I can convince you to drop it?" I said as we all sat around the table.

"Hmm, I'm considering it."

"I can't believe it." Spencer's eyes bulged.

"I've considered it. If you want to keep it from me, it means it's something I really want to know."

"Where does that logic come from?" I asked, fully aware that she actually did have a point.

"Experience."

I realized that if I didn't explain, she would think exactly what I didn't want her to—that I'd spent the night in the lab. I knew how much she'd worried about me during that time, and I didn't want her to go through it again.

"My brothers were making fun of me because I didn't sleep last night. I was *entertained*." And that was about as much information as I was willing to give. No way in hell would I own up to spending the night with a woman. Yes, I was a grown-ass man, but this was my grandmother. I had boundaries.

"Good for you," Grandmother said. "Nice to see you took my advice." I stared at her.

"Wait, what? What advice? What did I miss?" Spencer asked.

Penny chuckled. "You're such a gossip."

"It's a family trait I've learned to accept," Spencer replied.

"Wait, Grandmother is playing matchmaker again, and we didn't know about it?" Jake asked.

I'd expected Spencer to join in the harassment, but not Jake.

The doorbell rang.

Grandfather said, "I'll answer that." Then he looked straight at me. "Colton, son, I'm sorry, but you're going to take one for the team today."

"What team?" I asked, bewildered.

He went out to answer the door. By the sounds of it, Gabe had arrived with Cade and Meredith. The three of them came into the living room at the same time as Grandfather.

"Sorry we're late. Waking up early is not my thing," Cade said. He sat down, looked around the table, and asked, "So what's new?"

"Let me recap for everyone who's just arrived. Colton had a sleepless night, and no, he was not stuck at work. My money's on the fact that he was with someone, and Grandmother was just about to tell us that she's been continuing her matchmaking efforts with Colton, unbeknownst to all of us," Spencer said.

"Oh, thank God," Gabe said. "I was worried when you all were so quiet. I thought you might be planning something for me."

"I can multitask," Grandmother replied, looking straight at him.

My brother swallowed hard. "Yeah, I walked right into that." But then he looked at me with interest.

Cade had a shit-eating grin. It was a knowing expression. He and Grandmother exchanged a glance.

"It's that consultant who just started in your office, isn't it?" he asked, and there was a round of gasps at the table.

"Wow," Gabe said. "Damn, that escalated quickly."

"Boys," Grandmother chastised, "can you be a little more respectful?"

I laughed. "They're just learning from the master, Grandmother."

She pressed her lips together. "Look, I just made a comment. That's all."

"No, come on. Admit what you did," Cade told her. "It was the same thing you did with me and Meredith, right? You planted the idea in his head."

"You boys all have free will, but when I have a feeling about something, I don't like to keep it to myself. My feelings turn out to be accurate from time to time," she added with a wink.

Grandfather sighed. "Boys, I want you to know that I never have anything to do with whatever your grandmother is saying, okay?"

Grandmother glanced at him. "Way to have my back, Abe."

"You know I usually do. I just don't condone all of this. Although," he said, "it did work out for you three." He looked at the couples.

"Exactly," Grandmother exclaimed.

Just another Saturday in the Whitley family. We never talked about the weather or mundane things like that. We went straight to the personal stuff.

"So, Grandmother is onto something, right?" Spencer asked.

"Look, I'm not sure what all of you are used to—" I began.

"That's because you zoned out for like two years," Spencer said, "but go on."

"But I'm not going to share any details with anyone," I informed them.

"You don't have to share anything," Grandmother said.

I stared at her. "Now you're taking my side?"

"Honey, when I start a project, all I want is to give you a push. You have to work things out for yourself"—she glanced at Spencer—"without anyone giving him a hard time."

My grandmother operated in mysterious ways, but thankfully the conversation moved away from me.

But the truth was that Zoey was at the center of my mind. Even though we'd been up the whole night talking, I wasn't nearly done with all the questions I had for her. I had a burning desire to know every detail about her life, about *her*. We hadn't spoken about the future or the office situation because, honestly, that went against everything I stood for. I had to fight every instinct, but there was no going back now.

Zoey was mine.

Chapter Fourteen

Zoey

On Monday morning, I was a bit jittery when I went into the office. I was still tired even though I'd slept in yesterday. But that wasn't the only reason I was on edge. I wasn't sure how I'd react when I saw Colton. The night we'd spent together was amazing, but I had no clue what that meant for us. Still, work was work, so I sat at my desk, lit a lavender-scented candle, and opened my inbox, knocking out the first few emails.

By lunchtime, I was starting to get a bit suspicious. I hadn't heard Colton's voice at all. So while I went to get myself a coffee, I stopped by Darla's desk. His calendar showed he was in a meeting all day, but I hadn't heard him arrive.

"Hey, is Colton in a meeting?" I asked.

"Yes, but not at the office. He's at one of our producers.'"

"Oh. All right."

"He's not coming to the office the whole week."

My stomach bottomed out in disappointment. I wouldn't see him at all this week? I couldn't believe the wave of sadness that just rolled over me. I went back to my desk, pouting as I focused on my inbox again.

My stomach somersaulted when I saw an email from Colton. The subject line said **Urgent**, but the body only said **Check your messages**. But I had my phone right next to me.

Holy shit! It was in Airplane Mode. How did I manage that?

I was suddenly giddy, and I took it off Airplane Mode, but in my excitement, I tapped it twice and managed to activate it again.

Ah, get a grip on yourself, Zoey. He just messaged you. And chances are it's work related.

But I didn't think it was, because he could have just emailed me.

When I finally managed to take it off Airplane Mode, I waited for a few seconds until I had both internet and a phone signal, then realized I had four unread messages from him. I was in seventh heaven right now. I hadn't even realized how much I'd been hoping he would write to me until this very moment.

He'd sent the first message early in the morning. *Damn it. I'd had it on Airplane Mode all this time?*

Colton: Hey, I've got a last-minute meeting crammed into my schedule for the whole week. I'll only be at the office on Friday. I want to see you. Are you free in the evening?

The next one was an hour later.

Colton: Are you free Friday evening?

Colton: I've got a surprise for you for lunch on Friday. Let me know when you get this.

And just a few minutes ago, he sent me a question mark.

In my haste to reply to the messages, I dropped the phone in my lap. *Oh, if my brothers could see me now, they'd make fun of me forever.* Taking a deep breath, I typed.

Zoey: What kind of surprise?

I sent it quickly and then realized he'd also asked about the evening. I did want to see Colton, but my friend Tom and I had scheduled drinks on Friday a while back, and I knew he was looking forward to it. It had been a while since we managed to catch up because he was super busy. I couldn't wait to see what was going on in his life.

Zoey: I already have plans for dinner on Friday.

Then I got an idea and typed again.

Zoey: But maybe we can meet after? I'm not sure how long it'll take, though.

Colton replied a few seconds later. This was so exciting. I'd forgotten what it felt like to flirt... especially when it was forbidden.

Where did that thought come from? Nothing about this was forbidden. We were two adults who... well... I didn't know what we were doing, but I was thoroughly enjoying myself.

Colton: Let me know when you finish, and if it's not too late, then we can still meet up. As for lunch, I've made reservations at a Greek restaurant in the area. I'll send you the details.

I smiled, putting the phone to my chest.

Wait. He'd never mentioned that he was going to join me. I was confused now.

Zoey: So you're taking a break on Friday for lunch and joining me?

Colton: No, it's just for you. I'd originally planned to join you, but you can enjoy it even without me.

The rest of the week flew by. Things were strange at the office without Colton. I couldn't explain why, but it felt like a different place altogether. He and I texted back and forth every day, and I tried to keep the flirting to a minimum.

I failed.

On Friday, right before lunchtime, I realized I had no idea where the reservation was.

Zoey: Send me the address of the restaurant and I'll go eat for two.

I wasn't even joking.

Colton: I can't wait. Send me a picture.

Zoey: Will do.

He sent me the location right away. The reservation was in one hour.

At lunchtime, I burst out of the office and walked at a brisk pace. Once I reached the restaurant, I took stock of my surroundings. The facade was painted white with blue shutters.

Stepping inside, I could already feel myself relaxing. This was the perfect lunch place. The only thing that would have made it better was if Colton was here.

A young waiter approached me. "Hi, do you have a reservation?"

"Oh, yes. I think it's under Zoey, or maybe Colton Whitley."

The boy smiled as if I'd just told him that Christmas came early. "This way. Mr. Whitley was in contact with us. I'll take you to your table."

We stepped to the right, and I realized the restaurant extended into the adjacent room as well. It was smaller and cozier. He led me to a table. There was a huge bouquet of roses on it.

"That's for you, courtesy of Mr. Whitley," he said.

I stilled, nodding. I had no idea how to react. I wasn't expecting this.

Sitting down, I inspected the card that was with the flowers. I opened it, expecting to see some typed letters, but it was handwritten. I was sure it was Colton's handwriting: **Have fun. I wish I was there with you.**

I couldn't believe he'd done this.

The same waiter returned and said, "This is our menu. We even have your favorite dessert."

My mouth dropped. "How do you know what my favorite dessert is?"

"Because Mr. Whitley made sure we had it before he made reservations. I'm fairly certain that if we didn't have it, he would have convinced us to make it. He's a very persuasive man."

"Oh yeah." I completely agreed. "All right, I already know what I want. Pork skewers with a Greek salad."

"Of course. Right away, miss."

After he left, I couldn't stop staring at my flowers. They were gorgeous. I couldn't even remember the last time I'd gotten flowers. Did the corsage from prom count?

I snapped a picture of them and sent them to Colton.

Zoey: Thank you.

That was all I said because, honestly, I was at a loss for words.

Colton: Are you enjoying yourself?

Zoey: Yes. You?

Colton: Hell no. I'm trapped in this meeting from hell instead of being there with you.

My heart was beating faster. I was feeling sassy again, so I decided to taunt him. I sent a picture of my legs. It was nothing indecent, just enough to show I was wearing a skirt.

Colton: I'm two seconds from bailing on this meeting. Is that what you want?

I was acting out of character, but I had a burning desire to see him. No! I had to behave.

I put the phone down and took a deep breath. *I will behave.* If I told myself that enough times, maybe I'd actually go through with it.

I opened my eyes and wrote back.

Zoey: No. Focus on your meeting. I promise I won't tempt you with any more pictures.

Colton: You don't have to. I'm imagining you naked in my bed... and the kitchen counter and the couch.

I could feel my good intentions practically melting away. But no, I couldn't tempt him. I was here to eat lunch; then I'd go back to the office and finish my workday. Then I was going to tell Tom that we couldn't stay for too long tonight. That was a good compromise. I would catch up with my best friend and see Colton afterward.

I texted him right as the food came.

Zoey: My lunch is here. Tonight, I'm meeting my best friend. I'm going to do my best to finish my evening plans around nine or ten. How does that sound?

Colton: Fuck yes.

I replied quickly.

Zoey: Don't distract me during my lunch.

Colton: Or what?

Hm, that was a good question.

Zoey: I don't know. Let's not find out. I feel like we're in dangerous territory.

Colton: We definitely are.

I was giddy all through lunch, which was delicious. The Revani cake was truly the cherry on top. It was a sponge cake doused in syrup. The lemon flavor was very pronounced.

It transported me right back to my vacation. The only problem was, once I was done eating, I fell into a carbs coma. How was I supposed to go back to work now? But a girl's got to do what a girl's got to do. I had bills to pay and couldn't flake out.

When the waiter came to clean the table, I asked him, "Could you please bring the bill?"

"It's already taken care of."

I stilled. "What?"

"Mr. Whitley left his card information with us when he made the reservation and specifically asked us to charge everything on it."

"Well, I'll leave the tip th—"

"Oh no, ma'am, Mr. Whitley compensated us more than generously, but thank you. We're just happy to have you here."

Oh, Colton. I was going to make it up to him. He was spoiling me, and I was going to spoil him right back.

The afternoon dragged on. I drank three coffees to no avail. Not even the sugar rush from my dessert was helping.

I grinned every time I looked at the flowers. I'd put them in a vase with water and had them sitting on the corner of my desk. Several people had eyed them curiously, but no one asked anything. And if they did, I'd just tell them I bought them for myself.

When six o'clock came around, I burst through the door, carrying my huge-ass bouquet carefully as I headed to the Haymarket station.

I was meeting Tom at a restaurant near Fenway Park. I got there first and put the flowers right on the table so he could see them first thing when he arrived. I couldn't wait to get his take on this whole situation.

My phone beeped just as I was about to order. Colton was calling. I answered right away.

Look at that, I managed not to drop my phone. Progress.

"Hey," I said. *Why does my voice sound like that?*

"Hey, beautiful. Did you leave the office already?"

He'd gone to the office after all and I'd missed him? Damn it. "Yes, I'm already at the bar, waiting for my friend. How was your day?" I asked.

"Long and exhausting."

"You still want to meet later? We can postpone if you're tired." I didn't want to seem needy because it honestly wasn't like me.

"No way. Where are you, and when should I pick you up?"

"I can meet you at your place," I said.

"I don't want to waste any time."

I was dancing in my seat with joy. "Okay, I'll text you the address."

"Perfect. Let's catch up later," he said.

"Great. My friend is here," I said right before hanging up.

Tom strode toward me, checking out the arrangement of flowers. "What's that?"

"That is a long story. Now, sit down and tell me everything. How's Alicia feeling?" His wife was pregnant and on bedrest, which was one of the reasons we hadn't been able to meet before now.

"She's happy to finally have me off her hands. I think you might hear from her begging you to make this a weekly thing or something. She said she's tired of me hovering over her."

"But she's feeling all right?"

"So far, so good. But she still has to be on bedrest."

"And how are you feeling?" I double-checked.

He shrugged. "Let's order something to drink. Honestly, I can't wait for the baby to be here. Pregnancy is hard on her body. And work is more stressful than ever."

"I'm sorry you're having a rough time."

"It is what it is. So, what's going on with you? What do you want to start with? The job or the flowers?"

"It's complicated because they're related."

He raised a brow. "Now I'm intrigued."

While we ordered cocktails and food, I told him everything.

"That's unexpected," he said once I finished.

"I know, right? Well, I mean, I don't want to get ahead of myself, but the man is putting in an effort."

"It's good. Means he really likes you."

"That's good because I like him too."

"So, then there's just one question. Why the hell didn't you cancel tonight?"

I frowned. "Tom, I wanted to catch up with you. I knew you were looking forward to it."

"I was. Though if I'm honest, it's a good thing we're not staying out late because I can't leave Alicia alone for that long."

"You're a great husband."

We spent the evening chatting away, and I couldn't help but marvel at how the conversation had changed over the years. When we were in college, it was all about jobs, then about mortgages. And now, well, it was different.

At ten o'clock, we stepped out of the bar.

"I'll stay with you until he comes. Gives me a chance to meet him too," Tom said.

I grinned. "Oh yeah. Please take notes and tell me your impressions later, okay? I might have some lust goggles on, and, as we know, those are not always very objective."

"Don't worry, I can be." He took out his phone and started laughing.

"What?"

He showed me a picture. I leaned in closer to see. It was a huge belly with a scary grin drawn on it.

He chuckled. "Alicia's having fun."

"What's this?" Colton's voice came from next to us.

I looked up. He stared at Tom and me with a stony expression.

"Colton," I said. "This is Tom."

"You were on a date?"

I blinked, taking a step back. "What the hell?" I replied.

Tom cocked a brow. "Dude, take it easy."

"What do you mean, take it easy?" Colton asked, looking straight at me. "You told me you were meeting your best friend."

"Yes, Tom *is* my best friend."

Colton shook his head. "And you expect me to believe that?"

"Yes, I do."

Ah, damn it. It was way too good to be true, huh? The dreamy guy apparently had deep trust issues. I was pissed.

"Why would you even tell me where you were meeting?" he went on.

I scoffed. "Are you serious right now? You're making a scene because you don't believe what I'm telling you?"

He ran a hand through his hair. "*He's* your best friend?" Colton asked, his voice dripping with disbelief.

"You know what? I don't owe you any explanation." I turned to Tom. "Can you please take me home?" I felt like an idiot, holding my bouquet of flowers. I'd been so excited to see Colton, and he was being a total jackass.

"Sure," Tom said. He looked at Colton, "You're really barking up the wrong tree here. I'm married, and Zoey has been my best friend since college. She'll be the godmother of my daughter. Your loss, dude."

"Zoey—" Colton started.

"No, I really can't deal with you right now," I interrupted. I turned around and followed Tom blindly. I had no idea where he'd parked.

"I *cannot* believe him," I said when we finally reached his car. I put the flowers on the back seat and then climbed in the front passenger seat.

Tom gunned the engine. "You never mentioned to him that I was a dude?"

"No, I just said *best friend*, and he jumped to conclusions."

The car lurched forward, and Tom remained silent.

"Why aren't you saying anything?" I asked.

"The way he jumped to conclusions was annoying, but I have to say, we men are simple creatures, and sometimes our instincts get the better of us."

"You're defending him? Now I'm going to get pissed at you too."

"No, I'm just trying to imagine how I would have felt back when I first met Alicia if I saw her getting cozy with a guy."

I scoffed. "We weren't getting... Okay, I was all over you, but just because I wanted to see the picture. Stop defending him."

"I'm not. Really, that's your call. But just my two cents, the guy seemed really into you. Plus, you know, the flowers. I'm seriously considering that the flowers and the attitude cancel themselves out."

I crossed my arms over my chest. "I hate that he jumped to the worst conclusion. He must have a shitty opinion of me."

"I don't think he was being very cerebral, to be honest."

"You're my best friend. You're supposed to be on my side."

He grinned. "You're right. I won't say anything more on the subject."

CHAPTER FIFTEEN

COLTON

What the hell did I just do?

I took in a deep breath, trying to calm down. Adrenaline pumped through my veins. Rationally, her explanation made sense. I believed her, but I'd reacted like a fucking idiot.

I couldn't leave things like this. I knew she was pissed, but I needed to talk to her tonight and apologize. Maybe make her see things from my perspective. I couldn't even understand it myself, but that was another matter altogether.

Getting in my car, I put her address in the GPS—I'd saved it last weekend when I dropped her off at home. I couldn't just show up at her door, though. I had to call her first.

Starting the engine, I figured I'd make a plan while I drove there. I couldn't understand what had gotten into me. I was always levelheaded, never one who jumped to conclusions. And I never lost my temper.

I was almost to her place when it dawned on me that maybe she hadn't come home at all. Maybe she was still with him.

Damn it, I had to get myself under control. He was her best friend. The guy was married and was going to have a kid. Why the hell was I still on edge about it?

When the GPS informed me that I'd reached the destination, I called her. I was fully expecting her not to answer, but she did.

"Still in fight mode?" she asked.

I deserved that. "Zoey, I want to apologize."

"Damn right you do. Wait, you do?"

The fight went out of her voice, but I knew she was still angry with me.

"Listen. I'm actually in front of your building. Are you home?"

She sighed. "Okay, come on up."

Yes. Fuck yes. "I'll see you in a minute," I said before disconnecting the call. This was better. I needed to see her while I explained.

I needed to see her, period.

I watched her building with a critical eye. I hadn't paid attention when I dropped her off, even though I'd walked her to the door, because I'd been too captivated by her. But now I realized there was no doorman. *What the hell?* I wasn't a snob, but I thought a doorman was needed in every building for security.

She lived on the fourth floor. I only knocked twice before the door swung open. She'd changed into a golden dress.

"Are you going somewhere?" I asked.

She tilted her head. "I was going to take myself out for another drink."

"In that outfit?" I tried to control myself, then said, "Everyone and their brother will hit on you if you go out dressed like this."

She put one hand on her hip. "If that's how this conversation is going to go, there's the elevator. I thought you were going to apologize."

"Jesus, I was going to apologize." I cleared my throat. "I *am* going to apologize. May I come in?"

She hesitated, gnawing at her lower lip before stepping back. "Okay, but just so you know, you're on probation."

"I deserve that."

The second she closed the door, I turned around, facing her. She crossed her arms over her chest. "I'm listening."

I decided to be completely honest. "Look, I'm not sure what happened out there. I think I was just blindsided because I expected to see you with a woman, and then you were there with him, and you seemed kind of close."

"He was showing me a picture," she interjected.

"I know. But my mind immediately went to... a scenario that just tore through me." I hadn't meant to phrase it like that, yet it was exactly how it felt.

"Colton..." Her voice was soft, but then she tightened her jaw as if she was steeling herself. "That's no excuse for basically thinking I was out on a date right before I was about to meet you. How could you think that of me? You seem like a guy who's got his shit together. How could you just jump to that conclusion?"

"I don't know, Zoey. I'm not myself when it comes to you. I don't *get* angry." I stepped closer. "I don't get jealous. I'm not hotheaded and impulsive. I'm sorry you had to see that side of me."

"Can you promise not to doubt me again?" she asked.

I drew in a deep breath and said, "Yes," realizing it was actually true.

She narrowed her eyes. "Are you sure? Because I'm not a pushover, Colton. I'm not going to accept jealous rages."

"There won't be any. But I needed to clear something up first." I touched her neck with the back of my hand. She didn't pull back, so I cupped her cheek next. "You and I are exclusive, okay? No one else."

She parted her lips, nodding. "It goes both ways." Her voice was stronger now.

"Obviously." I drew my thumb across her upper lip. "I haven't even looked at another woman since I meet you," I told her.

"Do you mean that?"

"Fuck yes. You're on my mind all the time." I walked her backward until I pressed her against the door. "*All* the time. These past few days, I didn't recognize myself. Same goes for tonight, but in a different way."

"That's dangerous," she whispered. She knew I liked things a certain way. Losing control of myself was unthinkable. And yet I was willing to take that risk for her.

She tilted her head forward, kissing my wrist, and said, "Okay, you're not on probation anymore."

I started to laugh. "Glad I passed the test. Did I pass with flying colors?"

Her eyes flashed. "Oh no, you *barely* passed. You're going to have to do a lot more to get those flying colors."

"Challenge accepted."

I sealed my mouth over hers. Her taste was addictive. I moved my lips to her shoulder, going farther to the right and then down her arm. Goose bumps appeared on her skin.

"Colton," she murmured.

"I've been dying to do this for days," I confessed. "It's all I could think about."

"Don't say that. Now you're putting ideas in my head, and I won't be able to concentrate whenever I see you."

"That's fine by me." I smiled against her skin, continuing my exploration, moving to the other shoulder. She sucked in her breath every time I touched a sweet spot.

I brought my hand to her zipper, lowering it, and drew my mouth downward. As soon as I uncovered an inch of skin, I explored it with my lips. I wanted to do this all night long. Even longer than that.

When I finished unzipping her dress, she pushed her straps down until the fabric hung on her hips. I groaned at the sight.

"You're not wearing a bra." I barely recognized my voice.

She smiled. "No, the dress has sewn-in cups, so it wasn't necessary."

I didn't bother pushing her dress down any farther. I needed to taste more of her.

I lowered my head, and as soon as my mouth was level with her nipples, I drew the tip of my tongue around one. She gasped, arching her back. I moved to the other breast, but instead of drawing a circle, I took it in my mouth. Zoey went wild. She grasped the back of my head, pushing herself against me. I nipped and licked her nipple until it was completely hard, and then I moved to the other one while I kept my hands firmly on her ass cheeks. I loved feeling her muscles contract as she was internalizing the pleasure.

I was hungry for her. I wanted to taste her skin and her pussy.

I yanked her dress down with a tug. She gasped, stepping out of it. Her panties went down next. I needed to see every part of her. She sucked in her breath when I traced my thumb over her pelvis in a spiral downward, teasing her. I stopped just above her clit, drawing a circle slowly.

"Colton!" She put both hands on her belly, sucking in her breath even more. Then I lowered my finger, brushing her clit. Zoey whimpered, throwing her head back. I pressed her thighs together, skimming my thumb over her opening but not dipping my finger inside at all. She whimpered even more.

"Please." Her voice was uneven, a mere whisper. She was already at my mercy.

"I will make you come tonight, Zoey, but on my terms."

"Yes, yes," she said, looking flustered.

I kept her thighs apart while I put my face level with her pussy and pressed the tip of my tongue against her opening.

Then I dipped the tip inside, gauging her reaction. She trembled lightly. I wanted to explore her, but I needed a better angle. I looked at her coffee table and put my hand on it. It seemed sturdy enough.

"Lie down here, Zoey. On your back, legs spread wide for me."

She licked her lips and immediately lay down, resting on her elbows, and spread her thighs wide. I pulled her toward me so her ass was right at the edge of the table. Her eyes were trained on me.

"You like to watch," I concluded.

She nodded, and I feasted on her pussy without any mercy, without restraint.

I taunted her clit with my tongue and lips before dipping my tongue inside her. I alternated between giving her my fingers and my tongue. My cock strained in the waistband of my pants, but I didn't want to undo them yet.

I made eye contact with her while I was licking her. That seemed too much for her. She averted her gaze every time. She was sassy, but she could also be shy. I hadn't expected that. I paused when I felt her come too close to the edge, instead kissing the soft skin on her inner thighs. She rolled her hips back and forth.

"Colton," she murmured, but her voice was laced with discontent. She couldn't take the pressure anymore. She scrunched her eyes closed and pressed her lips together.

Then I gave her the release she craved. I worked her clit with my mouth, her G-spot with my fingers, and she was done for.

She thrashed around beautifully. I pulled back, watching her. She straightened one leg, then bent it again. Then she lifted her ass before putting it back down on the table, going completely still, as if her pleasure had run its course. Her hair was damp at the temples. I could watch her for hours, just drink in every part of her. But I also needed to be inside her.

I didn't want her to get up, as she was clearly still feeling the after-effects of her orgasm. Instead, I put my arms under her knees and back and lifted her in my arms.

"Where's your bedroom?" I asked.

She pointed to the left, and I went into a dark corridor.

"Just walk straight," she said.

I passed a door that probably led to the bathroom and headed straight to the bedroom. My erection was painful. I needed to free it immediately.

Once I stepped inside the bedroom, I clicked the light on with my elbow and placed Zoey on the bed. She pressed her thighs together before spreading them again. "I'm going to memorize the next few seconds forever," she murmured.

I cocked a brow. "Why?"

"You taking off your clothes for me? That's going to be memorable. And I suspect it's going to be the only time when I don't completely lose myself."

She was losing herself in *me*. I liked the sound of that.

I didn't even bother undoing more than the first three buttons of my shirt before I pulled it over my head. Then I focused on my pants and underwear.

"Hm. I'm torn because I want to ask you to go slower, but on the other hand, I want you inside me right now. So hurry up."

I laughed and then said, "Fuck. My wallet's in my jacket. I've got a condom there." I took two steps toward the door.

"Wait. Are you clean?"

I snapped my head to her. Her eyes were wide.

"Yes, just had a physical."

She nodded. "Me, too, and I've got an IUD, so if you want—"

"Fuck yes, I want," I interrupted, and in a fraction of a second, I was next to her in bed.

She laughed. "I should have led with that if I knew it would get you here so fast."

I lay down on one side, propping myself on my elbow. Zoey put her hand on her stomach, moving it up to her breast and then her neck. She tilted her head toward me, and I captured her mouth, kissing her.

I basked in her scent. She smelled amazing. I lowered one hand down the side of her body right to her hips, and then I slid it back to her ass, cupping one buttock. When I pulled her on top of me, she gasped, and I put her hands on my shoulders, steadying her.

I touched my crown to her clit, rubbing it lightly. Holding her hip with one hand, I kept her ass suspended in the air at the angle I wanted it, then moved my hips in a short motion, just teasing her clit. She trembled in my arms. Then she put her hands on the sides of her waist, looking down between us. I dragged my cock from her clit down her slit to her entrance, then pushed it back up just a little. Her thighs were shaking in earnest now. She didn't know it yet, but I was going to make her come with my cock before I even slid inside her.

I watched her face while I moved with precision. Her gorgeous green eyes widened with shock before she cried out my name. She came hard, and I couldn't wait any longer. I slid inside her and stilled, feeling her tighten around me while she completely came apart. She was squeezing me so hard that I was getting dangerously close to the edge already. The skin-on-skin contact was driving me insane, and feeling her muscles work through the orgasm was out of this world. I felt like I was a part of her.

"Colton," she gasped when she started to come down from the cusp.

I was still keeping her suspended in the air with my hands as I started to move inside her from below. I pulled out and then slid back in, pressing my thumb on her clit, keeping it there as I watched her fall apart right in front of my eyes again. She hadn't even finished coming from the last orgasm and I was already heightening the anticipation again.

The sensations went bone deep, unlike anything I'd experienced before. How was this much pleasure even possible?

My mind was completely blank. I had to remind myself to breathe. When I felt her muscles relax around my erection, I knew she could take more. She could take everything I wanted to give her, so I increased the pace. Zoey gasped, then arched forward, pressing her hands on my chest. She moved her hips, clearly wanting free rein. I allowed it, wanting nothing more than to see her chase her orgasm.

She came first, and her cries triggered my own orgasm. I'd never experienced anything so intense. I thought my body was on fire. My senses were overwhelmed. I didn't know what was real or not, except Zoey. She was real. She was mine. She was perfect.

Once she was soft in my arms, I patted my chest. "Lie down on me, beautiful."

She rested her head on my chest. I was still inside her, and I didn't plan to move. I wrapped my fingers in her hair. It was silky and damp and smelled like cherries. Her breaths still came out in short pants. I massaged her upper back, moving four fingers down to the middle and then up on her spine before touching her shoulder blades.

"I get an orgasm *and* cuddles? You're Wonder Man. Wait, that's not a thing, is it? I always get my superheroes confused."

"What?" I asked. "You're not making sense."

She looked up at me, smiling. But she was sleepy. Her eyelids were hooded. "I've just decided that you're better than all the superheroes combined."

"If you say so. An orgasm is all it takes?"

"Three, and yes, that gives you superhero status."

I kissed her forehead before we went to the bathroom to clean up. After we slipped under the covers, I brought her right against my chest again.

"Colton?" she murmured.

"Yeah."

"You passed with flying colors."

"Good to know." I pressed her closer to my chest.

"You like me here, huh?"

I raised my eyebrows. "I like you riding my cock best. But I like this too. I want to do it all night long."

She lay down on top of me so my cock was right under her pelvis. "Hmmm... I want to tease you some more, but I can't keep my eyes open."

"Go to sleep, Zoey. I'm right here."

She was out within seconds.

Chapter Sixteen

Zoey

I yawned, moving about in my bed before opening my eyes wide. It was still semidark outside, but I could see the first rays fighting their way across the morning sky. It took me a few seconds to focus on Colton. He was sitting right behind me on the bed and smiled brightly.

"Good morning, gorgeous."

I yawned again. "Why are you so alert? Did something happen?"

"The sun rises in ten minutes. Want to go see it?"

I grinned. *Holy shit, he's romantic.* That was another thing I wasn't expecting besides that weird jealous outburst. But I liked this side a lot. Honestly, once I'd calmed down, I kind of liked that other part too—not that I would ever admit that to him. The thought that he wanted me all for himself filled me with joy.

We got out of bed. I felt surprisingly good. Then again, it was past six o'clock.

Colton held my hand tightly, leading me out of the bedroom and into the living room. My jaw dropped. He'd put out two cups of steaming coffee and breakfast made from all the stuff I had in the fridge: sliced tomatoes and some cheese, toast, and bacon.

"You planned this for seeing the sunrise?"

"I woke up before you and realized it was coming up quickly, and I wanted to share it with you."

"Colton, this is amazing."

We each took a cup of coffee and stood in front of the window. He was behind me, one arm wrapped around my waist. We were both butt naked.

"You know, I actually never catch the sunrise even though it's not even that early," I admitted.

"Neither do I," he said. "But I wanted to share it with you."

I lost a piece of my heart to him right then. This was a special moment for both of us. "I bet it's gorgeous at your place too."

He kissed up the back of my neck. His lips were wet from the coffee. "You can come by anytime and watch it. We can pamper ourselves in the jacuzzi while we do that."

"You've got a jacuzzi and I missed that? Hmm. Must pay more attention next time I'm at your place."

We were both silent as we watched the sun come up. I was lucky that the buildings in front of mine weren't too high. There were taller ones in the distance, but we could still see the yellow rays and then the sun.

This moment, right here, was pure magic. The sunrise, Colton's arm around me, his breath against my cheek. It felt more intimate than anything we'd done last night. My heart skipped a beat and then two more. I had a feeling that Colton would have no trouble at all making me completely lose my heart to him. I wasn't sure how I felt about that.

When he'd kissed me the first time, I was ready for a sexy fling with this broody and mysterious man. But I wasn't counting on anything else.

Once the sun was up and I'd finished my last drops of coffee, I turned around to face him and kissed his chest. Then I pushed myself up onto my toes, kissing his Adam's apple.

"You're too tall," I complained, setting my cup down and then lacing my hands behind his neck, tugging him toward me so I could reach him. "Now that's better," I said, kissing up his neck and jaw.

I let him go, moving past him and looking at the table. He sat down on the couch, and I meant to sit next to him, but to my astonishment, he pulled me into his lap. I nearly fell over, but he secured me with one hand on my back.

"That works too," I teased as I grabbed a plate. "You don't want to eat?"

"Later. Now I just want to watch you."

I rolled a slice of cheese, eating it up quickly. "I hadn't realized I was so hungry."

"We exerted a lot of energy last night, and I need you well fed."

I elbowed him. "Why? You have plans?"

"You know it," he said. While I swallowed a second slice of cheese, he asked, "You got anything planned today?"

I shook my head. "No, you?"

"Later in the evening." He brushed my tailbone with his fingers. "I'd like to spend the day with you. The whole day."

My heart skittered and my stomach leaped. The thought of having him for myself for a full day was exhilarating. I nodded vigorously, shimmying on top of him.

"All yours," I said. "The whole day."

His eyes flashed. "Good. I was half expecting you to argue me on it."

"Hmm, why?"

"Because you like keeping me on my toes."

I tilted my head, considering this. "That's right. I let you off the hook far too easily last night, didn't I?" I took a sip from his cup of coffee because mine was already empty.

He straightened, pinning me with his gaze. "Happy to grovel some more."

"That's more like it," I concluded.

Just then, a phone beeped.

Colton

"Yours or mine?" Zoey asked.

"It's mine," I said. "Let me check."

I went to the hallway, grabbing my phone from the jacket I'd worn last night.

"The office wouldn't call you on a Saturday, would they?" she asked.

"No, I don't expect anyone to work weekends."

"Hmm. But if *you're* working, it means you make others work."

"I don't *make* them work. They just have stuff to do."

"Mm-hmm, keep telling yourself that."

I looked at the screen. "It's Grandfather. Let me see. Maybe Grandmother did change her mind and wants us to go by today." She'd canceled at the last minute yesterday, saying she forgot that she was seeing a friend. Maybe the friend canceled on her.

"Hi, Grandfather."

"Colton," he said in his brisk voice.

"Something wrong?" I asked.

"Listen, don't panic."

Why do people ever start sentences with that? I clenched my jaw. Zoey probably realized something was off because she put a hand on my chest. It was surprisingly calming. I put my hand over hers, pressing it deeper into my skin.

"I'm listening."

"I brought your grandmother to the hospital. She wasn't feeling great yesterday, and this morning she had a headache that was so debilitating she couldn't even get out of bed."

"What hospital are you at?"

"A small clinic here in the area."

"I know it," I said. It was a boutique facility with astronomical prices but excellent care. I passed it every time I went to see them. "Did the doctor say what's wrong with her?"

"No, not yet. They've ruled out anything life-threatening, so that's good."

I felt some semblance of relief pulsing through me.

"I'm going to drop by and see what I can do to help."

"There's no need. I've just spoken to the doctors. They won't tell me any more until they know more."

"Can she receive visitors?"

"Yes."

"Then I'll come by, and I'll take you home once she's discharged."

"That could take hours, son," Grandfather added.

"That's not a problem. Is this why she canceled the lunch today?"

Grandfather hesitated. "Yes."

It took all my willpower not to berate him for not taking her to the doctor yesterday. That was the last thing he needed. He was worried enough.

"I'll see you soon," I said and hung up.

"What happened?" Zoey asked.

"Grandfather took Grandmother to the hospital. She's been having severe headaches. I'm going to check on her. I'm sorry to spring this on you. I'll call you as soon as I'm out of there."

She bit her lip. "You're so tense."

"I'm worried. Though it does help to feel you close to me," I admitted. I was still holding her hand over my chest.

"Want me to come with you and be your moral support?" she asked with a grin.

"Yes. Fuck yes. If hospitals don't bother you."

"I don't mind. And I want to see Jeannie too."

"Fuck, you're so... I don't even know how to describe you."

She smiled again. "You don't have to. I can figure out what you're thinking just by the way you're looking at me."

Knowing she wanted to be by my side stirred things inside me. But I could barely work it all out for myself, let alone explain it to her. So I just kissed her forehead and then pinched her ass. 'Cause why the hell not? I liked taking her by surprise.

She started laughing. "Come on, let's head over there. Which hospital is she at? Mass General?"

"No, it's their smaller satellite hospital near my grandparents' house. I want to make sure she's taken care of. It's well equipped, but it's small. I don't know if they have everything they need there."

"I'm sure your grandfather would have taken her somewhere else if he thought they weren't doing a good job."

"Yes, but Grandfather is also ninety." I paused. "Whatever you do, don't tell him I said that."

Zoey smiled. "I promise I won't. Let's get dressed."

Chapter Seventeen
Colton

We arrived at the clinic forty minutes later. I'd never been inside it before. It only had two levels and a small reception area manned by one guy.

"Hello! I'm Colton Whitley," I said. "You received a patient named Jeannie Whitley this morning."

"Sure. Please go upstairs and join the others."

I took Zoey's hand, leading her up the staircase. I didn't want to bother with an elevator, as it might slow us down. "I think my brothers are here."

"Oh?" Zoey asked. "Do you want me to, I don't know, wait downstairs until they're gone or something?"

"No. It's as good a time as any for you to meet them."

"Okay." Her eyes flickered.

"What's that look?" I inquired.

"Nothing. I've always wondered if your brothers are like you."

I chuckled. "You'll find out today."

I heard my grandfather's voice before I saw him, then stopped in my tracks. My half brothers were here too. Maddox, Nick, and Leo were pacing the hallway. They bore only a slight resemblance to my brothers and me. We all had blue eyes, and theirs were green and brown. They had also inherited our father's dark brown hair, whereas my brothers and I were a few shades lighter.

Grandfather was sitting, looking distraught. My entire body tensed. They all glanced up when they saw me.

"Colton!" Maddox exclaimed, then glanced at Zoey.

"Zoey, these are my half brothers." I introduced all of them by name. She shook hands with each of them. "Grandfather, any news?"

"No, they're doing tests. They think it's simply dehydration." He shook his head. "Sometimes she gets so involved in what she's doing that she forgets to drink water."

I relaxed a bit. "That doesn't sound so bad."

"They gave her an IV with electrolytes," Maddox said. They usually took everything in stride, but he sounded concerned.

I tensed again. "She needs an IV?"

"Right."

Maybe this was more serious than it sounded. "Did anyone talk to a doctor recently?"

"I did," Leo said. "They said she'll probably need to stay a few hours until the IV is empty, and then she can go home. I'm going to stay here and wait until that's happened, then drive her and Grandpa home." Leo glanced at Grandfather. "Actually, you know what? Why don't you and I go home? Then Nick or Maddox can bring Gran once everything is over."

I appreciated that more than I could say. Grandfather wasn't fit enough to sit on these uncomfortable chairs for hours on end. I was grateful that my half brothers were here too. Their concern for our grandparents made me look at them in a whole different light.

Nick and Leo reminded me of my youngest brother, Gabe. They were quick with a joke and lightening up the situation, and they usually played off each other. But right now, even they appeared very concerned.

"We already went in to see Gran. You can go too," Maddox said, then walked my way.

"Do the rest know?"

He nodded. "Yeah. Grandpa called everyone. Gabe is on the way. I came as soon as he called. I wanted to make sure this was the right place for Gran and that she didn't need a bigger hospital."

Zoey sat next to Grandfather, and they began chatting under their breaths. Grandfather nodded and seemed a bit more energetic than before. I couldn't believe she'd already had such a positive effect on him.

Then Grandfather looked up at me. "Colton, why am I just now meeting Zoey?"

I cleared my throat. "I was waiting for a good moment."

"And you thought that was when your grandmother was in the hospital? She's going to have a field day with this. You know," my grandfather told Zoey, "I really thought she was barking up the wrong tree with this."

"What do you mean?" Zoey asked.

Maddox looked at them with interest.

"She came home from Colton's office, declaring that she thinks there's finally someone who can... well, challenge Colton. I couldn't believe she was right again."

"No shit," Maddox said. To my amusement, he sounded a bit panicked. Then he turned to me. "She mentioned that to me, too, but I thought... You know what? Never mind. We don't want to scare Zoey away with tales of our insane family dynamics."

"I agree," I told him. "Can we go see Grandmother now?" I asked Grandfather.

"Yes. She's surprisingly awake, but the doctor did tell us not to overwhelm her. You can go in. We already saw her, so we won't go in again for now."

"All right."

"It's the room down the hall on the left."

"I can wait here," Zoey said, "if you'd rather go in alone."

"And risk Grandmother's wrath?" I asked.

Both Maddox and Grandfather started to laugh. Zoey got up from the chair, smiling.

"You managed to lift his mood in just a few minutes," I told her when we were out of earshot of Grandfather and Maddox. "How did you do it?"

"I shifted the focus to positive stuff, like how much I love Jeannie's work. Instead of him thinking his wife is sick and in a hospital, he had to focus on the times when she was healthy and full of energy."

"That's very smart," I said.

"So your grandmother thought you needed someone to challenge you? Did she say that when she was in your office and I missed it?"

"No, but she's been saying that on every other occasion for years," I clarified.

"Then let's give her a show, shall we?"

"What do you mean?" I asked her.

"Let's take everyone's mind off things. Just follow my lead."

"Sounds good."

Grandmother looked well. I'd been dreading the moment I saw her. I wasn't a fan of hospitals, but she was relaxed and even had some color in her cheeks. She had on headphones, which she immediately took off when she saw us. "Colton, you came with Zoey."

"Are we bothering you?" Zoey asked.

"Not at all. I was listening to an audiobook. I wanted to read, but the doctor said I shouldn't. Honestly, I'm not even sure if I could. I'm afraid the headaches could start again."

"You have to take it easy, Grandmother," I said. "And drink more water."

She narrowed her eyes at me. "Tell me you didn't come here to berate me."

I ducked slightly forward and straightened again. "I didn't come *just* for that."

Zoey sat at the side of her bed and looked at me over her shoulder. "Hey, be nice to your grandmother. That's no way to talk to someone who's in a hospital bed." She winked at me.

What was that about? Oh right, that plan she has.

My grandmother smiled brilliantly. "Attagirl. I'm so happy my prediction turned out to be true."

"You don't know that," I said, somewhat affronted. I knew Zoey had a plan to take Grandmother's mind off being sick, but I had some pride too.

"Ha," Grandmother exclaimed. "Want to tell me why you two are together on a Saturday? And before you ask why I know you were together, it's because you both showed up here."

"It could be any number of reasons," I challenged.

Zoey looked at me over her shoulder, winking again. "Is that so? You're not going to own up to your grandmother to what we were *really* doing?"

She was great at this! Grandmother was having a field day.

"Fine, Grandmother. You were 100 percent right. We were on a... date."

"That's good to know." The smile on her face was addictive. That Zoey could do this for her, for our family, was huge in my book.

"Now, I know you said not to berate you, but you need to take it slower," I urged.

"It's a headache."

"Grandfather said you get them when you overwork yourself because you forget to hydrate."

"He has a big mouth," she muttered.

"Grandmother, you know he only cares about you. "

She pursed her lips and shook her head. "You're right. I only had a few headaches here and there, and I didn't realize they were getting stronger and more frequent. I'm going to take better care of myself. I'm determined to live to see every single one of you give me great-grand-kids."

"What? Every one of..." Zoey stumbled over her own words.

"Don't mind Grandmother," I said.

"Oh yeah, do mind me, because I'm very serious," Grandmother insisted, eyes twinkling.

Zoey glanced at me, and for once, she didn't look sassy. She seemed a little panicked. I should have warned her. But this was fun to watch. I'd never seen her caught off guard.

She turned to Grandmother again. "Jeannie, whatever gets you motivated to stay healthy is good."

"That's what I say all the time," Grandmother replied. Then she yawned.

"Okay then, we should go," I said.

Zoey immediately rose from the bed. "It was nice seeing you again, Jeannie."

"Don't be silly. Seeing me on a hospital bed can't be a highlight, but don't worry. I'll get better in no time, and then I'll have you all over to our house."

That was going to be catered, and I wasn't going to take no for an answer. But I wasn't going to bring it up now.

We stepped outside into the corridor. Grandfather and Leo had already left. Maddox and Nick were talking to Gabe, who must have just arrived. He looked up at me, and then his eyes fell on Zoey. Judging by his grin, he knew who she was.

"Well, well, what do we have here?" he asked.

"Gabe, this is Zoey. Zoey, this is my youngest brother and a pain in the ass."

"He took the words right out of my mouth," Gabe said, winking at her. "I was going to use the exact same introduction."

Zoey laughed. "Do you want to go see your grandmother?" she asked. "Better hurry because I think she's going to nap soon. She seemed a bit tired."

"Sure," Gabe said. His smile fell. "How is she?"

"She's good," I assured him. "Just tired."

"Okay, good. By the way, our brothers will arrive soon."

After he left, I wanted to ask Nick what he'd found out from the doc, but Maddox said, "Did you by any chance look at that email I sent you a few weeks ago?"

Zoey cleared her throat. "I saw a coffee machine downstairs. I'm going to make myself one. Colton, you'll let me know when we're ready to go?"

"Sure," I said. Only after she left did I realize she'd done it on purpose to give us privacy.

"Yes, I read it," I told Maddox. "Wanted to ignore it and delete it."

He nodded. "I thought about doing the same. But then I figured if he didn't hear from us, he might ask our grandparents."

Fuck, that had never occurred to me.

"Do they know about it?" I asked, putting my hands in my pockets.

Maddox cocked a brow. "I'm not an imbecile. Of course not. I didn't forward them the email."

"No, but there are other ways they could find out," Nick said. "Don't get your panties in a twist, brother." His tone was mocking.

"Let's meet up at my office one evening," I said. Maddox looked stunned. This was my way of waving the white flag. I'd been at odds with them for years, and I was man enough to admit there was no reason for it. Besides, we needed to talk about this. "I'll send you all a calendar invite."

Nick burst out laughing, then said, "Wait, you're serious?"

I frowned. "How else are we supposed to find time?"

"You can just text us," Nick said slowly, like I was being dumb on purpose. "I'll make a WhatsApp group," he continued and immediately took out his phone. "Who knows how much time we have before you change your mind and decide not to be cooperative."

He wasn't completely wrong.

"I think we should do something for our grandparents too," I added.

Maddox nodded. "Yeah, I was thinking about that. But for now, I don't think there's a reason for you to stay here. Go entertain that knockout you've got waiting for you at the coffee station. We've got this."

"I want to talk to the doctor too," I said.

"Don't," Nick replied. "He got annoyed when Gabe and Maddox tried to talk to him and said he'd only speak with us when he had something new."

"Okay. Call me if our grandparents need anything," I told them.

"You can trust us on that," Maddox exclaimed, and I realized I truly could. They'd shown up here even before I did. They'd spoken to the doctors. They were on top of this.

"Thank you very much, for everything today. We'll stay in touch."

"Sure," Maddox replied, eyeing me suspiciously.

I didn't blame him. My history of keeping in touch with them was nonexistent.

I headed downstairs, finding Zoey by the coffee machine.

"Hey!" she said when she noticed me, then turned her phone to me.

"What's that?" I asked. The picture she had pulled up looked like some sort of bottle.

"It's a smart water bottle. Apparently it tells you if you've drunk enough during the day."

"I'm not following."

"It's for Jeannie. Maybe this will help her stay hydrated. It's easy to forget to drink water."

I couldn't believe she'd researched this.

"I think she'll appreciate it. *I* appreciate it."

"Of course. Every bit helps, right? I mean, obviously, if you don't keep it with you or you drink other things, it doesn't work."

"I didn't mean the bottle. I appreciate what you did."

"So, what's the plan? Are we sticking around?" she asked.

"My half brothers are on top of everything, so for now, let's go back home."

"Do you ever just call them your brothers?"

"No," I immediately replied. "It's a reflex, honestly. For so long, I've just been angry at them, even though it wasn't their fault that Father was... an asshole."

"They seem like great guys. I like how they rallied around Jeannie."

"Yeah, I liked it too."

Zoey had also made an effort to lift my grandmother's mood. And now she was looking up at me like just being here with me was enough to make her day better. I wanted to find out what I needed to do for her to look at me like that every day.

We heard footsteps behind us, and I knew my brothers must have arrived. Jake and Cade walked up first, and Spencer was right behind them. None of my brothers had come with their better halves. Maddox, Gabe, and Leo also came from upstairs.

"Relax," I said. "There's nothing wrong. The situation is under control."

I saw the change in them at once. Jake lowered his shoulders. Cade craned his neck as if it had been stiff, and Spencer just nodded. He had dark circles and a permanently exhausted look on his face. But then again, he had a small child, so that was to be expected.

"So what's the news?" Jake asked.

Maddox spoke. "First of all, they're keeping Gran here under observation and gave her an IV. Leo's already taken Grandpa home, and as Colton said, everything's under control."

That was when my brothers seemed to notice Zoey. She was looking at them with a smile.

"Everyone, this is Zoey. Zoey, these are my brothers Jake, Cade, and Spencer."

As they shook hands with her, it dawned on me that their reactions were very toned down. I would have expected at least Spencer or Cade to crack a joke or give me a shit-eating grin. Then I realized Gabe was exchanging a glance with Cade. I was willing to bet anything that our little brother had given them a heads-up. I was grateful to him for it.

"Nice to meet you, Zoey," Jake said. "We've heard about you."

"You have?" Zoey asked, stunned.

"My grandmother might have mentioned you in passing." That came from Cade. He winked at her and then added, "She used that tactic, too, to bring me and Meredith together, but I guess I never learn. She always has a plan."

Zoey laughed. "I'm a bit overwhelmed."

"Don't worry, so are we," Gabe said. "Anyway, Zoey, thank you for being here for Grandmother. With you here, she's got something else to focus on and won't turn on us anytime soon."

The mood had significantly lightened in the past few minutes. Knowing Grandmother wasn't in grave danger was a relief to us all.

"Now, how do we want to play this?" Jake asked.

"I'd say we take it one step at a time," Maddox said. "First, let's see what the doctor suggests. Right now it's just about hydration."

"I agree with him," I said. "All right, I don't think there's any point in meeting up tonight, then."

We were going to hang around at Gabe's bar in the evening, but none of us was in the mood for that anymore.

"Agreed. Okay, guys, let's go upstairs and check on Grandmother," Jake suggested.

We bid my brothers and half brothers goodbye, and then I was alone with Zoey.

"Should we buy some goodies and bring them to your grandmother once she's home?" she asked.

I shook my head. "No, she's going to need her rest. The doctor said not to overwhelm her. I suggest we wait until she gives us the green light to visit her. And in the meantime, my brothers and I will take turns checking on them. Jake's driver is already helping them with groceries. I'll check in with Grandfather tomorrow morning to see if they need anything."

"I think it's so endearing that all of you are coming together and taking care of them."

"I didn't think I'd say this, but I'm grateful that my half brothers are in Boston too."

She smiled brightly. "I'm happy you're seeing the positive side of this. Do you wish you were closer to them?" she asked.

"I always figured it would make my grandparents happy if we were closer. But I never really thought about what *I* wanted."

"Food for thought, huh?"

Zoey was exceptionally good at seeing right through me and wasn't afraid of asking the difficult questions and challenging me to do some introspection. I didn't have any answers—yet.

"All right, so what's the plan?" she asked.

"My family will stay for a bit, and they'll keep us posted. Grandmother will flip out if we all stay here, so I'm going to focus on you today."

"How are you going to do that?"

"What do you want to do?"

"We could spend the day outdoors, maybe at a park. I'm afraid these sunny days will be gone before we know it."

I nodded, taking out my phone.

"What do you think about a hike at the Cascade in Melrose?" I asked her.

She blinked, jerking her head back. "Wait, you just looked that up?"

"Yeah," I muttered. That wasn't totally true. When she'd mentioned camping a while ago, I'd done some research, and the Cascade popped up as a possible day trip.

"Okay then," she said, "I'm all yours. I can't believe you're going to be mine all day."

The idea of belonging to someone, of giving anyone power over me, was foreign to me, and yet I liked hearing Zoey say that. I liked the idea of being hers.

Chapter Eighteen

Zoey

Zoey

We went to my place first and then Colton's to change into comfortable clothes for our day out. The drive to Melrose only took half an hour.

"I've never been here," I said, looking around. "I can't believe we're so close to Salem too. I've always wanted to go." I'd seen a few signs along the way.

It looked very colorful, with leaves ranging from green to yellow. We parked just off Washington Street. The trail was close by.

"This looks so dreamy," I said after we got out of the car. "Have you been here before?"

"No. I jog a lot, but I'm not into hiking."

I frowned. "So wait, what are we doing here, then?"

"You said you enjoy being out in nature."

"If we weren't surrounded by other cars and incoming hikers, I would jump your bones right now. Just thought you should know."

He grinned. "Keep that thought for later."

He took my hand, and we went straight onto the trail. It wasn't too easy to traverse, as there were lots of roots and leaves, making the walk a tad challenging.

"Oh look, people brought their dogs too. I've always wanted a dog, a Lab maybe. But I need a bigger place first." I took in a deep breath. "I love the smell of the forest."

Colton wasn't saying anything. He was looking at me. "I like seeing you like this, all relaxed."

"I like enjoying the present."

"Something I've yet to learn. My mind is constantly on other things."

"I hope not work."

He nodded. "Sort of. I was thinking about Browning."

"Oh, his name rings a bell. I've seen a few emails from him asking about updates."

"Browning is my mentor. He's been with Whitley Biotech for about twenty years and knows the business forward and backward."

"He worked with your dad too?"

"Yes, but he was actually a good friend of Mom's. After everything went downhill, he was sort of like a father figure to me. I can't wait to introduce you to him, although he's rarely at the office these days."

"I can't wait to meet him, whenever that may be."

I was thrilled that he wanted me to meet his mentor.

A few minutes later, we reached the Cascade. It was beautiful, but I couldn't help feeling a bit disappointed. I'd hoped this would have taken us longer. Maybe there were more trails around here we could take.

Colton stood behind me, wrapping his arms around my waist as we watched the waterfall. There were quite a few hikers around us, and more were arriving. But we were nestled in a nook among the greenery, shielded a bit from view.

"Thanks for bringing me out here," I murmured.

"Thought you might like it because you said you enjoyed going camping with your parents."

"Thanks for listening to what I say."

"How could I not?"

I laughed softly. "I don't think I've ever dated someone who took what I said seriously."

Colton turned me around. "What do you mean?"

"My last ex seemed to think I was a piece of decor or something. No matter how many times I suggested we do stuff and even offered to arrange it, he never had time. Honestly, I don't think he liked being around me that much."

"Why were you even with him?" he asked.

"I thought... I don't know, that relationships are supposed to be worked on. After the guy with the whole Tinder thing I dated someone who forgot about my birthday."

"What the hell?"

"We hadn't been dating for long, but still. It made me feel like I was the last thing on his mind, and I have too much self-respect for that. He admitted I wasn't a priority for him."

I pasted a huge smile on my face.

"And that doesn't bother you?" Colton seemed perplexed.

"Of course it does. I just don't like to admit it, or dwell on it."

"Zoey, it's fine to be bothered by things and have expectations of people."

I frowned. "You think I don't have expectations?"

"Am I wrong?"

I frowned, considering this, then wrapped my hands around the back of his neck even though there were plenty of people around us. I wanted to be close to him, and I couldn't care less. I wasn't into PDA, but right now, I wanted the world to know I was with this man.

"I don't know. I'm always thinking that if I don't expect a lot from people, they can't disappoint me. Maybe that's why I never expected much of my relationships."

He nodded, threading his fingers through my hair. He really seemed to love doing that.

"I wouldn't know. The last relationship I had was years ago. I don't even remember how it ended."

"But you're not a big believer in relationships, are you?" I asked.

He let go of me, and we sat down on one of the big dry rocks. I liked hearing the water all around us.

"I've always focused on Whitley Biotech. And after how my parents' marriage ended, that wasn't a box I wanted to check."

"I understand that." Watching your whole family disintegrate would probably leave you with deep scars. "You know what's interesting? My parents are super happy and in love, and somehow I've never dreamed about a big wedding or even fantasized about relationships. I'm not sure that we always want to walk in our parents' footsteps. I think I was always focused on my career. I wanted to have a solid financial situation before I even considered having a family." Saying that out loud made me realize that perhaps I *had* been influenced by certain experiences in my childhood. "I love my parents, but I want my children to feel financially secure. That's always been a heavy weight on me and my brothers. I want to give my kids whatever they want and need—within reason."

Colton smiled. I uncrossed my legs.

"You are a generous soul, Zoey."

I opened my mouth, but I didn't manage to say anything because a splash of ice-cold water startled me. I jumped to my feet. So did Colton.

He stepped in front of me the next second, taking the brunt of the water. Several teenagers were laughing. One had pushed another in the water, and he was not amused. He was shouting something about pneumonia.

Damn, I wouldn't want to be him. The water looked dreamy, but it wasn't nearly warm enough to be in it.

Colton and I moved farther from the edge. When he turned around, I grinned. His T-shirt was plastered to his abs.

"I would feel sorry that you're wet and probably cold if I wasn't so amazed by how sexy you are."

He laughed. "Conflicted much?"

"Very much."

I licked my lips, fighting to keep my hands to myself. I definitely couldn't feel him up in public, even though no one was paying attention to us.

"I think we better get back," I said. "I wouldn't want you to catch a cold."

He grinned but didn't say anything. He was probably onto me. I mean, I wanted his sexy body, too, but in my defense, I wanted to get back home so he could change into something dry.

Once in the car, he turned on the heat.

"Will you look at that. It's not even as soaked as I thought," I said, pouting.

"Want me to pour a bottle of water on top of my head?"

I playfully swatted his shoulder. "It's all your fault for being so sexy. You're putting ideas in my head. Are we going home?" I asked eagerly.

He grinned. "No, but interesting to know that's what you want to do."

"So, what *are* we doing?" I asked.

Again, I was torn. On the one hand, I wanted to see what else he had planned. On the other, I kind of wanted to be alone with him. I felt closer to him after we'd both shared such intimate things in front of the waterfall.

He gunned the engine, and as the car jerked forward, I noticed the address he'd put into the navigation app on his phone.

"We're going to Salem?" I asked.

He winked at me. "Yeah. You said you want to go."

I felt warm everywhere. I had so many fuzzy feelings inside me that I couldn't even explain what was going on. I'd never felt anything like this.

"Thanks for this day," I said. "I wouldn't have taken you for a spontaneous kind of guy."

"I'm not usually, but I'm doing my best for you."

I spent the rest of the car ride looking up info on Salem and talking his ear off about the various details. I couldn't hide my excitement; I was practically dancing in the seat.

Once we arrived, I looked around curiously. The hair at the back of my neck stood on end, probably because I mostly associated it with the Salem witch trials. We passed a gorgeous flower shop inside a building with pink wood. The one next to it was white, and the next ones were pink again.

"Oh, look up there—hot air balloons. I've always wanted to try one."

We even passed the Salem Witch Museum, a building in a Gothic style with a wrought-iron fence.

"What do you want to start with?" I asked. "There are walking tours starting every hour, but maybe we should go to the museum first. It's going to get more crowded later in the day. There was already a line at the ticket counter when we passed it."

"The museum it is, then."

He found a parking spot easily enough. After getting out of the car, I inspected his T-shirt. Damn—it wasn't wet at all anymore. But I'd get plenty of opportunities to see him naked later.

We went straight to the museum, standing in line. Colton wrapped his arms around me in a sexy bear hug. I grinned, shimmying my hips against him. He grunted, a very small and weak sound, but I heard it.

Ah, how can life be so amazing?

I was here with this fantastic man who'd whisked me away on this impromptu trip. Even though just this morning, he'd been worrying about his grandmother.

"What are you thinking about?" he asked.

"That you're a fantastic man," I whispered.

"You really think that?"

"Well, yeah. You're perfect."

He stiffened a bit.

"I just like making you happy," he said.

"See? That's the perfect thing to say," I whispered back.

I had no idea what Colton and I had, but it was more than a fling. And my heart was immensely happy about it.

CHAPTER NINETEEN

ZOEY

Let it be known that I wasn't prone to daydreaming. And yet, for the past few weeks, I'd done that a lot... even at the office. *Especially* at the office. All it took was hearing Colton's voice. If I accidentally saw him, I moved way past daydreaming, and my heart started fluttering. My stomach too.

One afternoon, I got an idea. A dangerous one. Colton had blocked his calendar with "science time" until late in the evening today. He told me that was code for wanting to work without any interruptions. But I had a hunch that he wasn't going to mind mine. I'd make it worth his while.

On one of my coffee breaks, I googled nearby lingerie stores. I was wearing lace underwear but needed a finishing touch. I wanted garters.

I found a store that was only five minutes away. Shortly before they closed, I jogged out the door of our building and headed over there. *Fingers crossed that they have what I need!*

I'd had a very sexy dream about everything we could do in Colton's lab. To my intense joy, I found a pair of black garters. By the time I reached my office again, everyone else had left.

Time to put my plan into action.

I closed the door to my office and slid on my garters. You wouldn't know I was wearing them just by looking at me because I appeared perfectly professional.

I schooled my features as I left my office in case anyone else was still here. I went into Colton's office first, only to find he wasn't there.

Yes! This was my lucky evening. He was in the lab, and we were going to have super-forbidden but delicious sex there.

I walked briskly to the elevator, still working on schooling my features as I went one floor down and then down the corridor to the lab. I knocked three times at the door. There was no answer.

"Colton?" I called. There was still no answer. I knocked again, but I was met with silence. I plastered my ear to the door. There was no sound. Clearly, he wasn't here.

Hmm. The only other place he could be was in one of the meeting rooms. I couldn't imagine why he'd want to go there. He had plenty of space in his office, but he did say once that he liked to switch spots because it got his brain going. Maybe he'd needed a change of scenery.

I headed back up the stairs, working up a sweat, and then I had to stop and readjust the garters. One of them had slipped down. In my haste to clip it back together, I realized my palms were sweaty. I straightened up and headed into the biggest meeting room, walking with quick steps. The door was closed.

I knew it! He was inside.

I shimmied my hips, working up a seductive smile, then opened the door wide.

Only to come face-to-face with all his brothers and half brothers.

Colton looked up. "Zoey, did anything happen?"

Shit! I wasn't prepared for this scenario. I wasn't sure if my poker face was working.

"H-Hey," I said, stammering a bit. "I didn't realize you had a meeting. Your calendar had 'science time' on it."

"Zoey, hey," Jake said.

"Hi, everyone!" On any other day, I'd make chitchat, but right now I was too embarrassed to say anything. They might not know the intention behind my visit... but I did. "All right then, I'll leave you to your meeting."

"Wait, why did you come by?" Colton asked.

I swallowed hard. *Don't blush, Zoey.* "It can wait until tomorrow. Have a good evening, everyone."

There was a chorus of "Good night" as I closed the door and breathed out a sigh of relief.

Crisis averted.

Colton

I stared at the door even after Zoey closed it, wanting to go after her. I had an inkling she'd come here for a reason, and I wanted to know what it was.

"Earth to Colton," Jake said.

I snapped my gaze away from the door. I'd asked everyone here, and I didn't want to waste their time, but still, my mind was on Zoey.

"Let me just do one thing first," I said. I took out my phone, sending Zoey a quick message.

Colton: Is everything okay?

I put the phone on the table with the screen up so I could see notifications. Then I focused on my family. They were all sitting at the table.

"Thank you for coming here tonight," I started.

"We couldn't say no to a calendar invite, could we?" Maddox teased.

"Don't mind Colton," Gabe said. "He likes to do things a certain way."

"Enough small talk," I said.

"Dude, we just began," Nick protested.

"Yes, but he wants to be quick about it," Maddox said.

Gabe winked at him. "Someone's waiting for him. I don't think for a second that she came in here for a business purpose."

Spencer and Gabe were quick to joke, as usual. Cade cleared his throat. It wasn't easy to know how he'd react—sometimes he took things in stride, yet sometimes he was dead serious.

Maddox looked at Leo and Nick, cocking a brow. Nick cleared his throat. Leo held up his hands in self-defense. Clearly, Maddox had an influence over his younger brothers. I hadn't spent enough time with him to figure out the dynamics yet.

I stared at my youngest brother. "Leave Zoey out of this. I'm not going to engage in locker room talk with you."

Jake cleared his throat. "We're here for a purpose."

I was grateful that he could be the voice of reason even when I wasn't.

Spencer ran a hand through his hair. "Yeah, please make it quick. I haven't been able to sleep the past two nights. Ben's had a fever, so I only have a very limited capacity to focus. I can't waste it on stupid banter."

Maddox nodded. "All right, so you all know about Dad's email."

"Did you speak to him?" I asked.

"No, I told all of you that we'd decide together how to move forward, and that's exactly what I'm doing. I don't want him to think he can pit us against one another," Maddox said.

"Why did he just email you, though?" Cade asked.

Maddox shrugged, looking at Nick and Leo. "I think I'm the last one he was in contact with. I reached out once. It was a long time ago. I don't even know why I did it. Anyway, after that, I never wanted to hear from him again."

"I say we completely ignore it," Jake said.

"I agree with him." I added quickly. No one else seemed to, though, because there were no nods of approval around the table. "You all disagree?" I asked incredulously. "You want to help him out?"

"No," Gabe replied quickly and glanced at Leo, Maddox, and Nick. I suspected they'd already talked about this among themselves. My youngest brother was as close with our half brothers as he was with us. "We just think there's a risk he might reach out to our grandparents if we completely ignore him."

"That's my fear too," Maddox said.

"Are we sure he hasn't done that yet?" Cade asked sharply.

I was surprised he wasn't on Jake's and my side on this one. He'd taken Dad's infidelity very hard.

"Grandmother hasn't said anything," Jake replied. "I questioned her a lot, and I know she wasn't just hiding something. So you all think we should just give him money?" He sounded affronted. I felt the same way.

Maddox rested his head in one palm, looking at us sideways before straightening up. "I think I should talk to him."

"Dude, what?" Nick asked, clearly taken off guard. "You didn't mention that."

"He wrote to me. It would be weird if anyone else talked to him. But I actually want to know more about why he needs the money. Does he plan to reinvest it? Is it to pay off debt? I don't know."

"What makes you think he'll be honest with you?" Gabe asked. He seemed worried; I'd never heard him sound like that.

"Maybe he won't be," Maddox replied with a frown. "But I don't think there's any harm in asking. I wouldn't agree on blindly handing him money."

"I wouldn't agree on giving him any money at all," I stated, though with less conviction than before. What if he went to our grandparents for help? I couldn't even believe that a grown-ass man was asking his sons for money. But he was.

"Look, the last thing we need is for him to cause any ruckus," Nick added, putting both hands on the table and lacing his fingers. "I've scoured the Australian media. He's not making waves there, thank fuck. But you know how things are here. If they get so much as a rumor about him, it could backfire on us."

"You're right." I hadn't thought about that. We'd all worked hard to restore the Whitley reputation. I didn't want to see it trashed again, but I couldn't find it in myself to give him anything.

Spencer yawned. "I'd hoped we'd agree on something tonight."

"Spencer, go home and sleep," I said. "We won't reach a conclusion tonight. If we do, I'll let you know."

He rose from his chair immediately. "I'm going to go with whatever the majority wants. Honestly, I'm not in the mood to process all this right now."

I didn't blame him. With a small child, he had limited energy, and our brother was very good at prioritizing.

Once he left the room, Jake rose from his chair and paced the room, looking out the window. "I say we do whatever it takes to just make sure he stays out of everyone's lives."

"I agree," I said grudgingly.

Maddox nodded. "All right. Still, we don't know much about this, and I'd like to do some checking first. I'll also tell him that I've shared this with all of you so he doesn't get any ideas."

"Good," Gabe said.

"I'm going to try and call him right now," Maddox said, immediately putting his phone to his ear.

With nothing to do but wait, I checked my phone. I had a new message from Zoey.

Zoey: I'd planned to surprise you with a sexy idea, but I totally misread the situation.

Holy fuck! I took a deep breath and exhaled sharply. Damn it, I couldn't believe I was here with these bozos while she was there, waiting for me. *What sexy idea did she have in mind?*

Colton: Are you still at the office?

She immediately replied.

Zoey: No, I'm already home. I'll probably fall asleep soon. It's been a long day. Come to my place tomorrow morning if you want :)

Disappointment rolled through me. I put the phone down, glancing up at the group. Cade was watching me with a suspicious expression and wiggled his eyebrows.

"So, we were right."

I pointed at him. "Don't start."

Maddox lowered his phone, shaking his head. "He didn't pick up. I suggest we all go and let Colton get on with things. I'll get back to you once I hear from him."

"I agree with you," I said.

Jake and Cade exchanged glances. Gabe was grinning. Nick whistled.

"Good for you," Leo said after a while.

He and Nick were the first ones to get up, and then the rest followed suit.

I texted Zoey again.

Colton: Are you still up?

I walked out of the meeting room, too, intending to head straight to her apartment tonight. But she didn't reply, which meant she was probably asleep. Damn it, I needed to see her tonight. I wanted to tell her about the meeting. Not only so she knew I didn't brush her off for nothing but also because I wanted to share this with her.

Instead, I headed to the lab. I had too much energy to sleep, and the work was endless, so I'd better put it to good use.

Chapter Twenty

Zoey

I swung my hips to the left and right, pumping my fist in the air while I drank my morning coffee. I couldn't believe I'd fallen asleep at nine o'clock, but I felt super refreshed this morning.

Colton was going to drop by soon. I already had a text from him when I woke up. He'd sent it late last night, which meant he went to bed thinking about me.

I was going to show him exactly what I'd planned for him last night.

After drinking my coffee, I put the garters under my pink glittery dress. It wasn't appropriate for the office, more of a clubbing dress, but still, you couldn't see the garters unless I bent down, which I didn't plan to do.

At 9:20 a.m., my doorbell rang. Out of habit, I looked through the peephole, thinking it was Colton, and gasped. Holy shit, my brothers were here.

I took a step back, quickly glancing in the mirror. They'd immediately get suspicious if I opened the door wearing a sexy dress at this time of day. I darted to the bathroom, grabbing my fluffy maroon robe and putting it over me.

Shit. You could still see the top of the dress. It wouldn't do.

The doorbell rang again.

"Just a minute!" I yelled. Running to my bedroom, I took off the dress, putting on the first thing I grabbed, which was a homey cotton dress, then threw the robe back on.

I just had to make sure not to undo the belt of the robe because this dress was so short, you could see my garters. The last thing I did before I opened the door was text Colton.

Zoey: My brothers showed up here unexpectedly. Save yourself and don't come over just yet or they'll eat you alive. I'll text you when they're gone.

I put my phone on the console next to the entrance before flinging the door open. Dean was holding coffee cups, and Alex had bags of delicious treats that smelled amazing.

"What are you doing here?" I asked.

Dean was looking behind me. "Are you hiding someone?"

"No," I said very quickly. I mean, I was, but not in the way he thought.

"We brought you breakfast. Thought we'd surprise you."

"Yeah, we haven't caught up in a while," Alex said.

"Come on in." My voice was high-pitched.

"Are you sure you're okay?" Dean asked.

I nodded and welcomed them to the living room.

"Let me grab plates," I said.

I took three from the kitchen, bringing them to the living room and putting them on the coffee table that I also used as a dining table. When I sat down, I pulled my robe tighter so it covered me completely. *Why didn't I take the garters off?* My brain wasn't up to speed this morning.

"Thanks for bringing breakfast."

"You look well rested," Dean said.

I nodded. "I fell asleep super early last night."

"So, how's work going?" Alex added.

"It's good."

"Whitley treating you all right?"

I swallowed hard. "You could say that."

"What's that supposed to mean?" Dean asked.

I looked at my brothers with a grin. "We're going out."

"Why didn't you tell us?" Alex inquired.

I picked a donut out of one of the bags, eating it over my plate. "Because it's still at the beginning."

"We want to meet your boyfriend," Dean said.

I blinked, putting my plate down. "We are not referring to him as my boyfriend, okay?"

"Oh, fucking hell, I knew it. He's taking advantage of you," Alex said, getting to his feet and pacing around. Clearly, he had no interest in the goodies he'd brought. That was fine by me. It meant I had more for myself.

"No, he's not," I said patiently. "I'm very happy with how things are. Look, I'm not one to rush into things." I shrugged.

"I want to talk to him," Alex said.

"You will. In, like, a million years."

I crossed and uncrossed my legs before realizing I wasn't supposed to do that. I quickly covered myself again. Luckily, my brother hadn't noticed.

The doorbell rang just as I was about to reach for a second donut. I froze.

"Are you expecting someone?" Dean asked.

Please let it be the postman. Please let it be the postman.

Did I forget to press Send on my text message?

I swallowed hard, getting up from the couch and heading straight to the door, looking through the peephole. Yep, it was Colton.

This is going to be a bloodbath.

"Who is it?" Alex asked.

"It looks like you'll get your wish after all," I said. "It's Colton."

I spoke loudly, hoping Colton could hear me from the other side of the door, and then I swung it open. He looked exhausted and was carrying a blue gift bag.

"What are you doing here?" I asked him. "Didn't you get my message?"

His eyebrows shot up. "No, my phone's battery is dead."

"My brothers are here," I said under my breath.

And by *here*, I meant they were right behind me. They'd teleported from the living room or something.

Colton looked up at them as he stepped inside. Alex's and Dean's eyes fell on the blue bag, which Colton set on the table.

"What's that?" I asked him.

"A present for you."

I clapped my hands, smiling broadly. "I'll open it later. Colton, this is Alex and Dean."

"Nice to meet both of you," Colton said.

To my relief, they behaved themselves as they exchanged pleasantries. Then we all went to the living room.

"They dropped by with breakfast. Help yourself," I told Colton.

"I'm not hungry," Colton said. "I grabbed something on the way from the office."

I stared at him. "Why were you at the office?"

"I was at the lab until late at night, and I ended up sleeping there."

My mouth dropped open. That would explain why he seemed a bit stiff. I thought it was a reaction to my brothers. I was going to take care of him as soon as we were alone.

"So, Colton, my sister told us you two are dating, but you refuse to be called her boyfriend. Would you mind explaining to us how that's not taking advantage of her?" Alex asked.

I nearly dropped my donut.

"Alex! You can't talk to him like that," I said.

Colton cleared his throat and took my hand, kissing the back of it. "I've got this," he said.

Okay, that wasn't the reaction I was expecting. Not sure what I thought—maybe that he'd bolt or punch my brother.

He looked at the two of them calmly.

"Zoey and I don't want to put pressure on ourselves. The second she tells me she wants me to be her boyfriend, I will be more than happy to let the world know. But until then, we're both good. I understand you want to protect her. As her brothers, it's your right. But know this: I'd never take advantage of her."

My brothers blinked.

Alex nodded. "All right, that's a reasonable explanation."

"I can't believe you two," I said. "Why are you behaving like this?"

"We're just looking out for you, Zoey," Dean said in a soft tone.

"I'm not having it," I informed them.

Colton chuckled.

"What?" I asked him.

"I don't have sisters, but if I did, I'd probably act exactly like this too."

"Good to hear that, man," Alex said, his voice warmer than before.

Oh really? That's what it takes for them to warm up to Colton?

On the other hand, I wasn't going to look a gift horse in the mouth.

"Right, I think we'll catch up another day," Dean said.

Alex looked like he wanted to disagree, but Dean cocked a brow at him.

"Yes, don't be a stranger, Zoey," Alex added.

"I'm not," I protested, although I'd abandoned them a bit since I'd started spending more time with Colton. I was going to fix that.

Colton and I went with them to the front door. I opened it quickly, not wanting them to change their minds. I loved my brothers dearly, but they were being impossible today.

After they left, I closed the door and grinned at Colton. "I'm really sorry about that."

"You have nothing to be sorry about."

I looked behind him at the bag containing my present. "Can I open this now?"

"Sure, I bought it for you."

"Between you and me, I think showing up with a present helped win my brothers over."

He chuckled. "The only one I wanted to impress was you."

I opened the bag and gasped. "You brought me something from Tiffany's?"

"I passed by and saw it, and I thought it would look great on you."

I glanced at him over my shoulder. "You just bought something on a whim from Tiffany's?"

I untied the knot with trembling fingers, then just as carefully unwrapped the paper. It was so pretty that I didn't want to risk damaging it. I opened the box, admiring the gorgeous necklace. It had five teardrop-shaped stones, each a different color.

"I love it," I said.

"Want me to put it on you?"

"Yes. Thank you, Colton."

Once he'd hooked the clasp, I looked at it in the mirror, undoing the belt of my robe so I could see it better on my skin. "Colton, you don't have to buy me gifts."

He stepped behind me, bringing his mouth to my ear, looking at me in the mirror. "I wanted to give you something that would always remind you of me."

I grinned. "I'll wear it all the time." It was understated, so I could even wear it at the office.

He groaned, taking a step back. "What are you wearing?"

I whirled around, glancing down at myself. Yeah, with my robe open, he could totally see my garters.

I laughed, licking my lips. "Funny story. My plan last night was to come into your office wearing these and seduce you. I felt like we could break a few rules. Actually, my original plan was to seduce you in your lab."

His eyes flashed, and his pupils dilated. "Go on."

"This morning, I put them on because the plan was still to seduce you. I had to improvise when my brothers came, and I covered myself up with the robe."

He groaned again, stepping closer. "So, this is all for me, yes?"

I nodded.

"Say it," he commanded.

"It's all for you, Colton," I whispered.

Colton

She looked like a goddess with the necklace, the short dress, and the garters.

"You're the most beautiful woman in the world," I told her.

She opened her mouth, and I stepped closer, tilting her head back slightly. I covered her lips with mine, kissing her slowly, savoring her, losing myself in the way I'd needed to last night. The work in the lab had been completely unsatisfactory. For the first time since I could remember, work hadn't provided the relief I sought. This was what I needed.

She tasted like sugar and apricot jam. I took off her robe completely and drew my fingers from the back of her hands up to her elbows and then farther up to her shoulders. I desperately searched for the dress's zipper. It wasn't at her back.

Finding it on the side, I yanked it down, pushing the dress to the floor. Then I groaned. She was wearing a bra without straps. It was black, just like her panties, which were connected to her tights. Then I realized her panties were completely transparent.

"Fuck, Zoey. You wore this at the office?"

She swallowed hard. "Yeah. As I said, the plan was to seduce you in the lab. I thought I'd make an extra effort, hence why I also went and bought garters."

"I needed you last night," I confessed.

She widened her darkened eyes and ran her hand through her hair. It was exquisite, reaching down her back, and wild. It was about to get wilder still.

"Why?" she asked.

"I met with my brothers and half brothers because they wanted to discuss our father. Maddox is trying to get in touch with him."

"What did you decide?"

"Nothing yet. Our goal is to keep him from reaching out to our grandparents. Anyway, after they left, I texted you."

She pouted. "I fell asleep."

I ran my thumbs over her clavicle and then farther down her chest until I reached her bra.

"I went to the lab. It usually helps me forget, calms me down."

"But not last night?"

"I didn't need work. I needed you."

She gasped, putting both hands on my face. "Colton, I'm always here for you. I'm just putting it out there, but if something like that happens again, feel free to burst through my door and wake me up. I promise I won't mind."

"Fuck, don't say that twice or I'll take you up on it next time."

"I hope you will," she said.

I kissed her again, needing to be as close to her as possible. My hands were all over her body. I needed to take her farther into her apartment or I was liable to fuck her right here against a wall, and that wouldn't do.

I pushed her all the way to the center of the living room, and then we stumbled over something. I jumped to one side, keeping one hand on her lower back, steadying her.

"Whoops," she said with a laugh. We'd nearly knocked over the table.

"Are you hurt?" I asked.

"Not at all," she replied.

I needed to get her naked. "You look sexy wearing these, but I want to rip them off." I bent down on my knees, unclipping the garters from the tights and pulling them down. Then I looked up at her, darting out my tongue and licking once over her panties.

She gasped, putting both hands on top of my head, steeling herself.

"Colton," she whispered. "Give me some warning."

"No, you're so beautiful when you don't expect it."

"I wonder why," she murmured, gasping again as I licked from her entrance up to her clit.

"Because you can't brace yourself," I said as I kissed down the front of her thighs.

"Hmm, you're an expert on pleasure."

I'd taunted her enough. Now I wanted to taste her bare skin. I yanked down her panties and went up to my feet. She made to reach behind herself.

"No, I want to do it," I said.

She dropped her hands and braced them at her sides. I found the clasp easily and undid the bra. Since it had no straps, it fell right down to her feet, her breasts spilling out of it. Her hair was covering the left one, so I pushed it to one side. I pressed my thumbs below her nipples.

She shifted her hips back and forth, groaning. I rubbed my thumbs straight across her nipples, and she gasped.

I smiled wickedly. Damn, she was already so on edge, but so was I. Her hands were on my belt the next second, undoing it and then pushing my pants down.

I took my hands off her, needing to quicken the process. I wanted all my clothes out of the way. Kissing her and touching her wasn't enough—I craved as much skin-on-skin contact as possible. My need for her was deep and all-encompassing. Having her once wasn't enough to satisfy me, but we had the day to ourselves.

"Someone's in a hurry," she said once I'd gotten my pants and underwear out of the way. I dropped my shirt too.

"I am. I want you so damn bad," I said.

I started kissing her shoulders, walking her backward again until we reached the living room wall, nestled between her bookcase and a plant. Then I kissed along the side of her body, down to her hips, and back up. I wanted to touch her pussy and her breasts at the same time, so I grabbed my cock at the base, rubbing the tip against her clit.

"Ooooh." Her voice trembled when I drew circles around her clit.

My left hand went to her breast, cupping it. It was slightly bigger than my palm, and it drove me crazy.

All my plans went out the window when she tilted her hips, and I slid an inch inside her. I was a goner. A grunt tore through me, and then I slid in all the way. I needed her in another position. I wanted to bury myself inside her to the hilt, but I didn't want to fuck her against the wall.

I put a hand on the bookcase, moving the books on top. They fell to the floor with a thump. She didn't protest. I lifted her ass onto it without sliding out of her.

"Are you comfortable?" I asked.

She nodded. "Yes. Yes. I want you deeper." She put her hand under her left knee, tilting her leg up at an angle. I watched as my cock disappeared inside her.

"Colton!" she cried.

I put a hand on her lower back and the other one at the back of her head as I buried my nose in her hair and tasted her neck. That was exactly what I wanted: to be inside her and wrapped around her. I wanted to get my fill of her, but I was starting to realize that wasn't going to be possible. No matter how often I had her, I'd always need her.

I thrust in and out, soaking up her sighs of pleasure. She broke out in a sweat. The skin at the back of her neck was humid.

Fuck yes. All because of me.

I increased my pace, blind with need. The way her pussy felt around my cock was insanely delicious.

A sound broke the air. I stilled.

"What was that?" she asked, and then I realized it came from the bookcase.

I lifted her off it, taking a step back right as it crumbled. She gasped and then burst out laughing.

"I'll get you a new one," I said.

"Later," she murmured and placed her mouth over mine.

I carried her to the wall. It was all I could do. My thrusts became faster. I was even more desperate for her, chasing my release like a madman. She wrapped her legs tightly around me, but I slid a hand between us, pressing my forefinger and middle finger against her clit. Small shocks ran through her body. I felt every single one of them. She wasn't going to last long. Neither was I, but feeling her desire course through both our bodies made me feel connected to her on a level I didn't think was possible. Then she grew so tight around me that she nearly brought me to my knees. She exploded, gasping, clenching her muscles and digging her fingers into my shoulders, pressing her nails against my skin. She was wild, and I loved it.

I looked down at her, taking in the details. She was always beautiful but even more so now, engulfed in pleasure.

I went over the edge unexpectedly. One second, I was drinking her in; the next, my climax hit with unexpected strength. I jerked my hips forward like I wasn't in control of my thrusts anymore. I was moving on pure instinct and need. The relief was tremendous, and yet I craved more of her.

Chapter Twenty-One
Colton

O n Monday morning, we went to visit Grandmother at her home.

"Won't she be overwhelmed with everyone here at the same time?" Zoey asked as we approached the front door.

"No, it's just us. I coordinated with my brothers so we wouldn't crowd her."

"You coordinated? Oh, that's so cute. What did you do, make a WhatsApp group for it?"

"We already have one."

"Oh, right. My bad," she said. Then she patted the small bag she was holding as we stood in front of the door and I knocked.

"I brought her a small 'get well' gift. I hope she likes it."

"Damn it, why didn't I think of that? Can we tell her it's from both of us?"

"No," she said. "This is me. All me. Besides, trust me, even if we do say that, she'll know."

Zoey was probably right. Grandmother would be pleased that Zoey did something so kind.

Grandfather opened the door. "Hi, Colton, Zoey. Nice to see you again."

"And you, too, Mr. Whitley."

"Please, call me Abe."

"How's she feeling?" I asked in a brisk tone.

"She's good."

"Is she taking it easy?"

"Yes. I'm onto her. She's trying to get away with things, but she can't. Honestly, I'm having a lot of fun."

"Why?" I asked as Zoey frowned.

"Payback for how much she warded over me the past few years."

I glanced at Zoey out of the corner of my eye. Her mouth hung open. She still had a lot of things to learn about my family. Sometimes my grandparents managed to surprise even me. I didn't know my grandfather was one for vendettas.

"Come on. Don't party out there without me," my grandmother called from the living room, and we all headed there.

"Zoey!" she exclaimed when she saw us. "Oh, it's so nice of Colton to bring you again."

"Of course," Zoey said. "I wanted to see how you were feeling. And I brought you these," she said, setting the bag next to Grandmother.

"What's this?" she asked.

"My favorite romance novels. I've read them about a million times. They always put me in a better mood, especially when I'm sick and can't do much else besides read."

Zoey was right. Grandmother would never have believed it if we'd told her that I'd pitched in on the present too.

"Thank you, Zoey! Everyone usually brings flowers, and then what am I supposed to do with so many of them? Romance books! Now *that* is going to keep me occupied for a while."

"How are you feeling?" Zoey asked as Grandmother took out a book.

The dude on the cover was mostly naked. Grandfather jerked his head back. It took a lot of effort not to laugh at him.

Grandmother looked at the rest slowly, turning around each cover as if she wanted to give my poor grandfather a heart attack—all the guys were half dressed —before putting them back. "I would like to say I feel just fine, but my headaches are still popping up if I overdo it. I can read though. I just can't move around a lot. Luckily, Abe here is hot on my heels no matter what I do."

"That's great," Zoey said. "You know, I think it's easier for most of us to let others care for us because we're not used to caring for ourselves."

"I guess I never thought about it like that," Grandmother said. "Now, what can we get the two of you? I made some scones earlier."

A vein pulsed in my temple. "You what?" I asked.

"Oh, young man, don't use that tone with me. The doctor didn't say I was bedbound. He said movement is important for circulation, but he advised I stay around the house because everything is familiar. at least until I get my strength back."

"He did say that, actually," Grandfather said. "And she wasn't overdoing it," he added quickly, anticipating my next question.

Zoey gave me an exasperated look. I had to tone this down or everyone would turn against me.

"I'll bring them from the kitchen if you tell me where they are," Zoey offered.

"I'll come with you," I said.

Grandmother nodded. "Good, you do that. Colton knows his way around the kitchen."

"How come?" she asked me.

Once we were out of my grandparents' earshot, I said, "My grandmother used to cook these elaborate dinners, and my brothers and I would clean up afterward. At some point, after Grandfather had a health scare, she agreed to hire a cleaning service. Maybe I can convince her again."

"I don't know your family that well, but I think you might be pushing it."

I started to laugh. "You've read them well, although I do have to say, both of them are surprisingly impatient today."

The corners of her mouth turned down. "I think it's normal. They're probably both on edge."

The scones were done but still inside the warm oven. We took them out, put them all on a plate, and brought them to the living room.

"So, when are the rest of your grandkids coming?" Zoey asked, sitting next to my grandmother, who lit up at the question.

"The rest of the boys are coming today and tomorrow. I don't know why you all insisted on coming separately. I'm perfectly capable of talking to everyone at once."

"Yes, but too much noise and hustle and bustle can induce headaches, remember?" Grandfather said. He sounded genuinely concerned. Could be the humor he'd shown us earlier had simply been to cover up the fact that he was worried. Damn it, why didn't I see through it?

"I remember," my grandmother said, but she didn't fight him further, which was a sign that she agreed with him.

"Do you plan on maybe going on a vacation or something?" Zoey asked. "Some fresh air would do you good, but I don't know what your restrictions are on traveling."

"The doctor actually mentioned that it wouldn't be a bad idea," Grandfather said.

"I was toying with the idea of asking Jake if he'd mind us going to Martha's Vineyard," Grandmother added. "But in a few months. I'm not up for it right now."

"He's got a vacation apartment or something there?" Zoey asked.

"He's got a beautiful house. It's quiet, and the journey isn't very difficult," I replied, already liking the idea. When she was at home, Grandmother seemed possessed by the need to do something. Maybe a getaway would relax her.

"I'm sure Jake wouldn't have anything against it," I said. "I must say, Grandmother, I'm proud of you. You're taking this more seriously than I thought."

"Of course. I want to get better fast. If not, who's going to matchmake the rest of your brothers?"

Zoey gasped and covered her mouth. "Oh, I'm sorry. That was such an inappropriate reaction. I was just..."

"Shocked?" I finished for her.

"Yeah."

Grandmother waved her hand. "These youngsters don't know what's good for them. They'll see things differently once they're my age. Looking back, you'll be able to realize that having someone to share the joys and sorrows is the most beautiful part of life."

Before I met Zoey, I would have discarded Grandmother's affirmation as nostalgic and wishful thinking. I wouldn't have taken her seriously. Yet now, I knew 100 percent that she was right. I couldn't imagine my life without Zoey in it.

"Jeannie, not even a health scare can keep you away from matchmaking." Zoey sounded a bit nervous.

"Oh, honey, it's what keeps me going. Sometimes in the morning, I get up and think, 'Well, Jeannie, you've now lived almost a century. What's going to be different about today?' Then I realize I still have four grandsons to matchmake, and I get to work."

"Jeannie, honestly," Grandfather said.

"There's no use berating her," I informed him.

Grandmother whistled. "See? Even Colton learned that lesson faster than you did."

Usually, I was all for curbing Grandmother's enthusiasm. But I had to admit, she wasn't exactly meddling. She simply saw things differently. She'd known Zoey for a hot minute before realizing she was just what I needed. I was confident enough in my manhood to admit that if Grandmother hadn't pointed it out, it would have taken me a long time to realize it.

Grandmother yawned.

"Time for Zoey and me to go," I said.

"I agree," Zoey added, getting off the couch.

Grandmother made an attempt to get up too.

"No, no, no. It's not necessary," Zoey told her. "Abe will see us out."

"Exactly. Woman, stay put. You've been on your feet enough today." He sounded stricter than I was used to hearing him with Grandmother, but it seemed to do the trick. She smiled and waved at us.

"I'm very glad you two stopped by," Grandmother said.

Zoey grinned. "I'm glad you're feeling better, Jeannie."

"Have a good day, Grandmother," I said, bending down to kiss her cheek before we walked out of the living room.

Once in the hall, I turned to Grandfather. "Listen, that cleaning service you had when you were sick—"

"I'm working on it," Grandfather said abruptly, his voice low. "I'm taking baby steps."

"Abe, don't go around bad-mouthing me," Grandmother called from the living room.

"Hell," Grandfather exclaimed. "That's not what I'm doing," he called back to her.

"I heard something about a cleaning company!"

"We're all on Grandfather's side," I said loudly.

"Don't you play games. I know all of them, okay? I invented some of my own too."

Damn. I'd praised her too quickly. She was far more stubborn than I thought.

"Listen. I've got a plan," Grandfather said. "But you stay out of it."

"I will," I assured him.

"I know how to get Jeannie to agree with me, but she needs time to do that. Hammering on a point usually has the opposite effect."

"I'm starting to learn that," Zoey murmured.

"What are you all still gossiping about?" Grandmother asked.

Grandfather walked backward, pointing at the door.

Zoey was silent as we stepped out of the house.

"What are you thinking?" I asked her.

"That you're all very endearing. How you make plans and look after each other."

"But you're used to that with your brothers."

"It's a bit different. This is intergenerational. Since my parents are always on the road, I don't get a chance to look out for them."

"And they don't get the chance to dote on you," I added.

She shrugged, but her eyes were vulnerable. "That's fine. I miss them a lot, but I think it's also what made me so independent, you know? Everything I ever experienced made me who I am today." She pushed a strand of hair behind her ear.

"It's perfectly all right to admit that you want things."

She narrowed her eyes as we leaned against the car. "But wouldn't that mean I'm ungrateful or unhappy with my parents and my upbringing? Because that is not true."

I considered this. "I think several things can be simultaneously true. That you had a great childhood, but you also wouldn't have minded being spoiled a bit."

"Yeah, that's the right word. I don't really think I realized that until now. I don't want to sound whiny."

"You don't. I want to know everything that's going on inside here." I tapped her temple. "And here." I tapped her heart.

She swallowed hard. "Thanks!" Then the corners of her mouth twitched. "But keep all those swoony things to yourself for now or I won't be able to focus at the office."

"That doesn't sound too bad."

"Oh, yes it does. Because I have a call with my boss in an hour, and I'm supposed to report on... you."

"Mmm, and what are you going to tell him, exactly?"

"That we're making progress. That covers everything, huh?" She grinned.

I leaned over, biting her neck.

"Not even close."

CHAPTER TWENTY-TWO
ZOEY

I loved the necklace Colton gave me so much that I wore it at the office every day. Since the weather was getting colder, I usually wore dresses with higher necklines, and my necklace was hidden underneath the fabric. But this particular Friday, I was wearing one with a V-neck, and my necklace was very visible. I was wearing it proudly, so when Sandra and I went out to lunch, which we hadn't done in a while, I didn't even think about covering it.

She kept looking at it nearly our entire lunch and, at the end, said, "Oh, I'm sorry, girl, but I have to ask. Are you dating a billionaire?"

I jerked my head back. "That's such an odd question."

"It's from Tiffany's, right?"

"Yes."

"That necklace costs something like ten grand."

I stilled. "What?" That couldn't be possible. I blinked incessantly.

"You didn't know?" she said.

"No. I don't know jewelry prices." My voice sounded more robotic by the second.

"Really? I always google the price of stuff when I get it."

I'd never thought about doing that, but now I was thinking that maybe I should have. I would never in a million years have accepted this if I'd known how much it cost.

Colton just dropped that kind of money on me?

Sandra frowned. "You don't look happy."

"Um." I cleared my throat. "I'm just... I don't know. It's a very expensive gift." I touched it absentmindedly. "I wouldn't have accepted if I knew."

She smiled sympathetically. "Clearly, you have a man who likes to spoil you. There aren't many of those around, so enjoy him."

I gave her a strained smile. I needed to talk to Colton.

Sandra and I spoke a bit about her boyfriend for the rest of the lunch, but my mind was still on Colton. I could hardly focus all afternoon.

As the evening rolled on, I couldn't wait and texted Colton. He hadn't been in his office all day and had put "lab day" on the calendar.

Zoey: Are you still in the lab?

Five minutes later, he replied.

Colton: Yes. Do you want to come here? You can keep me company. I'll probably spend a few more hours here.

I couldn't turn down that offer. I was going to see my sexy man in his white coat.

I turned off my computer, since it was already late and I didn't plan on coming back to my office. Then I hurried down to the lab, wondering how to bring up the subject. I was always upfront, but I didn't want to sound ungrateful. I just couldn't understand how he dropped that type of money without... I don't know. Asking me, I guess. Although, he didn't need to ask me how to spend his own money.

Ugh, this is perplexing.

The door to the lab was open.

"Close it after you come in," Colton said. There were two whiteboards full of formulas. There were even some solutions in glass containers.

"What's that?"

"My lead scientist was here until just now, playing around with something."

"He's gone?"

"Yes," Colton answered. "So, what's wrong?" he asked, looking at me intently.

I was playing with my necklace. Clearly, he could tell something was off. I shifted my weight from one foot to the other. This was a foreign sensation to me; I usually didn't get tongue-tied. I didn't mince words.

"The necklace looks gorgeous on you."

"Yeah, about that," I said, biting the inside of my cheek and smoothing my hand over his white coat. "I went to have lunch with Sandra today, and she mentioned that this costs a lot."

He frowned. "What do you mean?"

"Colton, this was ten thousand dollars."

"I don't understand. What's the problem?"

"I didn't know it was that expensive."

"What difference does it make? I saw it and knew you'd love it. That's why I bought it. I didn't even think twice."

"You dropped that much money on an impulse purchase?" I double-checked.

"Yes."

For the first time since Colton and I started going out, I realized we had wildly different concepts of money. Even now, he was looking at me as if he couldn't possibly understand what the issue was.

"Colton, I'm not used to expensive gifts. I really appreciate it, but I can't accept it. I wouldn't have accepted it if I knew how much it costs."

He touched my jaw with his fingertips. "Zoey, I would have bought this if it was seventy dollars, or seven hundred, or whatever. It doesn't matter to me. All that matters is it's something you like and makes you happy."

"Colton, the things you say..."

"And I mean every word. I love you, Zoey, and I want to give you things you enjoy."

I grinned, put my hands on his shoulders, and then jumped him. Several seconds later, I heard the unmistakable ripping sound of fabric. He laughed, grabbing me by the ass and bringing me to the nearest table.

"That was my very enthusiastic 'I love you,'" I informed him. "Can't believe I ripped my dress apart. There's something about this lab."

Colton kissed me, hard, mirroring my desperation. When he deepened the kiss, I parted my legs, shifting to the edge of the table. The dress ripped even more, but I was too lost in Colton to care. Feeling his lips on my mouth and his hands on my body overwhelmed me in a way it never had before. We'd done far more wicked things, but this felt different. More intimate.

Groaning, he stopped the kiss.

"Let's get out of here," Colton said.

"But didn't you say you have to stay until late?"

"I'd probably have to sleep here to figure out why this formula isn't working, but I don't want to. I want to spend the night with you. The lab will still be here tomorrow. The work will be waiting for me."

"How scandalous. I'm keeping you away from work," I teased.

"Before, I would never have even thought about leaving the lab when I was at this point in the process, but you're changing me."

I smiled. "That makes me really happy." Things were changing for me too. Before Colton, I'd never thought about how my life might look in ten or fifteen years, especially not with a guy. But with Colton, I could see us years from now.

Maybe I'd come in here, trying to drag him home one day so we could spoil the two or three kids we'd have.

Where did that thought come from? It was a scary one. I'd always been happy with what I had, but I was now suddenly dreaming about having more.

And it had all begun with a kiss and a ripped skirt.

Chapter Twenty-Three
Colton

The next morning, I woke up later than usual. I immediately turned onto one side, intending to watch Zoey for a while before deciding how to wake her up. My favorite method was to go under the covers and kiss my way down her chest. By the time I reached her belly, she usually reacted.

But she wasn't in bed.

I got up, opening the door of the bedroom, and heard her voice from the living room. The place looked like it'd been robbed. Zoey's stuff was everywhere. Then I went into the bathroom to brush my teeth. She had hair products on one shelf and face creams on another. We spent more time here than at her place, and it showed. I fucking loved it. I never thought I'd say that, but I liked seeing signs that she lived here.

Well, she didn't live here—*yet*.

After cleaning up, I went directly to the living room.

"I'm so glad you could call me," Zoey was saying into the phone.

She noticed me, and her face immediately lit up with a huge smile. She gestured toward me, and I realized what she was asking. I nodded.

"By the way, Colton's here," she told the phone. I assumed she was talking to her parents.

"Oh, can we meet him? Hi, Colton. We can't see you," a woman's voice said.

Zoey chuckled. "Mom, that's because he's not in the camera frame yet."

I went and sat down next to her, focusing on the screen. Two people were waving frantically, looking anywhere but at the camera. I stole a glance at Zoey. She shook her head almost imperceptibly, pressing her lips together. Clearly, her parents weren't big tech aficionados. Her dad vaguely reminded me of her brother Alex, but Zoey looked nothing like her mom.

"We've heard a lot about you, Colton. It's nice to finally meet you."

"Yeah, her brothers told us about you," her dad said.

"But Zoey didn't?" I teased.

She elbowed me lightly.

"She did, but we figured our sons would have a more unbiased opinion," her mom added.

"That's very true," I said.

"All right, I don't want to keep you youngsters any longer. We don't want to disturb you," her mom said.

"How come you're even awake?" I inquired.

"We have a flight to catch."

Now that they mentioned it, I realized they were in an airport. They were each wearing an earpod.

"We had to wake up at three o'clock in the morning. We feel jet-lagged already," her mom continued.

"Where are you flying next?" I asked.

"Rome. We're doing a bit of sightseeing there before our next gallery."

"Have fun and send me lots of photos. Any idea when you'll be back?" Zoey asked. There was apprehension in her voice.

Her mom smiled. "Oh, honey, we got word from the gallery in Copenhagen that they might extend our showing for another month and keep our paintings there. They've asked us to pop in for some events."

Zoey smiled back. "I'm glad for you. Send me pictures from everywhere, okay?"

"Will do. I think we're going to board soon," her mom informed us. "Love you."

"I love you too." Zoey blew a kiss.

"It was nice meeting you, Colton," her dad said.

"Likewise," I replied.

After they hung up, I turned to look at Zoey. She sighed, putting the phone away.

"You miss them," I said.

She nodded. "Yeah, but I know the gallery season will be over soon and then they'll be back, so I'll have them all to myself." She smiled sheepishly. "I know I'm being very possessive."

I touched her lips. She was wearing her nightgown still. "I think it's nice that you want to be so close with them."

She yawned. "I didn't get to shower because they called and I didn't want to miss it. I should go now, maybe wash my hair too."

I pulled her onto my lap, kissing the side of her neck. "By the way, do you want to order a shelf or something? I noticed you don't have too much space in the bathroom for your stuff."

She stilled, looking at a fixed point on my chest. "You want me to order a shelf?" she parroted.

"Or something to help you organize things a bit more."

She swallowed hard. "And you wouldn't mind?"

I frowned. "Why would I? I'm asking."

She licked her lips. "I don't know, Colton. This is new to me."

I pulled her closer to me so her breasts were pressed against my chest. "It's new for me, too, Zoey, but I'm excited to explore this new stage of life with you."

She grinned, kissing one corner of my mouth and then the other. The gesture was so tender that it completely caught me off guard. She grinned, shimmying in my lap.

"Okay, then I guess I'm going to look around for a shelf. What do you plan to do today?" she asked.

I tilted my head. "I should probably go back to the lab, but that's not appealing at all right now."

"I wonder why."

"So do I," I teased.

"Does it have something to do with me?"

She batted her eyelashes. Fucking hell, she was cute.

I kissed the side of her neck. She shimmied some more, gasping when I pushed my hand under her nightgown, cupping her ass and then her pussy.

"Hey! You already want to do the dirty first thing in the morning, huh?"

"I always want that," I replied. "Fucking always."

"Hm, I could be talked into it," she said, but my phone vibrated on the kitchen island. I groaned.

"Wait, I'll bring it to you."

She jumped up from my lap and hurried to the kitchen, grabbing the phone and returning with it. She made to sit next to me, but I pulled her right back onto my lap. Zoey immediately smiled, leaning in to kiss my Adam's apple. When she straightened up, I looked at the phone.

"Fuck," I said.

"What is it?" Her voice was laced with worry. "Is Jeannie okay?"

"Yeah, this is about our father. Maddox finally talked to him and suggests we all get together to discuss it."

"That's smart. It's better than going back and forth over the phone." She pressed her thumbs on my forehead, tracing my skin from my eyebrows up to my hairline.

"What are you doing?"

"You've got frown lines. I'm trying to make them disappear."

My phone beeped with another message.

"What the hell?" I asked.

"What?"

"They're suggesting we all drop by Nick's fitness club. They moved their weekly tennis match with Spencer and Cade. They think I can drop everything and just show up?"

Zoey cleared her throat.

I stared at her. "What?"

The corners of her mouth twitched, and then she smiled. "God forbid they suggest something spontaneous, huh?"

"That's not it," I said. "I like to plan things like that. It's a big conversation."

"Colton, honestly, if you don't feel comfortable, don't go. But... I don't know... I don't think family stuff needs to be scheduled in. And you do spontaneous stuff. You took me to Salem, and it was amazing."

I grinned. "You're finding this very amusing, aren't you?"

She nodded. "Yeah."

She put her hands on my chest, rubbing them up and down. The move was calming, but I considered her words. Before Zoey, I would have simply headed to the lab today and told Maddox we would need to reschedule. But I didn't want to go to the lab today. I'd planned to spend the weekend with Zoey.

"I'll do it. I'll go to the club, but only if you come with me."

"You're serious?"

"Fuck yes." I wanted her to be part of every facet of my life. I had this drive to share everything with her. I'd only ever been to Nick's club once before, and this time I wanted Zoey there with me.

"All right, that sounds like a deal," she said. "I do have some workout clothes here. I'll just grab them, and we can go," she said.

I stood up. "You really don't mind doing that on Saturday?"

She shrugged. "I'm game for anything. Unlike you, Colton Whitley, I don't plan my weekends, so I'm happy with whatever."

I put my hands on her back, kissing her hard while walking her backward until we reached the wall. I couldn't get enough of her. Even though she slept here often, I was inventing reasons just to see her. Sometimes to kiss her, sometimes just to watch her. This was an incredible feeling.

She grinned as she pushed me away. Her mouth was red.

"Come on, chop chop. We can leave the hot romantic things for later."

An hour later, we entered the fitness center. I wasn't a big fan of them; as far as I was concerned, going to the gym was a waste of time. The treadmill and weights section in my home were all I needed besides the ring.

"This is amazing," Zoey said, looking around. We'd brought our training gear with us. Zoey insisted we could train here after my chat with my brothers.

The fitness branch wasn't part of the original group of companies in Whitley Industries. Father set it up on his own, and Nick had transformed it by leaps and bounds.

I remembered reading the financial reports of all the companies in Whitley Industries back in the day when I first started at Whitley Biotech. The fitness branch was barely breaking even. Considering Nick had expanded it and it was now one of the top fitness clubs in the country, I was sure it was doing extraordinarily well financially.

We went straight to the reception desk where a woman sat behind a screen.

"Hi, I'm Colton Whitley."

Her expression immediately changed, going from polite to eager, smiling and looking at me and Zoey.

"Yes, Nick told me you were coming. They're expecting you. We can give you a small tour or you can head right to the locker rooms."

I turned to Zoey. "We can do a tour later."

"Sure. I'm curious. I want to see the fitness studio and check out everything."

I groaned. The prospect of checking out everything was daunting. "Come on, don't be such a grump," she said, and I laughed. "I know, not everyone can be a ray of sunshine like me. But you know what they say, 'Fake it until you make it.'" Her enthusiasm was contagious.

She was right. We could explore it together. At any rate, I wouldn't mind watching her work out. Even though it would probably be even harder for me to keep my hands off her. Whenever I saw her in tight spandex in the workout room at home, I immediately got a hard-on. I couldn't see myself doing much better in public.

"Anyway, he asked us to do anything to make you feel comfortable, so let us know what you need," the receptionist said.

I appreciated that. I was determined to make more of an effort with my half brothers. I was the one who'd been standing in the way all this time.

I'd only been here once before and had hung around with my brothers at the bar. Spencer had needed everyone's advice, and I wasn't one to sit out a family meeting if I could help.

The receptionist showed us to the changing room. Zoey and I agreed to meet in front. Five minutes later, I came out, looking around. There was a place to fill the water bottle I got from the reception area, so I went to do just that. Someone walked up to me, and I stepped to the right.

"Oh, hi. Thanks, such a gentleman. You can finish filling your bottle."

"No, be my guest."

"I haven't seen you around," she said with a smile.

"Only my second time here."

"I could show you around. I've been coming here for years. I know all the best spots."

"The best spots in the gym?"

"You know, where it's not too crowded," she said. "Where we can grab a drink, if you want to buy one."

I realized she was hitting on me. "I'm here with someone, so no thanks."

The woman took a step back, shrugging. "My bad. Didn't know you were taken."

She glanced at my finger and smiled, looking very pleased.

What the hell? Suddenly, I realized she was checking for a ring.

"I'm not interested," I repeated.

"All right, love," she said, turning around.

I shook my head, finally filling my water bottle. Then I heard a shuffle behind me, and looked over my shoulder. It was Zoey.

"Hey," I said, "when did you come up? I didn't hear you."

"No, you were talking to that woman," she said.

"You heard that?"

"Yes, I did."

"Why didn't you say anything?"

"I don't know. I was too surprised."

I walked over to her, giving her the full water bottle and filling her empty one.

"I leave you alone for a few seconds and you get hit on, huh?"

I looked up. Her voice was odd. "What's wrong?" I asked.

"Nothing. I don't know. It was a strange feeling. You didn't even flirt back."

I blinked. "Why would I? I didn't realize she was flirting until she flat-out asked me to buy her a drink."

She swallowed hard, draping her arms around my neck. "How are you even real?"

I moved my free hand from her waist up to her shoulder and then her neck. I had to keep eye contact because, damn it, she was far too sexy in these clothes. I spoke in her ear. "You're the only one who matters to me, babe. You're my everything."

She shivered. I was fighting my instinct to pin her against the nearest wall. Damn, it was a bad idea to be in public with her when she looked this delicious.

"Zoey, Colton, you're here. Oh shit, I didn't mean to interrupt." Nick's voice came from behind us.

I felt Zoey suck in a breath before I turned around.

Nick grinned. "Right. Far from me to want to cockblock anyone, but just so you know, we do have cameras everywhere."

Zoey blushed violently, which was even more delicious.

"Thank you for the information," I said curtly.

CHAPTER TWENTY-FOUR
COLTON

"This place is amazing," Zoey said.

"You've done a great job," I told Nick. "Where's everyone else?"

"We're just about to start our tennis match. You play?" he asked me. "No."

"We could come cheer for you," Zoey said.

Nick laughed, and then he turned serious again. "Wait, you meant that? I think Colton's going to shut that down quickly."

"We can join you," I said.

Nick's eyes bulged. He glanced at Zoey. "Well, aren't you the good influence on him? He's smiling way more since he met you."

I grunted.

"Oh, that I recognize. He's the master of the grunts," Nick said. "Come on. Follow me."

Zoey grinned at me, sending me an air kiss as we followed Nick through the gym. He pointed out the different sections: saunas, steam rooms, massage, and aromatherapy. Then we went down a staircase.

"It's in the basement?" I asked.

"Yes, we have some outdoors, but it's too windy this time of year, and that can influence the game. We've got rooms for ping-pong, racquet-ball and badminton, and tennis."

My half brother was clever for offering solutions year-round.

I realized that everyone was at the tennis court, even though only Maddox, Leo, Nick, Cade, and Spencer were playing. Gabe, Jake, and I had never played.

Jake was sitting on a chair. I went with Zoey over to him. He stood up, shaking my hand.

"I knew it," Jake said.

"What?"

"From the second you agreed to join us here, we figured Zoey probably talked you into it," Maddox said.

I glanced at all my brothers. "You have conversations about me behind my back?"

"No, just this one time," Leo clarified.

"All right, guys, now let's get to the game," Spencer said.

"How about we talk first?" I suggested.

"No can do, man. We booked the court," Cade said.

"Yes, but you know the owner," Nick replied with a wink. "I can arrange for us to use the court longer if you want to talk first."

"We can start by ripping off the Band-Aid," Jake suggested.

"Do you guys want me to give you space?" Zoey asked.

"Hell no," I replied.

"Damn, that was fast," Cade teased.

"I, for one, want to get rid of all the excess adrenaline I have first," Spencer said.

That was unexpected. Spencer usually took things calmly. Cade had always been the hotheaded one and Spencer the one to calm him down.

"Because right now my instinct would be to simply tell him to fuck off, and we can't have that," he continued.

Maddox cocked a brow and looked around the group.

"It's fine by me. We don't have plans for today," I said.

Cade looked at Zoey. "Who are you, and what have you done with Colton? This is definitely not our brother. Did he manage to clone himself, and our real brother is locked up in his lab?"

I laughed. "Not at all."

What a bunch of clowns.

"Is this your way of praising him?" she asked Cade. "I'm not sure if it's working."

Gabe whistled. "You show him, Zoey."

"Come on, let's play," Spencer said. "We can gossip later."

I watched him intently. It was true that he'd been tired ever since Ben came into his life, but I wondered if there was something else going on with my brother, if he needed more support than he let on. I knew jack shit about taking care of a kid, especially one as small as Ben, but I could offer my skills in other ways. Maybe I could take some of the workload off him at Whitley Publishing.

I didn't know much about tennis, but I did enjoy watching my brothers. They switched positions between sets, and everyone got to play.

Forty minutes later, Spencer said, "All right, I shouldn't have insisted on playing."

He lost spectacularly.

"Yeah, no shit," Cade said. He sounded annoyed. "Why were you playing so shitty?"

Spencer shook his head. "I haven't slept well in days. Ben's had colic."

"That sucks," Jake said.

"Come on, let's go out for a drink. You're getting a double espresso," Nick told Spencer.

"What are you thinking about?" Zoey asked as we all went up.

I kept her close, putting my arm around her waist. "I'm going to ask my brother if he needs help with the company or something, see if I can help out in any way."

She smiled. "You want to add more to your plate?"

"I can handle it," I assured her.

"You're a great brother. If you want, I could help with that. I can facilitate communications and so on."

If my brothers weren't with us on the staircase, I would have pinned her against the wall and kissed her until her legs shook. I couldn't believe she cared about me and my family enough to volunteer to help. She understood without me having to tell her how important this was to me.

She narrowed her eyes. "What exactly is going on in your head? You look like you're having... sexy thoughts."

"Fuck yes," I said.

"Elaborate."

As we came out from the staircase, Nick led us to the bar and relaxation area. There were plenty of people around, but they were all sitting on the armchairs and couches.

"Are you sure you don't want me to just go work out while you talk?" Zoey asked. "I don't want to intrude."

"Babe, you're part of the family as far as I'm concerned. I want you to know everything."

She smiled brilliantly as we all sat on the bar stools. They served no alcohol here as far as I knew, just concoctions of fruit juices that looked entirely unappealing.

"All right, everyone," Maddox said. "Ready?"

I nodded, wanting to get the gist of it and see if it could affect the Whitley name or our grandparents in any way.

"The debts he racked up are to banks and investors. I asked him point-blank if he'd asked shady people for money, and he assured me he hadn't. He didn't make any threats about going to our grandparents or the press."

"That's good," Cade said. His voice was tight.

"I wouldn't put it past him to try and blackmail us," Jake said.

I agreed with him. When it came to Father, my expectations were rock bottom.

Maddox cleared his throat. "He did, however, point out that he owned shares in Whitley Industries."

It was a minority package. A vein pulsed in my temple. Our grandfather had never transferred the majority package to him. Instead, he gave us grandsons our respective shares when we turned eighteen. But Father retained the minor package and had received dividends for years. Which, now that I thought about it, was a nice chunk of change.

"He's essentially asking us to buy him out," Maddox finished.

No one said anything.

I straightened up. "Fuck yes. I'd give him whatever he wants if he gives up his shares."

Even with his minority package, the amount of cash required to do this was astronomical. But I was certain we could come up with it. And it would mean Father was finally going to be out of Whitley Industries—and our lives—for good.

Maddox shrugged. "I feel the same. But he could have just led with that instead of saying he needed money."

"I bet he thought he could just convince us to give him money and he could keep his shares," Jake said. "See, he's still a fucking snake."

"You know, we don't always have to think the worst of him," Spencer said.

Yeah, there was my peacemaking brother.

"Yes, we fucking do," Cade replied.

Gabe, Leo, and Nick were silent.

"You three, where do you stand?" I asked. "For me, it's a no-brainer."

Zoey curled her arm around mine, and her fingers clasped my wrist. She gave me a meaningful look.

"Colton," she said, nudging me lightly.

"What?" I asked, waiting for the guys to answer my question.

"Bro, I think that's her way of telling you that you can't boss us around," Maddox interjected in a cautious way.

Jake was holding back laughter.

Gabe whistled. "But that doesn't mean he won't try, Zoey. You've still got a few things to learn about our brother."

Cade straightened up. "You know what? I'm with Colton on this one. We should all crunch numbers and see how much liquidity we actually need. We're talking probably something close to two hundred million."

Zoey stiffened next to me. I knew she wasn't used to this kind of conversation about money. I put my arm around her shoulders.

"Why don't we all check finances while everyone considers where they stand, and then we regroup?" I suggested.

As much as I wanted to get this over with, it wasn't something we could decide on the spot.

"Anyone else feel like we're rewarding him by giving him what he wants?" Jake asked in a tight voice.

"They are *his* shares," I pointed out.

Gabe looked at me. "That's his way of nudging us in the direction he wants."

"Yes, he's got a lot of skill," Zoey said. "I'm starting to learn that."

Leo winked at her. "You and us too."

Nick and Leo hadn't given an opinion either way. "What's your instinct telling you two?" I asked them.

"I've got to think about it," Nick said.

"I don't like to make big decisions before considering it," Leo added, "but your approach is good. We should check finances first. If that won't work out, then we'll have our answer."

I frowned, looking at Jake and Gabe. All of my brothers were doing spectacularly, but Whitley Biotech was a front-runner. Pharma had always been extremely profitable.

I cleared my throat. "Listen. Don't feel pressured. This doesn't have to be split equally, okay? Everyone just check how much cash you can spend, and I'll come up with the rest," I said.

"Now, wait a second," Jake began.

Everyone started protesting at the same time.

I was starting to learn more and more about my half brothers with this one conversation alone. They liked to have fun and mess around and sometimes seemed to not take things seriously, but that was only a first impression. They were cerebral, weighing pros and cons, and I appreciated that. They were very much like Gabe.

"For now, let's forget I brought it up," I said. "But keep it in the back of your minds."

There was a murmur of agreement.

"Maddox, thanks for doing this," Cade said.

Maddox nodded. "No problem. I won't tell him anything for now. I'll wait for all of us to decide."

"By the way," Leo said, "we should discuss this with our grandparents too."

That had crossed my mind as well. "I know."

Everyone else nodded.

It was one thing to protect them from Dad's antics, but buying him out of Whitley Industries was another thing altogether. They had a right to know and to veto it if they so desired.

"All right. Who wants to go play tennis again?" Nick asked. "I just got confirmation from my team that we can use one of the courts."

Leo, Nick, Cade, and Spencer immediately rose to their feet.

Gabe said, "No, man. I'm out. I'm sorry. I don't find watching so fascinating."

"Yeah, not my cup of tea either," Jake agreed. "I need to go, anyway. I promised Natalie I'd take her out after meeting you guys. She's at our grandparents' house with Meredith."

Jake left at the same time as the rest went to the court. Gabe was still here with us.

I got down from the chair and stood next to Zoey, threading my fingers through her hair, stepping closer so I could inhale the scent of her shampoo.

"All right," Gabe said. "I'm going to go too."

"Wait, I wanted to talk about Spencer," I said. "He seems a bit out of it. Think he needs help? I could take some things off his plate with the company."

Gabe laughed, throwing his head back. "Will you look at that? You and I do have something in common. I offered that. He bit my head off, so don't do the same."

"Okay," I said, feeling mad respect for my little brother because, hell, he had his hands full expanding the distillery.

"Time to head out. I'll think about this and let the gang know."

"It's a good thing Maddox has offered to take over conversing with Father. He's doing a good job at it."

Gabe shrugged. "I don't think it's as easy for him as he pretends it is."

"I think you're right," Zoey said. "He seemed a bit uneasy and like he was working hard to cover it up."

"How could you tell that?" I asked.

"I don't know. It's just a feeling."

Gabe pointed at her, then gave her a thumbs-up. "I think you're onto something. I'm going to figure out a way to bring that up to him, see how he's handling it."

Zoey sighed. "Wow. So taking care of each other is a family trait, huh? It's a very attractive one, by the way."

I cleared my throat.

She narrowed her eyes. "Please tell me you're not jealous of your own brother."

Gabe threw his head back, laughing. "You know, I have to give it to Grandmother. She really has a sixth sense. Zoey, you are exactly what Colton needed."

He winked, getting down from his chair. After bidding us goodbye, he left.

I focused on Zoey, wiggling my eyebrows. "How about working out now?"

"Hmm... do you really want to work out, or do you just want to ogle me?"

"I can do both."

"Of course you can."

My phone vibrated twice, which meant I'd gotten a new email. I'd forgotten to put it on Airplane Mode. I took it out, intending to just go into settings and then, obviously, went straight to the inbox.

Interim meeting was the subject line at the top of the inbox. Browning had sent me an email requesting a meeting to discuss the midquarter results. Strange. It wasn't unheard of. We just hadn't done it in a few years. Usually, when the company made profits, it wasn't necessary, and we were doing very well right now. Still, it didn't hurt to get together.

"What's wrong?" Zoey asked.

I briefly showed her the email. She looked at me questioningly.

"This is normal," I said.

"When does he want to meet?" she asked.

"Doesn't say. But it does say he'll be at the office on Monday, so he'll drop by. Want to join us?" I asked. "I'd like to introduce you to him."

She grinned. "I'd love that."

"All right. Now, how about that workout?"

Zoey pinched my abs. "Why does that sound like you're talking dirty to me?"

I pulled her even closer to me. "Because I am. This is foreplay, babe. Just foreplay."

Chapter Twenty-Five

Zoey

On Monday morning, Colton and I went together to Browning's office. He was on the fourth floor. Colton knocked at the open door.

Browning immediately rose to his feet. I guessed he was probably in his sixties but looked very fit.

"Colton, what brings you by? Oh, and you're Zoey, aren't you?" he asked.

I smiled. "Yes."

"It's great to meet you. I've heard a lot of things about you. So many, in fact, that I wasn't even sure you were real," he joked. "Colton is now actually responding to our requests and emails. Thank you."

"I just pointed out some tips and tricks," I said.

"Don't downplay your work," Colton replied.

"I'm not, but it's give-and-take. I share techniques with my clients, but if they aren't open to it, then it's all for naught." I clapped my hands together. "All right, well, I know you've got things to talk about. I'll see myself up to my office."

"You know, Zoey, you should stay," Browning said. "I'd like to hear more about your work."

"Browning, I actually stopped by to ask about that email," Colton said.

Browning darted his gaze to Colton. I sat up straighter, rolling my shoulders, putting up my guard. Something was off.

"Listen, Colton, why don't we agree on a meeting time?"

"If something's wrong, I want to know now," Colton said.

"Well, all right." Browning ran a hand through his hair. "Fine, fine, then let's talk about it now. Take a seat. You know what? Both of you, actually. Maybe Zoey will be able to help with the issue at hand."

"What issue?" I asked. I didn't like this.

He looked straight at Colton. "Look, you're a very smart man. I've watched you closely over the past years, and I've never seen someone work with so much dedication. People might call you a workaholic, but that's a key reason for your successes. You always give 200 percent."

"I don't see the problem," Colton said.

Browning looked away again. Damn it, why wasn't he speaking clearly? "Look, I've reviewed the documentation of your current work."

"And you found mistakes?" Colton asked, sounding affronted.

"No, not mistakes," Browning said. I had a feeling he was schooling his features and choosing his words carefully. "But you're not making as much progress as I thought you would. Based on your past work, you usually have more to show after two months. Now, far be it from me to tell you how to spend your free time, but I've heard that lately you're leaving the office much earlier."

"You're having me watched?" Colton asked. His voice was cold.

"No! Of course not. But you being a workaholic is a running joke. Is it possible that you've lost your focus?"

Browning turned to me. "Maybe you can help with that, Zoey. After all, you truly performed a miracle improving his communication with all of us."

I tried to keep my composure. Browning was way out of line. How the hell could he tell Colton he wasn't working hard enough? He was the hardest worker I'd ever met, *and* he was the CEO. If he wanted to take time off, he could.

"From what I can tell, Mr. Browning, Colton knows how to pace himself. It's not in my job description to regulate his free time. That would be *overstepping my boundaries* and my contract." I emphasized the words, hoping he'd pick up the hint.

He didn't. Instead, he turned to Colton. "Yes, yes, of course you can have as much free time as you want, but the point is... well, this particular research is progressing at a slower rate than usual. I'm not sure if you're aware of that."

"I'm aware," Colton said, rising from his chair. I followed suit. "I respect you a lot. Your knowledge is paramount. Your contribution to the company is something I will always value as well as your unflinching loyalty to my mother. But this will be the last time you question how I spend my time."

Browning held his hands up. "Okay. I didn't mean to"—he glanced at me—"overstep boundaries, as Zoey said. I just thought you might need a wake-up call. If this is deliberate, then my apologies. But if there's something causing you to lose your focus, then please..."

I felt chilled to the bone.

"Browning," Colton said coldly.

"I just have your best interest at heart, you know that."

"As I said, I respect you for a lot of things. But don't bring up this topic again."

"Understood," Browning said. "Zoey, it was nice meeting you."

"And you," I replied, but my voice sounded robotic.

Colton and I left Browning's office right after that, walking side by side in silence right up until we reached the door to Colton's office. Usually, I'd duck into mine, but I wanted to talk to Colton, so I stepped inside his. He closed the door.

"Sorry you had to hear that. I thought that was going to go a completely different way," he said.

"You know he was being completely unreasonable, right?"

Colton leaned with his ass against his desk, resting his hands at his sides on the edge. "Yes and no. He's right. I have worked at a slower pace than usual."

I walked to him with quick steps. "Colton, you were completely overworking yourself before. It wasn't a sustainable pace."

He looked up at me, shrugging. "I kept it up for years, and it got results. It's just that this damn formula has been eluding me, and I fucking don't know why. I just can't figure it out."

I closed my eyes, feeling his frustration. Then I opened them again. Stepping even closer, I put both hands on his shoulders. He was tense. "Yes, but half your family was on your case about being a workaholic. Doesn't that mean anything?"

He leaned over, kissing my left arm. "Yes, it does. But my motto had always been to give all I have to my work. Lately I haven't done that."

I narrowed my eyes. "You know what? Maybe Browning was right about the amount of work needed, but not in the way both of you think. You shouldn't be working more. You should be delegating. You have a team of brilliant scientists, and if something isn't working, maybe they can find the answer, or at least steer you in the right direction. Not every discovery has to rest on your shoulders."

"I work best alone," he countered.

"That's because you haven't tried any other way," I said, pressing my forehead to his. "And that really is something you should consider. At least try it, see if it works."

My heart rate was erratic. He swallowed audibly. I wanted to help him, but I didn't want to push. Nobody liked a bossy know-it-all.

He kissed down my arm again until he reached my hand and said, "I've always had this insane urge to work, you know? Like being inside that lab was the only time I felt at ease. Happy, even. That's changed lately." He held my hand. "Since I started spending time with you." He lifted his head, making eye contact. "Fuck, you're all I need," he said, standing up straighter and pulling me close to him.

My heart slid back into its place, but I was still feeling a bit uneasy.

He kissed my forehead. I felt in his body language that he was still tense.

There was a loud knock at the door.

"Can I come in?" The voice belonged to one of his lead scientists, but I couldn't remember for the life of me who it was.

"Sure," Colton said.

The second I stepped away from him, the door opened.

"Hey, Zoey. I thought I heard someone inside. Sorry to interrupt. Listen, Colton, can you come down to the lab? We're trying to do something, and we need your help."

"Sure, I'll come right away."

"Good," the guy said, then darted out the door, closing it behind him.

Colton took my hand, kissing it and squeezing my fingers. "We'll talk later, okay?"

I took another deep breath and nodded.

I was afraid he was considering what Browning said about cutting distractions out of his life.

And, well... the only distraction was... me.

CHAPTER TWENTY-SIX
COLTON

The rest of the week was insane. I spent more time in the lab than in the last month combined. At the same time, my brothers and half brothers reached a decision—they agreed to buy out Father. But we needed to speak to our grandparents first.

That was why, on Saturday, we all met at Spencer's house. His yard wasn't as big as the one at our grandparents', but he assured us that he had plenty of space for us all. He lived in a great neighborhood. He'd bought this house right after finding out he was a father, insisting he wanted his son to have a yard and a place to play outside. Before this, he'd lived in a bachelor pad much like mine.

We'd agreed to tell our grandparents today. They had a right to know if we decided to buy Father out. Grandfather had founded the company in the first place, so the two of them had to agree to it.

"He likes you so much," Penny exclaimed.

I'd been carrying Ben for the better part of the last half hour. Everyone in the family had been clamoring to hold him, but he'd cried when Jake and Natalie tried, then Meredith, then Gabe. He only seemed to like me.

And I was feeling fucking smug about that.

"He's so relaxed with you." Penny touched his small hand, and Ben smiled at her.

I was extremely happy that my brother had met Penny. He'd had the shock of his life when he found out his ex had had his child. He hadn't even known she was pregnant. She'd thought the baby belonged to the man she cheated on my brother with. But Spencer had done well by his son. That was my brother to a T—he could maintain calm even in a difficult situation.

Then he met Penny, and she cared about Ben a lot, basically considered him her son.

She and I came inside when Ben started fussing. I didn't know how to prepare his bottle. I watched Penny intently, memorizing all the steps. It seemed easy enough. Until now, the only ones in the family who'd had him for longer than an hour, and even overnight, were my grandparents. Before, he'd seemed small and fragile. I'd been afraid to even hold him for too long for fear that I might break him. But now he was bigger and sturdier. He was eating solids as well. I was looking forward to spending more time with my nephew.

Zoey came up to us. "Hey, you need any help?"

She cooed at Ben.

Penny chuckled. "You're trying to see if you can get Ben, huh?"

"You know it. I didn't want to insist before because everyone was already waiting in line."

"So you waited until there was no one around. Smart," Penny said.

I liked the ease between Zoey and my brothers' women. They'd only met today, but they seemed to get along.

Zoey stepped closer, looking at me eagerly.

I was planning to move Ben around anyway so he could take the bottle, but I transferred him to Zoey's arms. I watched him carefully, ready to take him back at the slightest sign that he wasn't comfortable. But the little guy immediately laughed at her.

"Hey, he didn't laugh at me," I said.

"Oh, and now you're jealous." Penny chuckled. "You know, I think the guys are too hard on you. You're not such a grump."

"Yeah, he is. Trust me," Zoey replied, smiling at Ben.

Something tugged inside me. I loved the sight of her with the baby.

"All right. Here's the bottle," Penny exclaimed, capping it and testing the temperature. "That's okay. Oh, Spencer is gesturing that he needs me outside. Do you want to try to feed him?"

"Sure." I took the bottle from her. I usually asked for instructions about everything regarding Ben, but this seemed straightforward. I tipped it, and the little guy began to drink.

Penny grinned. "That's it. Oh, you two are cute."

After Penny went outside, I kept a close eye on him, trying to gauge from his expressions if he was feeling okay.

"You can relax, Colton," Zoey said. "He's happy in my arms."

"You're really good at this. How are you enjoying the day?" I asked.

We'd been here for about two hours. Spencer and Penny had ordered pizza for everyone. They always liked to keep things simple. Everyone enjoyed pizza, and they didn't have to clean or cook. It was a win-win.

"Jeannie looks so much better."

I couldn't believe she cared so much about my grandmother. She even brought her the water bottle she talked about at the hospital. Grandmother accepted it reluctantly. I was certain that if my brothers or half brothers suggested it, she would have bitten our heads off.

She was right. Grandmother looked much better, although she hadn't yet made any plans for Martha's Vineyard. She also hadn't requested to hold Ben even once. In the past, she'd barely put him down or shared him with anyone else, so I took it as a sign that she hadn't fully recovered. But it gave me peace of mind that she seemed to accept that and was acting accordingly.

Half of my mind was still on my research. My lead scientist was in the lab today. I'd left him some formulas to play around with. I was trying to loosen my reins, but I wasn't too successful. I usually would have spent the whole weekend there, but my brothers and I decided not to postpone this any longer. We needed to speak to our grandparents.

"Okay, I think the little guy is done," Zoey said once the bottle was empty.

Spencer came in at that moment. "Hey, you two. Penny said you fed Ben. I'm gonna burp him."

"Can I do it?" Zoey asked in a shy voice. I'd never heard her sound like that.

"Are you sure?" Spencer asked.

Zoey nodded.

"Here. This is the cloth we use." He handed her one from the dining room table, arranging it on her shoulder. "He doesn't need burping as much as before, but he still gets a tummy ache if I don't do it at all."

Zoey kept Ben on her shoulder for a few minutes, and then Spencer looked at me.

"How about going outside and breaking the news?"

I nodded. "Let's do that."

Everyone else was sitting outside. My half brothers and Gabe sat nearest to Grandmother. Our grandfather was between Natalie and Meredith. Jake stood next to his wife.

"You know how I measure how well Jeannie's doing? By how much she's plotting, and I'd say she's up to 95 percent," Grandfather said.

"She's already got plans for the rest of the boys?" Natalie inquired.

"Of course," Grandfather assured her.

"So who's next?" Meredith asked.

I walked away from the conversation quickly. I did not want to be privy to that information. Then I'd feel compelled to tell whoever it was, and... well, let's just say, sometimes it was better if you didn't see things coming. It was certainly true in my case.

I cleared my throat. Gabe looked up; he'd been grinning but toned it down. Maddox seemed to immediately catch on and elbowed Nick, who was sharing something with Leo and Grandmother.

Leo also went quiet.

Grandmother narrowed her eyes. "What's going on?"

"How can you tell something's up?" Leo asked.

"You boys never stop giving each other a hard time even for one second. Now you're all silent." Grandmother looked around, then said, "Spill."

I nodded at Maddox. He was the one who'd been in contact with Father, so it made sense for him to lead this conversation.

I glanced around and saw Jake staring at us. I figured this had to be hardest on him. He'd been the one to discover the clues that led us to our father's infidelity, after all.

"All right, Gran, Grandpa, we've got to share something with you."

It still jarred me to hear him say Gran and Grandpa. They'd always been Grandmother and Grandfather to my brothers and me. Mother always insisted we use the proper form.

"Dad contacted me a while ago," Maddox began.

Grandfather turned white. Grandmother pressed her lips together.

"He needs a bailout," Maddox continued. "He started a business that went belly up, and he needs to settle some debts."

"And he dared ask you for money?" Grandfather asked.

I hadn't heard him sound so sharp in years. It was what I used to call his *office voice*, which I'd only heard a few times.

No one was speaking. Not even Ben was fussing in Zoey's arms.

"We all talked," Maddox said, pointing around the yard, "and figured that it's not a bad idea to buy out his remaining shares in Whitley Industries. And we wanted to hear your thoughts on that."

"We'll only do it if you agree," I said.

"I don't care," Grandmother said. "I agree with whatever feels right to you boys."

"Does Whitley Industries even have enough cash?" Grandfather asked. Of course his mind went directly to the business.

"Yes," I said. "We ran the numbers. We can afford it."

He looked around us, focusing on Jake. "You all want to do this?"

Jake spoke next. "Yes. That will solve the problem and also make sure he's out of our lives for good."

It wasn't as if we'd had anything to do with him since he left. He received money from his shares, but accounting took care of it. But this would be the end of our business dealings with him at all, plus any future contact with him. He could hang nothing over our heads. This would be final.

"Very well," Grandfather said. "If I'm honest, I think it's for the best too. This way you boys get control of everything. You're dividing the shares equally among yourselves?" His voice held an edge. I couldn't help but smile.

"Of course," Jake said.

"Colton is putting up most of the cash," Maddox stated, "so he should get the most shares."

"No," I said categorically. "Whitley Industries belongs to all of us, so we'll share it equally."

Grandmother smiled at me wholeheartedly. I knew how much this meant to her. But I wasn't only insisting on this because it would make our grandparents happy. Maddox, Leo, and Nick were Whitleys just as much as Gabe, Jake, Cade, Spencer, and I.

"That's why you boys brought us out here?" Grandmother asked and laughed.

"Well, not *just* for that. We've been figuring out a way to get you two out of the house," Maddox said.

"I agree with you boys," Grandfather said. He nodded at all of us.

"Okay, then. I'll give the lawyers the green light," I said.

Whitley Industries had a legal team that was almost unparalleled in the corporate world, so we didn't need to externalize this. I took out my phone, moving back inside while emailing the head of the legal department. He answered right away, saying he'd have everything ready for us tomorrow morning.

Then I noticed an email from my lead scientist and immediately answered it.

***

Zoey

Today was absolutely perfect. "Can you take a picture of me and Ben?" I asked Gabe because he was closest. We were sitting a bit away from the group, in the sun. It was too chilly anyway. Spencer had set up heaters in the yard, but we'd probably move inside soon.

"Sure."

I wasn't going to give Ben away at all today. He was mine. I couldn't stop kissing him. He was such a cute baby.

Gabe snapped a picture of me, and I immediately sent it to my parents, my brothers, and Tom, who replied first.

Tom: Hey, you've been holding out on me. You didn't tell me you were a baby person.

Zoey: I didn't know that either.

Up until now, I hadn't had a chance to be around babies at all.

Tom: Just a heads-up. I might ask you to babysit.

Zoey: I was going to offer anyway.

After I put my phone in my pocket, Gabe asked, "Well, where's Colton?"

I looked through the enormous window that peeked into the living room. "He's at the table, and he's got his work frown on."

"Is anything wrong?"

"He's a bit on edge," I said. And then the words tumbled out of me without my permission. "I think his mentor made him feel like he wasn't advancing the next breakthrough quick enough."

Gabe jerked his head back. "What?"

"He said that compared to previous projects, this was moving slower."

"That's because my brother has killed himself for years, basically working around the clock," Gabe exclaimed.

"I know. Colton says he's not paying any attention to Browning, but I don't know. He seems more stressed than usual."

"Do you think he's trying to revert to his grump self?"

"I'm not going to allow that."

"Good for you," Gabe said, clearly completely unhappy with Browning.

Ben began to fuss. I wondered if he could feel my turmoil.

"Hey, I can try holding him," Gabe said. It was really cute how eager the brothers were to take him.

"Sure, let's try," I said.

I transferred him to Gabe, and this time he seemed content to stay in his uncle's arms. I felt a little pang of jealousy. How was that even possible?

"I'm going to get another slice of pizza," I said. I'd had a few, but I wanted to eat one more. Besides, Meredith, Natalie, and Penny were at the pizza table, too, and I wanted to chat with them.

"Hey, we were wondering if you want another slice," Penny said. "It's just these four left. We should have ordered more."

"No, everyone is full," Meredith assured her. "If we get hungry, we can always order some more later. And by the way," she said, glancing at Natalie, who just nodded at her, "we just wanted to give you a heads-up. Jeannie has been mentioning the word *wedding* a lot. Don't be surprised if she mentions it to you as well."

My jaw dropped.

"I told you we were going to shock her," Natalie said.

"Yep, you were right," Meredith agreed. "We should have eased her into it."

"Wedding? But Colton and I..."

"We know. And she knows, but Jeannie has a logic of her own. We just didn't want you to get blindsided by her," Natalie said.

"You did well," I said. "It's always better to be blindsided by...you."

Penny laughed. "I like that you take everything in stride."

I liked them too. They were easygoing and clearly loved their men a hell of a lot. I glanced over my shoulder, but I couldn't see Colton anymore.

"Where did Colton go?" I asked.

"He asked me earlier if he could use Spencer's office. I think his lead scientist wrote to him. You can go up. It's on the second floor, next to the nursery."

"Thanks. Are you sure it's okay if I just wander through the house?"

"Please, we have nothing to hide."

"Hmm. Let's see if I can get him back out here with the family," I said, sauntering inside.

I went directly upstairs. I truly liked this home. It was decorated nicely, in shades of white and gray; it looked very minimalistic and still welcoming. The nursery was the exception. I peeked inside, and my heart just felt happy. It was full of colors and toys.

Then I walked in the room next to it. Colton was talking on his phone. The camera was on.

I didn't want to bother him, so I just waited by the door, but the lead scientist clearly noticed me, because he said, "I think Zoey needs to talk to you."

Oh crap. We hadn't made anything official at the office, though I wasn't interested in hiding it.

Since I didn't actually work at Whitley Biotech, I didn't much care what the team thought about me. Colton had made progress faster than I anticipated, so I was certain I wouldn't be staying on for much longer.

Colton looked over his shoulder, and his expression immediately transformed. "Right, yeah. Okay. We'll catch up later," he said.

"Look, you really don't have to come by today."

"I know, but we're going to make more headway if we do this together."

"All right."

He disconnected the call before turning around to me. I stepped inside, closing the door.

"I've come to whisk you away," I informed him. "The day is gorgeous, and you can't be cooped inside here."

"I was going to join you anyway," he said. Then he motioned with his finger for me to approach him, which I did. I went right in front of him, then decided to sit in his lap. I opened my legs wide, positioning myself right over his crotch. He groaned.

"Everything okay? Gabe is a bit worried that you'll give in to your workaholic tendencies again."

He shook his head.

"Something's on your mind," I said.

"My mentor was right," he replied.

My breath froze in my lungs. "What do you mean?"

"Usually, at this stage in the research, I would have been much further along in the process."

"Colton, this isn't a linear thing. Research is research. Two steps forward, one step back, and so on."

He nodded. "Yeah, only we've usually already done the two steps forward by this time. And now we've just done one. This needs more of my attention."

I couldn't help the small ball of anxiety forming at the base of my throat.

"Colton, you need to go easy on yourself. Let me spoil you," I murmured, leaning forward and nibbling at his ear before kissing down the right side of his neck. Then I moved to the left side, giving it the same treatment.

He groaned, placing his hands on the middle of my back and moving them slowly upward toward my shoulders. "You're making a great case."

"I know, right?" I teased even though I was feeling a bit uneasy.

His mentor was getting in his head. Still, I wasn't going to let him think I was a distraction. I mean, I was, but I was convinced that he needed it.

"Now look what you've done," I said.

He laughed. "What did I do?"

"I came here, just intending to convince you to come downstairs, and now I find myself seducing you."

"You find yourself," he teased right back. "You don't have a say in this?"

"Not when it comes to you. I see my sexy man and hormones take over my neurons."

I straightened up a bit, pulling back until my ass nearly touched his knees. "We're in Spencer's office. We can't get down and dirty here."

He wiggled his eyebrows. "We can."

"No, no, no. Damn it, don't tempt me."

He laughed. "You're all over the place, baby. You were the one tempting me."

"I told you, you make me lose my head."

I got up clumsily, smoothing my hands over my sweater and my jeans, as if that would solve anything.

"Come on. Let's go downstairs," I said.

He rose from the chair, taking my hand. Then he pinched my ass with both hands as we left the room.

I tried not to look too guilty as we joined the others outside. What was I thinking, climbing him in Spencer's house? The man was just far too irresistible.

We spent another hour with the group. The guys agreed to meet tomorrow morning to sign all the documents. I was impressed with the legal team's speed.

We were the first to leave later in the afternoon. Colton wanted to head to the lab.

"Hey, if you want, I can take a cab," I said.

"No, I'm dropping you off, babe."

"I'm meeting Tom downtown."

"Then I'll drop you off there."

"Thanks," I said with a big smile as we got in the car.

The drive only took fifteen minutes. Tom was waiting for me in front of the bar on Exeter Street.

"How long do you think you're going to stay at the office? " I asked Colton as the car slowed down.

"I'm not sure. Pretty late, I think."

"Call me if you think you'll make it in time for dinner."

"I'll call you either way, so you don't wait up for me."

He nodded, but I could tell he was already thinking about work. I kissed his lips before I got out of the car. Then, biting my lip, I added, "Colton?"

"Yeah?"

"I can deal with a workaholic boyfriend, but not one who ghosts me, okay?"

His brows narrowed. "What are you talking about? I'm not ghosting you."

"Good, because I would *not* have it," I said, flashing him a smile before walking away.

I couldn't wait until this evening. I was going to spoil him rotten.

Chapter Twenty-Seven
Colton

Colton

"I think we should call it a day," I said.

"You mean a night?" John, my lead scientist, pulled his glasses down, rubbing at his eyes. He and I were the only ones left.

Jesus, we'd spent the whole night here.

"I didn't pay attention to the clock," I said. "We're not going to get to the bottom of this today."

"We might make more progress if the whole team participated in this stage of research," he said carefully. He'd suggested this before, and I shot it down, but this was the first time I was considering it.

"Let's regroup Monday. Gather the other guys, too, so we can all tackle this together."

John looked stunned. "Wow. I didn't think you'd actually take me seriously."

"There's a first time for everything. Have a great rest of the day, John," I said.

After he left, I hung my own white coat by the door. That's when I noticed my phone. I'd put it by a table next to the entrance. The screen was lit up.

Maddox: Fucking hell, man. Where are you? Did you change your mind?

Fuck, I forgot we were meeting this morning to sign over the papers. He'd sent that to me half an hour ago. I saw messages from the rest of my brothers, too, but decided to call him instead. He answered immediately.

"I wasn't blowing you off" was the first thing I said. "I was in my lab."

"Yeah, the rest of the guys predicted that was the case." There were a lot of sounds in his background.

"Are you all at Gabe's bar?"

"Yeah, it's empty. We figured it's as good a place as any. Everyone else has signed, so we just need yours."

Pity this couldn't be done with the digital signature Zoey set up.

"I'll be there quickly. Half an hour or less."

"There's no traffic at this time."

"Sure," I said.

Maddox had been right—there was zero traffic. I stepped through the doors of Whitley Distillery and Bar twenty minutes later. For some reason, I'd expected them to be at the counter, but instead I saw Gabe waving at me from the other end of the room.

I headed straight there. My brother had made some changes in the bar. It looked good.

Leo, Nick, and Maddox were sitting on a smaller couch, my brothers on the larger one. I sat down in the free armchair.

"And he has arrived," Gabe said mockingly.

I held up my hands, "I owe everyone an apology. I went into the lab, and, well, one thing led to another."

"And yet you checked your phone," Jake said.

"I actually only looked at it after I sent my lead scientist home. We weren't going to finish anytime soon."

Cade whistled, glancing at our half brothers. "Just so you're on the same page with us, this is news. My brother has made a habit of sleeping at the office."

"All right, are we going to gossip about me, or are you going to give me the papers to sign?" I asked.

Maddox took out a thick stack of papers and put them on the table in front of me. I'd already gone through everything yesterday evening when the legal team emailed, so I signed without any hesitation.

This felt cathartic in some ways. Ryan Whitley was getting his money, and we wouldn't have to think about him interfering in our lives ever again.

"Now it's done," Maddox said.

"Fucking finally," I exclaimed.

"Does anyone else feel like we're rewarding him?" Jake asked.

I was surprised Jake was still beating this drum. I'd thought he finally understood the benefit of ridding Father from our lives.

"I don't think so," I said. "I mean, he did run it for a while."

"Not necessarily well," Gabe said in a clipped tone. He was usually more forgiving about Father, but he was right.

"True, but he did set it up so we could take over," Nick said. "A better question would be if he actually deserves this much money, but nonetheless, he did contribute to Whitley Industries being what it is today."

"I think we should all toast," Gabe said. "I'd propose tequila shots, but it's 9:00 a.m. Also, this occasion needs more than that."

"I agree," I said.

Gabe immediately brought out a bottle of champagne and glasses. He handed the bottle to Maddox.

"Want to do the honors? After all you're the one who spoke to Father," Gabe said.

"Sure. I'm going to send this through, and then hopefully I will never have to speak to him again."

Gabe was right. This hadn't been easy on Maddox.

"You really haven't been in touch with him all these years?" I asked.

"No," Maddox, Leo, and Nick said at the same time.

"Since we found out, all we wanted was to put as much distance between us as possible," Leo said.

"Everything was a lie," Nick pointed out in a cutting voice. "The excuses that he had to go to Boston for work, the bogus stories he told us every time we asked why he and Mom weren't married."

I had never, not once, put myself in their shoes. Things were different when we'd grown up. Couples having children together and not being married weren't common. I didn't even stop and think how their childhood might have been with everyone in Maine knowing their parents weren't married. And then to find out that your father actually had another family? They probably felt exactly like we did.

Maddox popped open the champagne bottle. We each took a glass.

"I think the worst part was seeing Mom fall completely apart," Maddox said.

I froze in the act of holding up my glass.

"I don't even know how she managed to pull herself out of it," Nick went on.

I'd refused to put myself in their shoes, but now I wanted to. In certain ways, we had the same life.

"It was a horrible situation for everyone involved," I said.

Maddox looked straight at me. "Yes, it was."

I held up my glass along with... all my brothers. "To Whitley Industries belonging only to the Whitley brothers," I toasted.

"Hear, hear."

After we'd all emptied our glasses, Cade gave me an approving nod. "You know, we really should give Grandmother all the credit there is for you and for Zoey. I know she just gave you a nudge, but man, you ran away with it."

"I did," I replied.

"This is a treat, especially because we know *exactly* how this day would have gone before Zoey." That came from Spencer. "First of all, you probably wouldn't have even shown up."

"And if you did show up, you wouldn't be in the mood to celebrate," Cade added, playing right off him.

"Speaking of Zoey," Gabe cut in, "she sounded concerned when I spoke to her earlier."

I frowned. "When did you talk to her?"

"How do you think we knew you were in the lab?"

"Oh, right," I said.

"She kept asking if you do this often or if you're mad. I had an inkling what she wanted to actually ask was if you were mad at her."

"I'm not. Did she say I was? Why would she think that?" I glanced around the room.

"Hey, don't look at us for answers. I didn't know about this conversation until he just brought it up," Maddox said.

Obviously, Gabe was the best source of information right now.

"Has she said anything about why she thinks that?" I asked.

"No, I think she was just concerned that you'd been locked up in the lab for, what—I think she said she last saw you fourteen hours ago. It sounded like she was counting."

"Fuck." I played back my last conversation with Zoey. "I know what this is about."

"What's wrong?" This came from Nick. Cade and Spencer also looked at me curiously.

"Oh, now you want to chime in," I said.

"Dude, they're the ones with the women in the group. If anyone's going to be of any help, it's them," Nick pointed out.

"Recently, I went to see Browning. I took Zoey because I wanted to introduce them. The guy basically told me that he thinks I've lost my focus because I'm not sleeping at the office anymore."

Gabe shook his head. "I know. Zoey told me. That's fucked. He's in no position to say that shit."

I stared at him. She'd talked to my brother about this?

"What the fuck?" Spencer asked. " I know you think highly of him, but that dude's got no right to do that."

"I do," I said, "and I told him that he's completely off base. But I think Zoey might believe that I think she's distracting me."

Jake shrugged. "Well, I mean, she *is* distracting you, dude, but that's for the best. That's exactly what you need. Someone to actually show you that there's more to life than work. Something that completely escaped you before."

"Like you weren't the same," Cade said, turning to him. "I like having my brother back."

Everyone gave a resounding "Hell yeah."

Jake shook his head. "I never denied that."

"But I didn't. I mean, I assured her that's not the case." I glanced around for a clock. "What time is it? I need to go over to her place."

Then I realized that I'd promised to call last night, and I hadn't. *Shit.*

"That sounds like a smart strategy. Strike while the iron is hot and all that," Gabe said.

"You've got to revise your strategy. No woman wants to hear that you're striking while the iron's hot," Spencer retaliated.

"I wasn't telling him to tell *her* that."

For so long, I'd carried this need to prove that I gave everything my best. Work was all I knew, all that mattered to me. Somewhere deep down, with every new medicine I brought onto the market, I was closer to saving someone... the way I couldn't do for Mother.

But meeting Zoey changed that fundamentally. I didn't need work or breakthroughs to feel fulfilled. I needed to be with her, and I needed her to know it.

"All right," I said, standing up, "we'll catch up another time. I need to go see Zoey."

Leo and Nick looked at Maddox and said, "Yep, you were right. Gran is going to have a field day with this."

Maddox waved his hand. "We're toast. Colton's a done deal."

And I was. Deep in my bones, I knew I wouldn't need anyone except Zoey for the rest of my life. And it was high time I made sure she didn't doubt that.

CHAPTER TWENTY-EIGHT

ZOEY

My phone beeped with an incoming call from Meredith. I immediately answered.

"Good morning, Meredith."

"Hi, Zoey. I didn't wake you up, did I?"

"No, not at all. I've been up for a while."

"Awesome. Penny, Natalie, and I thought it would be cool to go out today and enjoy the sunny weather. Care to join us? We'd love to get to know you better."

"Sure. I don't have any plans."

We'd spoken yesterday about maybe meeting today, but I hadn't made any commitment.

I was hoping for a certain sexy man to call, but at this point, I wasn't sure when that was going to happen. But it was better to be outside enjoying the day than moping around.

"Perfect," she exclaimed. "I can pick you up in... I don't know, an hour or so?"

"That's great. Gives me enough time to get ready."

I might be a morning person, but not on weekends.

"We can't wait."

"What are we doing?" I asked.

"Oh, a bit of this, a bit of that," she said vaguely.

It sounded like they didn't have a plan, but that was good. We could play it by ear.

I kept my phone next to me as I dressed and got ready for the day, but Colton didn't text or call. Clearly, he was still busy with work. My heart was growing heavier.

I touched my necklace, but I'd rather have him here by my side. I was totally head over heels in love, and I wanted my man.

Exactly one hour later, I went downstairs in front of my building. A black Range Rover pulled up in front of me. Meredith was driving, Natalie was next to her, and Penny was in the back. I opened the door to the back seat and climbed next to her.

"Hello, girls!" I said.

Meredith turned around, looking at me intently. "How's your day going so far?" she asked.

I shrugged. "It was just a lazy Sunday morning." I bit the inside of my cheek, wondering if I should ask if they'd heard anything from their guys about Colton, but I decided not to.

"Where are we going?" I asked.

"We thought about maybe a day trip to Salem." Penny was looking at me curiously.

That was an interesting choice. Did they know I'd already been there with Colton?

Oh, stop it, Zoey. You're going out on a day with the girls. Enjoy it.

"That's great. I was there recently with Colton."

Now I realized that Natalie was also looking at me in the rearview mirror. Something was off with all of them. Although, honestly, I didn't know them well enough to draw that conclusion. Maybe I was just making things up in my mind.

"Excellent," Penny said. "Then you can show us around a bit. Now, who wants to make a pit stop and buy some goodies for the road?"

I laughed.

"The road is only thirty minutes away," Natalie said.

"Exactly. We need sustenance," Penny added. "Something to make our road trip fun."

I smiled, feeling like I was truly part of a sisterhood. I'd never had that before, and I loved it.

We ended up making three stops: one for coffee, one for ice cream, and the last one for cookies at a bakery that Natalie loved. She sang their praises all the way there.

"Oh my God, they *are* amazing. You were right," Penny exclaimed, and we all munched on our cookies as we hit the road.

"How are they so good?" I asked. I was a veteran when it came to eating chocolate chip cookies, but these were on another level altogether. They weren't just soft—they were creamy, even though they didn't actually contain any cream. They were hands down the best delicious treat I'd had in a long time.

By the time we reached Salem, we had zero cookies left even though we'd bought enough to last us the whole day. It was honestly the perfect way to start a Sunday: by indulging in something delicious.

"All right, do you girls want to go look at one of the museums?" I asked. "Or, if you prefer, we can do a walking tour. They start hourly on Sunday."

"Sure, a walking tour sounds great," Meredith said distractedly.

"What's that address you gave the GPS?" I asked, realizing she was still following it. I'd assumed she'd just given a random address in the town.

"Oh, it's a parking lot," she said in a strange voice.

Meredith looked around carefully as she drove through the small streets. The town was already full of tourists today, but that was no surprise, considering how amazing the weather was.

Three turns later, we reached a parking lot. There was only one car in it: a familiar BMW. Colton stood next to it.

"What's happening?" I asked.

"I've been bursting to say something the whole drive," Penny said.

"And you deserve a medal for keeping silent," Natalie replied. "A few times, I was sure you were going to spill the beans, especially after the third chocolate chip cookie."

Penny pressed her lips together. "Delicious treats have a way of making me talk."

"I don't understand." My heart was going faster. "Wait, this was all a ruse?"

Meredith turned around, grinning. "Yes. Colton called this morning and gave a speech that made me swoon."

"Yeah, we didn't hear it," Natalie added, "but we're going to make Meredith reenact it for us just so we can swoon as well."

"Those are two words I never thought I'd hear in relation to Colton," Penny exclaimed. "Although, I do think the guys are a bit hard on him."

"This is where our involvement stops," Meredith added.

"If we hurry, we can catch the next walking tour," Penny exclaimed.

"Okay, girls, I'm off," I said, opening the door.

Meredith winked. "Have fun."

Penny nodded. "You'll have an amazing day. I'm sure of it."

My legs were shaking slightly as I got out of the car. I couldn't understand what was happening. *Why did we come here so Colton could meet me? Why not back home in Boston?*

Meredith pulled out of the parking lot right away. Colton walked forward, stopping in front of me. He looked damn gorgeous, and a bit tired. But even though he had dark circles under them, his eyes were glinting.

"Good morning, gorgeous," he said. "How did they treat you?"

"They're great." I raised a brow. "Colton, what is happening, and what are we doing here?"

He bunched my hair to one side, threading his fingers through it. "First of all, I know we had plans yesterday, and I completely bailed."

I exhaled sharply, biting the inside of my cheek. "You had work."

"True, but that doesn't excuse me for not reaching out to you. It was brought to my attention that you've been inquiring about me."

I sighed. "Gabe said that?"

"One thing you have to know about my brother: he will always rat everyone out. He doesn't do it on purpose. He even rats himself out."

"Good to know." I sighed. "I only spoke to him because—"

He put a finger on my lips, and I fell silent.

"You don't have to explain anything. I, on the other hand, want to tell you a few things."

"Like what?"

"Like how much I love you and how much you changed my life."

I narrowed my eyes. "Now you're just buttering me up."

"Yes, but it's 100 percent true. Before I met you, work was all I cared about. I sort of closed myself off to everything, including my family. But being with you, my life got a new dimension. You opened me up to it. I fucking love you for that. After my brothers and I signed the documents today—"

"I completely forgot about that. How do you feel about it?"

"Relieved. But that's not what I'm here to talk about." He moved one hand down to my shoulder, then onto my lower back.

I couldn't explain why, but I always felt extremely safe and protected when he touched my back.

"I don't want to ever give you a reason to doubt how much you mean to me," he continued, his voice soft but sincere.

"I didn't doubt it," I murmured. "I... I was just afraid that you took Browning's words to heart."

"Listen to me, Zoey. What do you know about me? I don't give a flying fuck about anyone's opinion. You're far too important to me for a throwaway comment from him to make me doubt what we have. What I feel for you."

"Oh, Colton."

"Actually, I stand corrected. I do take advice. Yours. I've spoken to my lead scientist and handed more responsibilities over to him."

I grinned. "Wait, you what? Holy shit. That is amazing news. Now, are you going to tell me what we're doing here?"

He nodded and whirled me. "Remember our last trip here?"

"Vividly," I said.

"You saw those hot air balloons flying."

I turned, inspecting our surroundings. There was a small cabin in the distance.

"We're going in a hot air balloon?"

"Yes," he confirmed.

I shimmied back against him, wrapping my arms clumsily around his torso in a weird reverse hug. Then I turned around and hugged him properly.

"I'm so excited."

"So am I," he said. "I can't wait to have you all to myself up there."

I didn't correct him. Was he under the impression that someone would let us fly a hot air balloon on our own? *Oh, Colton.* He had another think coming.

"Thanks so much for bringing me out here. It's my dream."

"I want to fulfill every single one of your dreams for our entire lives, Zoey. Most of all, I don't want you to ever feel like you're not the first thing I think of every second of every day, because you are."

Then he turned me back around, and put an arm over my shoulders as we walked toward the cabin. I assumed they sold tickets there or something. On the way, I gave him another awkward half hug from one side. I could feel his chest up under the pretense of trying to find a good angle for the hug.

"I know what you're doing," he said in a gruff voice as we approached the cabin.

Okay, so maybe I wasn't as subtle as I thought. I looked up at him innocently. "I'm just trying to find the most comfortable way to hug you."

"That involves tracing my abs?"

I grinned. "Absolutely." I looked over my shoulder. There was no one else behind us, so I groped his ass too. "And this is also extremely necessary."

Handwritten on a blackboard next to the entrance were several activities one could do, including a balloon ride.

A young man came out of the building. "Colton Whitley?" he asked.

"Yes," Colton replied.

"You're a bit early, but you're in luck because I'm ready for you."

"Great."

The man looked at us. "You're not really dressed in layers," he said.

I had on jeans, a T-shirt, and a light jacket, and Colton wore jeans, a shirt, and a suit jacket, but I could see what the guy was saying. I assumed that up there, the temperature would drop.

"We've got some universal-size jackets. I'll take them with us. I always need more layers than I think," he said, ducking inside.

Colton looked stunned, and I couldn't help but laugh. "You really thought we were going to be alone?"

He turned me around, plastering me against him. "Yes. I had great plans for us."

I was sort of starting to wish we were alone, too, even at the risk of flying into the boonies.

"I want you to be on your best behavior during the flight," I said, fighting to keep my voice even because I was melting under his hot and intense gaze. "I don't want you distracting me. This is a once-in-a-life-time event."

"No, it's not, babe. I can take you in a hot air balloon whenever you want to go."

Well, I just melted completely.

I smiled, wiggling my eyebrows.

"What?" he asked with a chuckle.

I put my hands on his chest again. To everyone else, it would look innocent, but I was touching his pecs. "I'm just thinking of all the ways I'm going to feast on you later on."

The guy came out a few moments later with jackets and blankets. "All right. Are you ready?"

Colton looked at me. He was smiling. I liked this playful expression on his face.

We were led around the building to the back, where I'd spotted the air balloon. It was quite a distance away. Colton and I walked with quick steps, anxious for this experience. Up in the sky, I could see one other colorful balloon floating around. How had I not noticed it before? Clearly, I'd been too lost in this sexy man and his swoonworthy ways to pay attention.

"By the way," the guy said over his shoulder, "I forgot to introduce myself. I'm Ron."

"Nice to meet you, Ron," I replied.

"So, which one of you is more excited?"

"I think that would be me," I replied, looking up at Colton.

He brought his mouth to my ear. "I love making you smile like this."

Once again, I wanted to jump his bones, but we weren't alone. He had such a strange effect on me. I was giddy by the time we reached the balloon.

"Wait, it's just the two of us?" I asked.

"Yes," Ron said proudly. "Mr. Whitley here requested a private tour."

"You can call me Colton," he said.

"Well, Colton here asked us to make it happen."

I felt even giddier than before as we stepped inside. It was big enough for ten people—at least that's what it felt like to me.

Ron explained security details, but I was only half listening. My heart was beating so fast that I could barely make out words.

A few minutes later, we took off. It was the strangest feeling. I'd never experienced anything like it. I sometimes got a bit sick whenever a plane started off the ground, but I wasn't even the least bit nauseous.

I looked out as we lifted farther away from ground.

"This is beautiful," I exclaimed.

"I agree," Colton replied.

Ron stopped talking as he maneuvered the balloon and we floated. I glanced at the trees below us. Some were green, but a lot were also golden and red.

"Are you cold?" Colton asked.

"Just a bit, but I don't want a jacket," I said.

I took a deep breath. The air changed as we went up higher. It felt almost humid, like dunking my head into water. I closed my eyes and leaned my head back against Colton.

I could swear that I felt his heartbeat against mine even though I didn't think that was truly possible because I had my back against his chest. But I felt deeply connected to him, especially when he interlaced our fingers.

Twenty minutes later, Ron started our descent. Colton kept his arms around me all the way down.

As soon as we stepped out of the balloon, Ron said, "Can I interest you in some champagne? We offer that with every ride. It's free." He sounded extremely proud. "But I know some guests don't want that in the middle of the day."

I wanted some champagne, but I wanted to be alone with Colton even more.

He put his arm firmly around my lower back, looking down at me. Since I was wearing sneakers, I had to tilt my head back more than usual to see him. I loved that he towered over me like this.

"Your call," he said.

I shook my head. "I'm good. We can go."

His eyes darkened.

"All right, then. It was great having you as my customers." Ron gave me two cards. "If you liked the experience, please leave a review on Tripadvisor or Yelp."

"I will," I said, carefully tucking them into my pocket.

We bid Ron goodbye and headed straight to our car. There was only one other in the parking lot.

"I loved, loved, loved that," I informed Colton as he opened the door to my car.

"I'm glad to hear it."

"What do you have planned now?" I asked.

"Get in the car first."

With a grin, I did as he said, mentally reviewing what lingerie I had on. Since I'd dressed for a comfortable day out with the girls, I wasn't wearing anything overly sexy, but most of my lingerie was sexy anyway. I couldn't remember if I had black or white lace, so I peeked at my bra.

Black. I had matching panties too. Colton always seemed to be more feral when I was wearing black lingerie.

As soon as he got in, he asked, "What do you think about spending the weekend out here?"

"Really?"

He nodded. "I found a cabin not far from here."

I smiled widely. "Wait, you planned for us to spend the night here?"

He grinned. "I thought we might want some time alone."

"Ah, and you figured we wouldn't be able to keep our clothes on long enough to drive back to the city? You're a genius," I exclaimed.

"Besides, last time we were here, you did mention that you think this place is great for a weekend getaway."

I was so in love with this man that I couldn't even see straight.

"Let's go. I'm excited." I trailed my fingers up his arm.

"What are you doing?" he asked as we drove out of the parking lot.

"You were right. I do have a hard time keeping my hands off you, and since I know we don't have a long drive, I don't have to exercise self-control at all." I leaned forward, moving my hands to the buttons of his shirt, drawing my finger around in a circle.

"Zoey," Colton said in a dangerously low and calm voice. "Keep doing that and I'll pull the car in a secluded spot and have you right now."

I straightened in my seat, keeping my hands in my lap. Although the idea of riding him here in the car was appealing, I did prefer to reach whatever location he'd reserved. I could be more creative when I had more space, and I wanted to explore him.

He put the address into the GPS on his phone, placing it under the radio. We drove through back streets that we hadn't seen at all last time.

A few minutes later, we arrived in front of an absolutely dreamy cabin. It was made of wood, but it had clearly been built recently because the windows were more modern. Even the coat of paint seemed fresh. What I loved most about it was the porch. The front of it was completely surrounded by trees, and now, in the middle of fall, a mix of orange and red hues interspersed with yellow and brown leaves. Here and there, I still spotted a few green leaves.

"Colton, this place is amazing."

"I thought you'd like it. When I looked on the website, they had photos that were clearly taken in summer, because the trees were green."

"*You* looked it up personally?"

"Yes. I wanted to choose a place you'd like." He grazed the side of my neck with the backs of his fingers.

"I could stay here forever," I murmured.

"If you like the inside, I can buy it for us, and we can come here every weekend."

My jaw dropped. He was completely serious.

"C-Colton," I stammered. "No. You don't have to buy something just because I... Oh, never mind. Let's go check the inside. I'm curious to explore it."

He brought his mouth to my ear. "I want to explore *you*."

I shimmied in his arms. Goose bumps broke out on my skin, but he didn't notice because I had long sleeves.

"That too," I agreed.

The inside was just as charming, all wood decor and large windows that made you feel like you were outside. It had a fireplace as well.

"This must be really cozy in winter," I said, pointing at the fireplace.

"We can come back here in winter too." He stood next to me, glancing around.

"This is the perfect day," I confessed.

He stepped in front of me, touching my cheek and wrapping his other hand in my hair. I loved when he did that. The way he held me was so damn sexy—like he couldn't wait to make me his.

That was all I wanted for the rest of the day.

And for the rest of my life.

Chapter Twenty-Nine
Colton

"Thanks for organizing all of this," Zoey said.

"Anything to make you happy." I meant it more than she knew. I was serious about buying this place. I didn't care what I had to do to make her happy. Nothing was too much or too difficult. Seeing her excitement in the balloon had been an amazing experience.

I brought my mouth to her cheek, then trailed my lips up her ear, nibbling her earlobe before tracing a line of kisses down her jaw and up her other cheek.

"I love you," I said. "Being here with you is all I want. It's all I need. Forever. You gave my life meaning in a way that nothing ever did. Certainly not work."

A light shudder coursed through her body. She was already on edge and sensitive. I moved my hands down her arms, but I didn't want to touch her over the fabric. I wanted her bare skin. But not yet. I had to pace myself. I wanted her desperately, but I didn't want to be too domineering.

I turned her around, kissing the back of her neck and making her shudder even more.

"Do you have goose bumps?" I asked.

"Yes," she whispered.

I pushed up her sleeves, bunching them at the elbow. Fucking hell. She really had goose bumps all over her arms.

I couldn't wait to get her naked. I'd wanted to sink inside her since this morning, and I could barely hold back any longer. I placed hot and wet kisses on the back of her neck, then on its side. I couldn't get enough of this woman.

Then I moved my hand from her hip forward to the waistband of her jeans and up to her chest. As I massaged each breast through her clothes, she shifted her body against me, moaning. She could already barely tolerate the feeling of the fabric against her nipples. I couldn't wait to see how she'd react when I used my tongue.

I grabbed the edges of her shirt, pulling it up. She held her arms up, and I tugged it over her head, throwing it somewhere behind me.

She was the most beautiful woman on the planet, and I was a lucky bastard for having the privilege of being the one to take off her clothes. I planned to be worthy of her for as long as I lived.

I walked in front of her as she sucked in her breath and then exhaled sharply. Her breathing was labored as I stood in front of her, drawing my finger from one clavicle to the other, then in an S-shape down to her breast.

"You're amazingly beautiful." I traced my fingers down one breast, deeper in the valley between them, and then moved up the other one.

Her goose bumps had spread to her belly. Wanting to see how far down they went, I popped open the button of her jeans and pushed them down her thighs. Then I dipped my hand into her panties, only touching her pubic bone.

"I like that you have goose bumps everywhere."

She dropped her head back, humming as I nudged my hand farther into her panties. I only brushed her clit lightly, but her body spasmed. I'd never get enough of bringing her pleasure, of watching her surrender to me completely. Normally, she was always ready to give as good as she got, and yet sexually, she liked to surrender to me. It was a damn turn-on.

I tilted forward, kissing the front of her neck—I couldn't resist it when she exposed it so beautifully for me. Then I took my hand out of her panties.

"No. Why?" she protested.

I smiled against her skin. She straightened up, lightly pushing me away.

"You're teasing me," she said.

As I stood closer and kissed her hard, sucking her tongue into my mouth, I felt her press her thighs together. This always turned her on instantly. I hadn't checked how wet she was before, but I planned to rectify that immediately.

I needed to get rid of all her clothes. Pausing the kiss, I worked on yanking her jeans off. She stepped out of them quickly. As I rose to my feet, she tugged at my shirt.

"I want this gone now." She undid the first three buttons, and then I pulled it over my head.

"That's more like it," she said. "Finally. I've wanted this all day."

She ran both hands over my chest before moving one to my lower back. Then she cupped my ass with one hand and grabbed my cock with the other.

I groaned. "Undo my belt, Zoey."

Her eyes widened. Licking her lips, she immediately got to work, and it didn't take long to get rid of it, yanking it with so much force that she pulled it out of the loops.

I removed my jeans and underwear while kissing her again. I was rock-hard, and my cock was trapped between us.

She moaned, bouncing up and down on her toes, rubbing herself against me. I knew she needed my cock, but she wasn't ready for that yet; I wanted to work her up to that point, and I wasn't going to hurry the process. She couldn't take me in yet, and I never wanted to take the risk of hurting her, ruining her pleasure.

I moved her backward until we reached the dining table. It was against the wall, right next to two huge windows. There was no chance of anyone seeing us, though, as the property was completely surrounded by huge trees.

I palmed her breasts, flicking her nipples with my fingers. She raised her shoulders to her ears, closing her eyes. I positioned my cock at her entrance so I could tease her. I rubbed the length of my erection against her clit, but I was careful not to slide in because I knew she wasn't ready yet. But she would be soon enough.

She moaned, her thighs shaking as I nudged her clit again. I loved watching her slowly reach the limit of how much tension she could take. I wanted to see her come.

I pulled away and crouched before her. This was my favorite way of making her climax: watching her come while I had my lips on her clit and my tongue buried inside her pussy. I moved my hands down, cupping her ankles and then trailing my fingers at the backs of her thighs, considering the angle.

"Put your left thigh here," I said, tapping my right shoulder. "I want you open wide and exposed for me, babe."

She nodded, lifting her leg. I secured it on my shoulder, sliding closer to her. Her breathing was even more labored than before. She was looking at me intently. She liked to watch, and I was going to give her a show.

I touched my cock, intending to only give it one good squeeze. But I couldn't stop. I needed more.

I darted my tongue out, licking around her entrance, barely nudging around her clit.

She jerked her hips forward. "Fuck yes." She was nearly rubbing herself against my mouth. That was how much she needed to come, and I was going to oblige her. But I'd thought of another angle.

"Put your ass on the table," I said.

She licked her lips, doing just that.

The table was at the perfect height. I kept both her thighs on my shoulders, and then I feasted on her, flattening my tongue against her entrance and then sliding just the tip in. She was drenched. I loved tasting her.

She pressed her thighs against my ears and then opened her eyes wide, quickly relaxing her legs. I was acting on instinct and drew circles on her clit with the tip of my tongue, watching her turn even wilder. She was rocking back and forth on her ass.

I used my hand to lift her bottom from the edge of the table. I didn't want her to feel any discomfort. Besides, with her butt in my hands, I had complete control over her.

I held her firmly while I licked her, moving the tip of my nose and then my lips against her clit. Her cries grew louder. She was shaking in earnest. I felt every shudder because her legs dangled down my back. Every single one of her tremors seeped into my body. I was absorbing everything, and it was glorious.

When a groan shook her, I knew I couldn't tease her any longer. She needed relief right now. I took one hand from under her ass and pressed two fingers on her clit while I drove my tongue inside her. Feeling her inner muscles clamp around my tongue was exquisite. Then I drew my head back, not wanting to overwhelm her. I kept my fingers on her clit, watching her as she rode out her climax.

Getting up, I wrapped my arms around her torso as she laid her head on my chest. She drew in deep breaths. They were labored, but in a different way than before the orgasm. I rocked her back and forth, feeling her calm down.

Then she pulled back a bit, tipping her head backward. I knew what she wanted. She needed me to kiss her. So I did, without any hurry, simply exploring her.

My cock was once again trapped between us. As I intensified the kiss, I felt her slip her hand between our bodies, squeezing my cock, and groaned against her mouth. That one touch unleashed something inside me. I was beyond ready, and kissing her was no longer enough.

I lifted her from the table. I'd spotted the door to the bedroom when we first came in, and I wanted her to be comfortable while I sank inside her. She wrapped her legs around me, putting her palms on my shoulders. I didn't stop kissing her as we moved, only looking behind her every few seconds to make sure I was headed in the right direction.

I passed the dresser on the way to the bed, and then she rolled her hips, touching the length of my cock with her bare, wet pussy. And I couldn't wait one second longer. I moved her up and down my cock while she planted her heels in the backs of my thighs. I still wanted more friction and more leverage so I could thrust even deeper.

I wanted to be a part of her. This desire to mark her as mine was primal. But instead of moving us to the bed, I ended up pinning her against the window, her ass resting on the windowsill.

She gasped. "It's cold, but I like it."

I thought she might. My body was hot against hers, and the cold window was the contrast she needed. I pressed my forehead to hers, looking down between us as my cock disappeared inside her. Then I pulled back, watching every inch as I pushed into her again. Her nipples flattened against my chest on every thrust. Our bodies were completely in sync.

She and I belonged together. In the bedroom and outside of it, for the rest of our lives. I knew she was the one for me in the same way I knew I was a Whitley. It was part of my identity: to be Zoey's man.

I pulled back a bit, watching her face transform. She was on the cusp, fighting to stay in the moment and be aware of everything. The next second, the fight went out of her, and she surrendered to the pleasure. She pressed her hand against the window, closing her eyes and crying out my name as she clenched around me so tightly that my orgasm hit me completely unexpectedly. One second I was watching her, and the next I was pulled into the vortex of sensations and lost myself in her.

I'd felt her heels glide from the backs of my thighs down to the backs of my knees while I buried myself inside her. Even after the wave of pleasure subsided, I stood like that, enjoying the way her heartbeat felt against me until I finally pulled us away from the window and set her back on the floor.

She smiled, laughing as she pointed at the bed. "We *nearly* made it to the bed."

"Don't worry. We'll make it there on our second time."

"Great. Because I was hoping we'd get to christen every single surface in this gorgeous place."

"We can start right away."

I pushed her onto the bed. She laughed, pulling me over her. I trapped her underneath me, sinking my nose into the crook of her neck and inhaling deeply.

I was simultaneously losing myself and grounding myself in Zoey.

CHAPTER THIRTY

ZOEY

Four months later

"I'm very excited to start the job," I assured my boss.

"You don't even want a break?" he asked.

"No, really, I'm good to go." I'd finished my placement at Whitley Biotech last week, much earlier than we expected. I was already looking forward to my next project.

"All right, then. I'll tell her you'll be there first thing Monday morning."

I smiled as I disconnected the call, then put down the box I was carrying, glancing around. I couldn't believe I was moving into Colton's apartment. I still remembered how judgy I was the first time he told me he lived here.

Over the past few months, we'd decided to wait until my placement in his office was completed before I moved in. Even though I didn't much care what people said about me, I didn't want things to be awkward for him. And watching me descend from the penthouse to the office would definitely have qualified as weird.

"Where do you want us to put these?" Dean said.

Alex was right behind him, and they were carrying three boxes each. Dad was here too. Mom was holding a bunch of dresses in her arms. She'd insisted I put them in hanging bags, and she was right.

"Mom, you can go right through to the bedroom and hang the dresses in the closet I showed you."

I glanced at the boxes. "Why don't you put all of those here in the living room, and I'll sort through them later?"

"Works for me," Dean said, setting down the boxes.

Colton joined us a few seconds later.

"Got the last ones in?" Alex asked, and Colton nodded.

Mom came back from the bedroom.

"Boys," Mom said. "If you brought up everything, then let's go."

"Why so soon?" I asked. "I figured you guys could stay for a snack or something. Colton and I only have plans in the evening."

We were going to Jeannie and Abe's house. They were leaving for Martha's Vineyard tomorrow and wanted to see us all before they went.

Mom looked sternly at my brothers and Dad. Alex opened his mouth, and I bet he was about to say he'd take me up on the offer, but Mom said, "No. We have something planned this afternoon."

I blinked. That was odd. I figured they'd blocked the whole day for this since we didn't really know how long it would take to bring up all the boxes from my apartment. Colton had offered to pay for a moving company, but I'd flat-out refused. That man liked to spoil me with extravagant gifts, sure, but I wasn't going to take advantage of his wealth.

I so loved that he was getting better and better at delegating. He had more time for himself, for me, and his family. And as a plus, his newest research project was progressing much faster than anticipated. Browning apologized profusely numerous times for overstepping his boundaries, but Colton didn't hold a grudge.

"Oh, right," Dean said.

"Of course. Well, see you. And call if you need help with anything," Alex said.

"We're all good," I assured them.

I glanced at Colton, surprised he wasn't insisting for them to stay. Maybe they'd shared with him what plans they had. Who knew? My parents were staying in the city and then traveling again next month, and I planned to enjoy as much time with them as possible. But today I had to unpack.

Once they left and Colton closed the door, I smiled, looking around.

"I want to pinch myself. I can't believe this is happening. I'm here. I finished consulting at Whitley Biotech, and I'm starting a new placement on Monday."

"What?" Colton asked sharply, coming up next to me. He put both hands on my shoulders, looking sternly at me. "You aren't taking time off *at all*?"

I shook my head. "No rest for the wicked."

"Who is it for?"

"Why does it matter?" I asked, a bit miffed about his question.

That glint in his eyes. Wait a second, I recognized it. Was that jealousy?

"Tell me about the guy," he said.

"What guy?"

"The CEO."

I burst out laughing. Guffaws reverberated through my body. I pressed my boobs against his chest, wrapping my arms around the base of his neck.

"Right. Well, as much as I would enjoy continuing this little jealousy show and see where you're going with it, the CEO is a seventy-four-year-old woman who's a veteran in her business but is stubbornly refusing to use technology properly. Everyone who works with her is at their wit's end. And my job is to convince her that adding a little tech to her life will make things easier. Between the two of us, I have full confidence I can do it. Considering my previous client was the grumpiest CEO I'd ever met, and I even won him over," I teased. Colton was fun to banter with.

"A grumpy CEO, huh? You seem to like him."

"I love him," I said, rising on my toes and kissing his jaw.

He relaxed a bit. I loved bringing out his inner caveman.

I narrowed my eyes at him. "But I didn't appreciate your full-blown jealousy scene. You need to curb that, boyfriend of mine."

He trailed his hands from my arms up my neck and twiddled his thumbs against my earlobes. "I'm so glad you're moving in."

"So am I," I whispered.

He kissed my forehead.

His phone beeped the next second. He took it out, checking it, and put it back in his pocket.

"I'm going to grab the last box."

"But my brother said you brought up everything."

"No, we had one more," he said, avoiding my gaze.

"Okay. I can get started unpacking."

The task was monstrous, but I was determined to get through it as fast as possible. Maybe it wasn't my best idea to have them all stacked here in the living room because it made the place look messy. But that motivated me even more to finish everything today.

I opened the first one. Ah, my books. Crap, I didn't think this through. I needed a bookshelf for them. I closed the box, putting it on the floor. It was super heavy too. I'd find a place for it later.

I'd started on the next box when I heard the elevator ding again and looked over my shoulder. Colton came out of it, carrying a gift box—red with a bow on top.

"Wait a second. Where did that come from?" I asked.

Sounds came out of the box.

Is that wailing?

"What's that?" I asked. It could be a sound machine. Maybe something that produced white noise.

"Something you've wanted for a long time," Colton said.

Ha! I mean, that list was endless. But then it hit me. The wailing... and the fact that something was *moving* in it.

"Holy fuck, Colton, is that a...?"

I took the box from him and started to undo the bow before I realized it was just decorative. I removed the top and squealed.

"Oh my God, you got me a Labrador!" The puppy was completely white and looked up at me, wiggling his tail. I immediately scooped him up, putting the rest of the box on the floor. I squeezed him to my chest and looked up at Colton. "This is the best day ever."

Colton stared at me with warm eyes. Then he stepped in front of me, kissed my forehead again, and lowered his mouth to the corner of my lips. "I love you. I'd do anything to make you happy."

"Does he have a name?" The little pup was squirming in my arms, then nuzzling my neck. *Oh. My. God.* I loved this little bundle more than anything... well, except for my amazing boyfriend.

"No. And it's a girl. You get to name her. She's potty-trained and even knows basic commands."

"How old is she?"

"Twenty weeks."

"That's a great age," I said. "It's not too soon. You spent enough time with your mom, huh?"

She licked my face, and I squeezed her in my arms again. "Do you want some water?" I said before realizing, "Oh, we don't have any doggie supplies."

Colton smiled. "I took care of everything. You'll find supplies in the cabinet under the sink."

I dashed to see, puppy in my arms, Colton hot on my heels. Then I turned to face him. "Hey, is this why my parents didn't stay? Did they know about this?"

"Of course they did," he said.

"But I mean... I could have enjoyed this little beauty even if they were here."

At the sink, Colton opened the cabinet and took out the bowls. He wasn't kidding. He'd bought puppy food as well. "We can choose a bed together for the dog, if you want," he said as he filled one bowl with water and one with food before putting them on the kitchen island. We'd move them on the floor later, but for now I wanted to keep her at our level.

"Did you hear that? You're going to get a bed today. You're going to be the most spoiled dog ever," I informed my puppy. Well, *our* puppy.

I was about to set her on the island when I saw she had a box hanging from the collar around her neck. How on earth did I not notice it?

"What's this?" I asked. "It looks like a small present." It was a blue box with a white bow. I looked up at Colton. "You bought our puppy something from Tiffany's?"

"You're so cute," he said.

Colton took the puppy from my arms, putting her on the island, and said, "You do the honors."

Is it my imagination, or is he a bit on edge?

I immediately took off the box and opened it.

Oh my God. It wasn't something for the puppy. It was an engagement ring!

I looked up at Colton, then back at the ring.

"Damn it. I didn't plan this right. I was supposed to get down on one knee," he said, berating himself.

He started to bend, but then the puppy started crying, and Colton instantly straightened up. Then he took the ring out of the box.

"It's so beautiful," I whispered. The diamond was huge. "*That's* why my parents left."

Colton smiled. "Zoey, I love you. I cannot put into words how much you mean to me. How much I care for you."

"Oh, I have an inkling. You're my dream man."

"And I will strive to be that every day for the rest of our lives. I'll show you the best I can be, how I feel about you."

He slid the ring on my finger. I cleared my throat. "You're not going to pop the question? I think that comes before putting on the ring."

He swallowed hard. I realized he couldn't get the words out. Then he cleared his throat and asked, "Will you marry me?"

I opened my mouth, but now it was I who couldn't speak properly. I finally managed a strangled "Yes."

Colton sealed the deal, placing his mouth on mine with a kiss that put all others to shame.

I loved this man with every fiber of my being. Our life was so damn perfect. He was getting better at delegating lab work thanks to the systems I'd put in place, so I had him more to myself. Now we lived together and were engaged.

A sound pierced the air, breaking the magic. I stepped back, glancing at the puppy. Colton had put her down and she'd walked to the far edge of the island, and now she was looking down, clearly afraid of what was below her. Colton scooped her up with one hand, easily bringing her to us. The puppy lifted her paw, aiming it at me.

"She likes you more than me already," Colton said. Then, to my surprise, he pressed her tiny head to his cheek.

Oh, this is so adorable.

Holding the puppy in one arm, he pulled me close with the other and kissed me yet again. This time, it was even better. I rose on my toes, putting my arms around his neck. He kissed me until my legs shook. I pressed them together, feeling heat pool between my thighs. And then I felt something fluffy push between us.

I stepped back yet again, laughing. The puppy was wedging her head between us, clearly needing attention.

Colton chuckled. "I figured we'd all need time to adjust to one another," he said, looking directly at the puppy, "but I didn't imagine you'd be a cockblocker from day one."

I burst out laughing, covering the puppy's ears. "Hey, don't tell her that. She'll believe you."

"I wasn't joking."

"Don't listen to him, little puppy. We love you already."

He snorted. "I'd love her even more if she hadn't interrupted my speech."

I narrowed my eyes. "You were kissing me."

"I was getting to the important part. This is the best day of my life, Zoey. And I look forward to spending every single day of my life with you," he said.

I smiled, sighing. "I'm going to make you the happiest man on earth. I promise you."

The puppy wailed again, and I laughed, looking down at her. "I didn't want to agree with Colton, but you don't have great timing, do you? But we love you anyway. Can we call her Liv? I've always liked that name."

"Sure."

We spent the rest of the day in bed and taking care of Liv. In the evening, we went to Jeannie and Abe's house. They were heading to Martha's Vineyard for a month so she could relax a bit.

Jeannie greeted us at the door. "Oh, come in. I'm so glad you made it. Congratulations on your engagement! And you brought Liv with you."

We'd FaceTimed before coming over, just to make sure it was okay, and Jeannie instantly noticed the ring.

She smiled at Colton. "You're going to make this woman so happy."

My heart sighed. I completely agreed with her.

"But don't think I'm off your back about those great-grandkids," she continued.

Colton put his arm around my shoulders. "Grandmother, give it a rest."

"Fine, fine. You're off the hook *for now*."

"Thank you. How gracious of you," he said in a sarcastic tone.

Everyone arrived in the next five minutes or so, and they all oohed and aahed over the puppy and my ring. I was a bit on edge because even though Colton had assured me she was potty-trained, I didn't want her to have an accident in Jeannie's house.

The food arrived twenty minutes later. We'd all reached a compromise. The boys were uncomfortable letting Jeannie cook for so many people, and she wasn't a fan of catering, so we'd decided to order in. There was a flurry of activity in the dining room as we all went to grab plates and put all the food containers on the table.

"Hmm," Jeannie said, surveying the order.

We'd gotten a bit of everything: Chinese, Italian, Mexican, even a few burgers.

"Hey, this is actually a great idea," Gabe said as we all sat down. He'd already filled his plate to the brim with something of everything. "This way we can eat a ton of stuff instead of just—"

Jeannie cleared her throat.

"Man, you trying to dig your own grave or something?" Maddox asked.

Gabe shrugged. "Sorry, Grandmother. I love your cooking. Didn't mean any offense."

"Relax," she said.

"You know the best part of you leaving for a month, Gran?" Nick asked.

Jeannie narrowed her eyes. "What's that?"

"We don't have to worry about any matchmaking plans while you're gone."

She started laughing. "I had a feeling that's where you were going."

Colton tilted closer to me, whispering in my ear, "Watch a master at work."

"Just so you know, I'll have more free time at Martha's Vineyard to think and make plans," Jeannie continued.

It was almost comical how fast Maddox's smile went from smirk to shock. Nick and Leo looked stunned. Gabe seemed to take everything in stride.

"But you three can relax for a bit," she said to my half brothers, then turned to Gabe. "I've got big plans for you once I'm back. I'm going to introduce you to all of my friends' granddaughters."

"Separately or all at once?" Gabe asked with what I thought might be fake bravado.

Everyone at the table started laughing.

Jeannie tsked. "Oh, this isn't a joking matter, young man. Although, if it makes you feel better, then by all means, don't take it seriously. Once I'm back, all bets are off."

"Aren't they always?" Gabe asked. "You know what, Grandmother? I'm looking forward to it."

Dear Reader, this is the end of the book. For a full list of Layla Hagen's books, please visit laylahagen.com

Made in the USA
Las Vegas, NV
18 October 2023

79283507R00144